WITH...

"I am free. I can kill without remorse and I feel no regret or sorrow . . . Evil has taught me good; good has shown me evil."

"The temperature in the room dropped about 10 degrees. I got a shot of adrenaline . . . There was an erotic sensation . . . and sharp, clawed fingers touched me. I opened my eyes . . . there was this mist and I saw demons flying . . ."

"I stood there and I looked at them. And my mother . . . there was blood running out the side of her head. I stood there, and I laughed."

"I loved my parents."

DEVIL CHILD

**Vickie L. Dawkins and
Nina Downey Higgins**

ST. MARTIN'S PRESS/NEW YORK

DEVIL CHILD

Copyright © 1989 by Vickie L. Dawkins and Nina Downey Higgins.

All rights reserved. No part of this book may be used or reproduced in any manner whatsoever without written permission except in the case of brief quotations embodied in critical articles or reviews. For information address St. Martin's Press, 175 Fifth Avenue, New York, N.Y. 10010.

ISBN: 0-312-91533-0   Can. ISBN: 0-312-91534-9

Printed in the United States of America

First St. Martin's Press mass market edition / May 1989

10 9 8 7 6 5 4 3 2 1

Note to the Reader

This book is the true story of the three murders committed by Sean Richard Sellers. However, some names have been changed as a courtesy to those involved to help protect their privacy. The following names used in this book are *not* the real names of the individuals depicted: Jim Mathis, Roger Landis, Sandy Barlow, Mack Barlow, Tara Duncan, Jere and Doyle Ricks, Sally Harjo, Jason Sellers, Solhad Muldani, Jennifer Highland, Rachel Dean, Sherry Taylor, John Paul Hinson, Mike Landry, and Debra Wilson. In addition, the characters given the names Scott, Lisa, Tracie, Lori and Dutch do not depict any specific actual individuals. Each of those five characters was created entirely by the authors and represents a composite of imaginary personality and physical traits and those of a number of individuals. Nothing those five characters say or do in the book should be taken to have been said or done by any specific real individual. Some conversations and situations have been re-created for dramatic effect.

To our parents. And to the memory of John.

ACKNOWLEDGMENTS

There are many to be thanked for their efforts in assisting the authors to reassemble this story. Foremost, we thank the relatives of Sean Sellers, who graciously set aside their grief to allow us to present an accurate portrayal of Vonda and Lee Bellofatto. To those who, for reasons personal and private chose to remain in seclusion, we find it impossible not to respect their wishes. The authors pray that no disservice has been done to the memories of the lives lost.

We laud the congeniality of the Oklahoma City Police Department, which stepped far beyond the bounds of kindness to aid in background research of this case history. In view of the hundreds of pages of legal documents, court transcripts, police files, photographs, lengthy interviews, and well-honed memories, a re-creation of this story would have proved difficult, if not impossible, without their guidance. Special thanks to the detectives assigned to the Bower and

Acknowledgments

Bellofatto cases—Bill Cook, Ron Mitchell, Bob Horn, and Eric Mullenix.

Many thanks to Linda Morgan, public information officer at the Oklahoma State Penitentiary, and former warden Gary Maynard, who allowed us the time necessary to conduct interviews with Sean Sellers. Thanks also to Robert Macy and staff of the Oklahoma County District Attorney's office; Caroline Emerson and David Lee of the State Attorney General's office; Bob Ravitz of the Oklahoma County Public Defender's office; and the Honorable Judge Wendell I. Smith.

Our gratitude is also expressed to Detective Curtis Jackson of the Beaumont, California, Police Department; Geneva Blackwell, Eric Blazek, Kim Alyce Marks, Barry Bilder; Ron Wolfe of the Tulsa *Tribune*; Nolan Clay of *The Daily Oklahoman*; Mike Peters of the Greeley *Tribune*; and Sapulpa, Oklahoma, police officer Steve Taylor for valuable information. Also, to Bettye and Jim Anderson, Tracie Dobbs, Lillie Cresap, Russell Higgins, Cathy Krans, Cathy Taylor, Peggy Fielding, and Frank and Marlene Quinn, who have lent staunch support and who answered numerous telephone calls from the authors—oftentimes in the dead of night. For Molly George, Darcy O'Brien, and William P. Wood, who believed in this project from its inception—thank you.

The authors extend their very special appreciation to our editor, Charles Spicer of St. Martin's Press, and to our agent, Jane Dystel of the Edward J. Acton Agency, New York.

A special remembrance is reserved for Robert Paul Bower, who never had the opportunity to make a mark on the world. He is not to be forgotten.

FOREWORD

THE SIGNS OF SATANISM ABOUND. AS SUNG IN the song "Possessed" by the popular group Venom, such "black"-metal music lyrics have been blamed for mind-bending channeling and teenage explorations into the occult. But music represents only a slice of the sinister force taking shape and gaining momentum among America's youth.

In an age of MTV and high-tech recording mechanisms, murder seems but another mechanical experiment for a bevy of today's fallen angels. Crime statistics of up-and-coming generations reveal that a vast number of teenagers search more diligently than ever before for that ultimate quick fix to rescue them from the problems of their formative years. Vowing to alleviate their disciplinarian problems and aid in peer acceptance, a forked-tongue "savior" awaits on street corners, back alleys, movie houses, and in public schools.

His name is Satan.

Recent history records only vague rumors of devil mongers and their clandestine deeds. Before the current outbreak of Satanism, crimes were crimes—some more baffling than others. However, as occult-related crimes increase, today's media and law enforcement are latching on to the devil's coat-tails. By the 1990s criminals linked to the devil will cover police blotters. Murder for sacrificial purposes and thrill killing for Satanic devotion will augment national statistics in a frightening symmetry.

Those who choose to believe that Satanic practitioners do not inhabit their town or city, do not shop in their grocery marts, do not occupy the car in the passing lane, might take note of some figures. In 1976 the number of active Satanists in the U.S. numbered nearly half a million. By 1985 that figure almost tripled. No community is untouched. No boundary is uncrossed.

Who, then, are these Satanists who invade our protective spiritual armor? They are business professionals, politicians, even priests. They deliver your mail, cut your hair, pump your gas.

They are your children.

As the occult ferments in the largest metropolitan cities and towns of the Bible Belt, people are at last recognizing the advent of the Left Path. To extinguish the fanatical appeal of demons who inspire our children, steps are being taken in the form of education to discredit these adopted black guardians of unholy fantasies. Occult investigation has become common. Reports of related criminal activity have proved beyond a shadow of a doubt that teenagers are finding a more titillating outlet for venting frustrations. Satanic rituals allow adolescents the unconscionable freedom to

2

murder and commit suicide en masse. The Satanic credo reinforces this emancipation: "Do what thou wilt."

The Cult Awareness Network, a non-profit Chicago group that educates the public on cult activities, receives more calls about Satanism than any other of cult behavior. A few years ago the network received approximately four to five telephone calls a month regarding Satanic groups, related stories and sightings. Today the number has increased to four or five per day.

Some experts estimate that thousands of people each year are slaughtered in Satanic sacrifices. Transients, runaways, abducted children, and babies conceived exclusively for the purpose of human sacrifice, are easy prey and among the most difficult to trace. In the thousands of covens and cults scattered throughout the U.S., secret pacts guarantee that human remains are never found. Facts emerge almost daily, according to those who have escaped covens, that sacrificial victims are burned, buried, mutilated, or cannibalized.

The infamous "Devil Child" in the pages of this work is but one facet of Satanic murder. The true account of Sean Richard Sellers is a psychological journey that looks into the mind of an intellectual prodigy and the mystifying terrain of the evil he embraced. For those who scorn the idea of his love for the prince of darkness, questions arise time and again: Could a demon force a seemingly normal sixteen-year-old boy to commit murder? Or did the devil only awaken an evil that existed all along?

This bizarre account, which to some might echo the fiction of an overimaginative horrormeister, is geared toward those who have not witnessed the raw truth: the millions of parents who cannot envision their child falling into such macabre trappings, and those who consider their child too intelligent, too religious, too sweet, or too moral to be captured by a devious entity.

For those who believe, and for those who don't—the entity you doubt, whose existence you deny, is alive and well in one form or another. Beware, lest it scare the "hell" into you.

Nothing in this world could ever mean more to me than you, Sean. I love you so very, very much, and would give my life for you without a second thought . . .

—Vonda Bellofatto, in a letter to her son, written the day she was murdered

ONE

March 4, 1986

LEE AND VONDA BELLOFATTO HAD TO DIE.

It began as a fleeting thought. One of those twisted, violent ideas that lingered in the eddies of his mind. And although the idea came and went as winter succumbed to spring, as the weeks raced in marathons, soon he could think of nothing else.

The sequence of how it all would happen played like still shots in his brain, frame by frame, flashing images of torn flesh, then the lifelessness of their bodies. Sometimes the gravity of it all—*the sheer reality of what he planned to do*—forced his mind to consider their lives. But the internal doubt was soon dismissed, and when the confusion receded, the thought returned.

Then, the idea became a well-constructed plan.

* * *

It was an excellent night for a blood ritual. A mundane and unremarkable Tuesday, late at night. The days had grown warmer with the onset of spring, but the nights still clung to a wintry chill.

Parading in front of his bedroom mirror, Sean reveled in his reflection. The mirror never lied. His shoulder-length dark blond hair and cobalt eyes were like that of a choir boy's—virginal and sensitive. And the innocence that masked his young face never failed to help him in times of need.

Another such time was drawing near.

Slipping into the pair of black undershorts, the pair he'd saved for this night, he pirouetted in front of the mirror, watching his hair dance wildly and his eyes blaze. There wouldn't be time for this sort of thing later. After tonight, he would have to become someone else—an affable son, a loyal friend. A victim.

With steps of assurance, he strode to the closet and removed the black robe from its hanger. Pride swelled in him as he stroked the fabric of the costume, which he had made on his mother Vonda's sewing machine. Every stitch had been lovingly sewn for the roles he had in store.

The robe slipped over Sean's head with a rushing sound, blanketing him with its bulk. The crisp material cooled his flesh, soothing the prickles of heat that had gathered on his forearms. The room glowed with warmth as he pulled the hood over his head. His brain teetered like a merry-go-round. The master would be pleased.

He watched himself in the mirror, searching the shrouded form for a sign of familiarity. Even in the darkness Sean could see his blue eyes dart from the hood's slits, then stare with a hollow gaze. The prophetic, throaty voice of Ezurate greeted him.

Whhhhrrrr . . .

In the bosom of his room he lit candles and incense, giving life to each as a priest prepares for Sunday mass —quietly and subserviently. The flames lunged, lapping his fingers with what must have been a hell-spawned fire. The wavering light gave a clearer definition to the display surrounding him. The silver chalice gleamed. The black sheen of the altar excited him. He was on home ground now.

He began as always, ringing the bell to clear and purify the air of all other sound.

"In the name of Satan, the ruler of the earth, the king of the world," he whispered, "I command the forces of darkness to bestow their infernal power upon me." Sean recited the invocation, facing the altar and the symbol of Baphomet that hung on his west wall.

He beckoned the master, calling to him by the infernal names in his bible, then drank from the chalice. Turning counterclockwise, he embraced his sword and summoned the four princes of hell: Satan from the south, Lucifer from the east, Belial from the north, and Leviathan from the west. Cross-legged on the carpeted floor, guarded by the candlelight, he flipped through the pages of his secret book—the keeper of his fantasies—his Book of Shadows, until he located the appropriate incantation.

Readying the paper that he had earlier seared to resemble parchment, he placed the knife and chalice atop his dresser, then loaded the .44 Smith & Wesson, which lay beside him.

The demon clutched his insides, yanking his innards with inhuman power.

Oh, great desolate one, spawn of the abyss, enemy to the weak . . .

Sean fondled the knife and raised the instrument until the tip of the blade pointed to the ceiling.

. . . send forth your most glorious blessing, and heal the wounds of one of your children . . .

Sean heard a moan. But it was not himself, only Ezurate, watching, approving.

Whhhhrrrr . . .

The tingle began as a malignant growth in the pit of his stomach, then traveled in waves until it consumed him. Skirting its way through his torso and limbs, he felt the demon enter his veins, commanding his blood to slow, his heart to thump silently.

Welcome, Ezurate.

Ezurate brought the knife toward him. The blade idled at Sean's wrist, as if awaiting instruction. The image in the mirror shifted and leaned over the dresser, mimicking Sean's every move. Ezurate smiled, pressed the tip of the blade into Sean's wrist, then dragged the knife across the skin. With one precise movement the demon sliced a shallow gash in the flesh. Droplets of blood formed in unison. A crimson rivulet oozed across his arm and dripped eagerly into the chalice.

Voices swirled in Sean's head, croaking their demonic cheers, urging him to squeeze his life into the silver goblet. Some of the voices he recognized— Ezurate's chant rising above the rest—but the others were distant to him, unrecognizable. Sean pinched at the wound, demanding more of the ink for the letter he would write. Having satisfied himself with the quantity, he suckled the flesh until the bleeding stopped.

Sean had not written a letter to his master for some time. But despite his carelessness, the master had been good to him. Never allowing his wishes to go unfulfilled, the master had sent Tara, the beauty who perhaps unwittingly introduced him to the "new life." The bond that united them hallowed tonight's communion.

But it was Angel who commanded his agility and deepened his allegiance to the master. In Angel, Sean discovered a soulmate—a sharer of his intimacies who knew just what he wanted, when he wanted it.

As he dipped his finger into the blood, he knew with certainty that Lee and Vonda *deserved* to die. That the sacrifice would finally make everything all right.

Forever.

The first words flowed smoothly, turning a tarnished brown as air dried the blood. Sean poured heart and soul into the master's letter, scrawling his signature at the bottom of the page.

"I renounce God. I renounce Christ. I will serve only Satan. To my enemies, death. To my friends, love. Regie Satanas. Ave Satanas. Hail Satan!"

He knelt before the candles and burned the paper. *Shemhamforash!*

Each preliminary detail had been administered without flaw. His concentration would now be fixed on the sacrifice. His time, dedicated to the beast.

Lee must be first.

Even in sleep, Lee might hear the most insignificant sound. He could pose a dangerous threat to the demon if awakened. Sean was pleased that he had disciplined himself against the frivolity of emotion. Vonda would be more difficult—if he allowed himself to wallow in sentiment. But the maternal bond had been severed long ago. Vonda would be an ignorant target, unaware of his motives. From a physical standpoint, she would be the easiest. There would be little struggle, if any.

Yes, Vonda would be last.

Sean again rang the bell, which signified the end of the ritual. "So it is done," he whispered. He stretched out on his bed, closed his eyes and fell asleep almost instantly. His dreams were undisturbed by the duty at hand, but Ezurate lingered in the foreground. The demon's cackles grew louder, until Sean woke.

He rose and prayed to Satan for guidance. It was time.

Sean disrobed. His hand wrapped around the butt of the .44. Lifting the revolver, he gripped and re-gripped the gun until it felt comfortable. Twirling about the mirror, he struck an imaginary pose, aiming at his reflection, and mouthed a silent *pop!* The gun looked handsome in his hand—almost *natural*—and he could feel Ezurate tugging at his gut.

Barefoot, clad only in the dark underwear, Sean moved with the stealth of an animal. Only the sounds of night converged as he entered the shadowed hall-way. The foundation creaked and whined. The wind whipped against the windows, whistling in the dark-ness. Ezurate followed.

At their bedroom door, Sean paused. He listened for the slightest movement. Only the pulse of sleep penetrated the early morning quiet. Lee's heavy exha-lation rose above Vonda's lighter breathing. Sean con-centrated, scanning the room as his eyes adjusted to the swallowing black.

He stalked the sleeping forms, drawing closer to Lee's bedside. There was no room for even the smallest error. No time to blink away the pellets of sweat that fell into his eyes and blurred his vision. Greedily, the demon pushed him forward. The .44 locked in Sean's hand as he raised the barrel to Lee's head.

Whhhhrrrr . . .

If for one second a tiny seed of doubt clouded his thinking, he dismissed the thought with glorious anticipation of what tomorrow would bring.

When Ezurate whispered, he cocked the hammer.

Sean had lots of school friends, but he always thought he was a little smarter than everyone else.

—Geneva Blackwell,
September 1987

TWO

OKLAHOMA NESTLES IN THE CENTER OF TORnado Alley and the Bible Belt. Summers are bearable, until the thermometer leaps to the 110-degree mark and relative humidities near 85 percent. Winters are mild, until the stinging cold seeps through the cracks and crevices and the wind chill takes a plunge to 30 below.

In spite of the weather extremes, Oklahoma entices millions of people into the confines of its borders, where the colorful history of cowboys and Indians is resurrected in museums and powwows. The aromatic influence, and affluence, of oil still pulsates, but the sagging economy has dimmed much of its glamor.

Although the oil boom plateaued in the late seventies and subsided in the early eighties, jobs were abundant for men like Jim Blackwell. Jim had devoted most of his life to the Texas and Oklahoma oil patches, where his love affair with the fields was threatened by the floundering petroleum business. Nevertheless, he was a seasoned oil man and, in the off periods, a jack-of-many-trades, which provided him with income in times of recession. While his skill as a diesel mechanic kept meat and potatoes on the dinner table, his dream to one day return to the oil fields never faded.

Jim's marriage, however, suffered long before the onslaught of the oil crunch. When his only daughter, Vonda Maxine, was two years old, the Blackwells divorced. Although Jim remained in Oklahoma, his "little princess" was whisked away by her mother to Corcoran, California—far from the cowboys, the Indians, and her father. And as Jim Blackwell attempted to reassemble the pieces of his life, the oil economy—and his dream—turned bleak.

A thousand miles to the west, little Vonda was growing up. A pretty, slender brunette, Vonda was a popular child—almost aristocratic in her manner. She learned to sew and crochet early in adolescence, and was inclined to seek out any type of craft that gave her the opportunity to use her hands. Vonda enjoyed creating her own works of art with papier-mâché or valentine cards, and sewing her own clothes. She particularly reveled in surprising her mother Geraldine and other family members with handcrafted gifts of her own design.

Vonda's greatest passion, both in her youth and adulthood, was undisputably her home life. Her craving for love and security clouded any career aspirations, and the desire to have a family of her own remained a priority. She adored her mother, who had remarried transplanted Oklahoman Carlos Lindley, who treated Vonda as though she were his own daughter. But she also cherished her yearly visits to Oklahoma, where she spent the summers with her natural father and his new bride, Geneva.

In vying for her affection, Jim and Geneva Blackwell lavished special attention upon Vonda. It seemed that she had the best of both worlds, and she adapted well to each visitation and homecoming. Vonda showered everyone with her friendly chatter and bubbling laughter.

At fifteen Vonda Blackwell met Jason Sellers, a stocky, would-be artist who charmed her with his talent and flashing blue eyes. Jason offered Vonda the chance to realize her fantasy of a family, and when he proposed marriage, the dream of living happily ever after glowed in her heart. Although money was tight, the two were united for better or worse. The idyllic marriage was further enriched when Vonda learned she was pregnant. And on May 18, 1969, when she was barely sixteen, Vonda gave birth to a son, whom she named Sean Richard Sellers.

She couldn't have been happier, but Jason's life was turning upside down. His adjustment to a wife, and now a baby, had put a crimp in his foot-loose style.

Sean was not an especially pretty baby, but when Vonda held him in her arms, she experienced an immediate mother's love—a contentment and joy beyond her wildest dreams. The realities of rearing a child were frightening, but the reward was an unparalleled sense of belonging. It seemed appropriate that Vonda would later call May 18 the happiest day in her life.

All the world's troubles and her own disillusionment with life seemed miles away when Vonda held Sean to her breast. Her every fiber centered on his needs, on his fragile dependency. But as her attention and nurturing took her further away from Jason, the friction between them intensified. Vonda's jaunts to Oklahoma stretched into longer and more frequent visits. When the Sellerses' marriage dissolved in 1972, Vonda returned with her son to Oklahoma.

With a newfound independence and a three-year-old son, Vonda matured rapidly, and took a small apartment in McAlester. She grew more attractive as she blossomed into full womanhood. She lightened her naturally brown hair to blond, but she was never pretentious, nor did the gratifying change in her looks alter her personality. Vonda remained friendly and genial, traits that were undeniable aids in landing employment. Although her skills outside a domestic environment were few, her enthusiasm and determination were priceless assets.

The first few years of struggle at fast-food chains, restaurants, and truck stops unveiled new realms with which Vonda had to cope. If she suffered from an aching back, fatigued legs, or sore feet after standing for hours on end, she didn't complain. On the job, her lips were always on the verge of a smile, and she was ready with a word of encouragement for patrons who sought her station. At the end of each shift she returned to her modest apartment, overjoyed to be reunited with her son.

If her dreams of the perfect marriage had been shattered, Vonda bounced back quickly. Her hopes for a close-knit family life never waned, and she was determined not to subject Sean to the dangers that had stolen his father. She expected of her son a higher standard of living, and moral discipline. Together they could—and would—conquer any obstacle the outside world had in store.

Above all else, Vonda couldn't ignore her irrepressible and constant desire to care for Sean; to ensure that he had plenty to eat, nice clothes to wear, a safe place to live, and that he never wanted for anything, even if it meant going without herself. Her little baby would have the chance for a *good* life. She wanted to protect him from suffering, from feeling the pain that she had felt.

Her fears kept her awake at night, creeping into the silence and loneliness of her bedroom. Many nights she took Sean into bed with her, not sleeping until he slept. Then she would suddenly awaken, afraid that she had rolled too close to him, cutting off his air.

As he grew in childhood, Sean's sensitivity emerged in ways that both delighted and saddened Vonda. One evening as they huddled together, Vonda read aloud E. B. White's *Charlotte's Web*. She neared the story's end, and when Charlotte's cycle of life drew to a close, Sean's blue eyes filled with tears. Vonda pulled him closer and tried to comfort him, and finally he settled into her arms and, still weeping, fell asleep. For Vonda, the fine line between real life and make-believe had all but disappeared.

Because of her loving discipline, the least of Vonda's worries was finding babysitters for her son. She departed for work assured that he would be the same good boy he was at home. Sean was sweet. Compliant. Intelligent far beyond his chronological years. He was, in his mother's eyes, the perfect child. And there was no greater reward than to watch his face light up as she picked him up after work and listened to the sitter's daily report. Did she realize how *smart* little Sean was? And, oh, what a *lucky* mother Vonda must be to have such a well-behaved child.

When Geraldine and Carlos returned to Oklahoma from California, Vonda's world was complete. Her mother and stepfather took up residence just seven miles away, in Arpelar. Jim and Geneva lived in Oklahoma City, where Jim worked as a mechanic. Vonda divided her time between her restaurant job in Savanna—a small community southwest of McAlester—her four parents, and her son.

But then her world turned dark. Vonda's mother developed a terminal brain tumor. When she died in April of 1974, Vonda was devastated. She cradled Sean in her arms and they cried in shared sorrow. A mother and her son. Sean's arms reached around Vonda, hugging her tightly, until she felt that she could go on, must go on. For her little boy.

The loss of her mother drew Vonda closer to her father and Geneva, who moved that same year from Oklahoma City to Ravia to be near Jim's aging mother. Vonda now spent her spare time with Sean, driving from McAlester to Ravia.

When a tall, dark, mustachioed Army recruiting sergeant in McAlester entered Vonda's life, her world— once again—turned completely around.

Paul Leon Bellofatto's move to Oklahoma during the final years of his Army stint might be deemed coincidence. To the more spiritualistic minded, the transfer—not of his own choosing—might be termed destiny. Vonda met and fell in love with Paul, nick-named Lee, when she was twenty-one. Lee, who was Italian, came from Boston. Divorced for several years, he was a former Green Beret who served in Vietnam. He was eleven years older than Vonda, an age difference that might have strengthened their relationship. Lee exuded the maturity and security that an assertive young woman with a small child found appealing. They began their life together in a McAlester apartment, where Lee proved to be the ideal mate for Vonda and the perfect male role model for Sean.

By the time Lee's tour of duty with the Army ended, the Blackwells, Vonda, Lee, and Sean had grown quite close. Jim and Geneva liked Lee Bellofatto and hoped that marriage was imminent. Jim, who had expertise as a mechanic, tutored his prospective son-in-law, and when Lee mustered out of the Army in the latter part of 1976, he happily settled into his new career as a mechanic and tow-truck driver in a McAlester garage.

On New Year's Day 1977, Vonda Maxine Sellers became Mrs. Paul Leon Bellofatto in a simple ceremony at the home of Vonda's aunt in Arpelar. Vonda was radiant in her wedding dress and veil. Lee made a striking appearance with his dark, curly hair, mustache, and tanned good looks. His father, who had traveled from Boston for the wedding, stood proudly at his side. Geneva recalls that the resemblance between father and son was uncanny.

Lee's love for Vonda was apparent to everyone. Much like his father, he was open with his emotions. His warm, caring nature and fondness of Sean revived Vonda's dream of a loving family.

In the late 1970s the economic recession shot across Oklahoma like mortar shrapnel, branching off into every direction. While Sean was too young to understand why there might be less milk and cereal for breakfast, Lee Bellofatto joined the ranks of the unemployed. But Vonda and Lee were not unduly distraught. Vonda's father, after all, was a man of clout and had an ability to persuade people. He was employed at a trucking firm, and like the loyal father-in-law he was, it was only a matter of days before he secured a cross-country driver job for Lee.

From her experience as a waitress at a Savanna truck stop, Vonda was keenly aware of the lonely, frustrating life of the truck driver. She would not allow *anything* to threaten the newly-discovered security that meant so much to her and Sean.

The answer was clear to her. She would become Lee's team driver. Her logic was two-fold: The truck would stay on the move while one driver slept, meaning more mileage and more money. Soon, they'd have that home they wanted—*their* home. They would have all the money they needed for Sean's upbringing and a sound education. There was only one small problem. What to do with Sean? He obviously could not endure the erratic routine of cross-country driving. Besides, he would soon be of kindergarten age.

Jim and Geneva, however, had a solution. The Blackwells considered it a privilege to care for their polite, well-mannered grandson during the three- to four-week periods Vonda and Lee would be out on the road. Sean would have his own room and grow to love the small-town ambience of Ravia.

If one drives far enough along Oklahoma's Highway 78 en route to Ravia, idle pump jacks can be seen on vast expanses of flat plain land—a picture story that requires no words. Ravia is a tiny town, tucked between its two sister provinces, Tishomingo and Mill Creek. Post–Civil War Ravia was a bustling town, consisting of two banks, three grocery stores, two drugstores, a post office, a depot, and a hotel. Once a thriving community, Ravia greeted its visitors with

COME GROW WITH US—A CITY ON THE MOVE, and a population of 792.

Today, Ravia's population stands at about 100. Its welcoming sign, rusted and crippled over the decades, tilts against a sloping embankment. A tour of its boundaries reveals the same post office, two service stations, two grocery marts, a senior citizens group community center, and a monument works and gift shop.

Over the years Ravia's Methodist and Baptist churches have been proud of their work in the saving of lost souls. In the bosom of the Ravia Church of God, where Christian teachings are strict, many of the wayward have been sanctified and filled with the Holy Spirit.

Children in the first to eighth grades attend Ravia's only school—simply named Ravia School—and move on to high school in the neighboring city of Tishomingo. Unless those who graduate go to work in one of the area's glass factories or granite works, they join the hundreds of others who flock to the larger cities of Oklahoma to eke out a living.

Sean's stay in Ravia lasted a little longer than anyone anticipated, especially Vonda and Lee. No one thought that his separation from his mother and stepfather would continue for four years. Nor did the fact that he would see his mother but four days out of each month seem to pose a problem.

Sean was a healthy, well-adjusted, sweet and normal child of above-average intelligence. He developed an exceptional talent for writing, and he sketched with a photographic eye that allowed him to re-create most anything from memory. He also held an enormous love for animals, and frequently rescued neighborhood strays, begging his grandmother for approval.

But Geneva noticed early on the rigid demands Sean placed on himself. He wanted to be the best at everything. In control of every situation. The leader. A winner. If he was unable to grasp the meaning of a concept or attain a particular skill, he abandoned the project. If he didn't perfect a task on the first try, it no longer interested him. Little League was one of those attempts that Sean soon retired to his personal archives. He had trouble hitting the ball. As a result, he never played the game again.

Geneva was employed two blocks from the Blackwell home. Her job at a little country store brought in extra income and gave Sean a grand excuse to ride his bicycle after school and on Saturdays. In retrospect, Geneva recalls that Sean posed no problems for anyone. At school, he got along well with other children, had many friends, and boasted grades that were above the norm. He never seemed particularly disturbed by the fact that his parents were gone for weeks at a time.

He did, however, seem elated at their return each month. During one reunion, Lee asked Sean how he would feel about taking the name Bellofatto through legal adoption. Sean was more than agreeable. He loved his stepfather. And Vonda and Lee decided that when time permitted, Sean would legally become a Bellofatto. That time, unfortunately, never arrived.

Before Sean entered the third-grade, the Bellofattos announced that they were moving to California. The couple, who had sent money for Sean's welfare, plucked him from Ravia School and away from Jim and Geneva, with the hope of making more money on the

West Coast. Sean, happy to be reunited with his mother and Lee, looked forward to the trip.

The family never suspected that the move to the West Coast would drastically change their lives. But deep in the recesses of Sean's mind something had begun to take shape.

Deep down I want power . . . the unruling [sic] power of the supernatural.

—Sean Sellers, an entry in his journal

THREE

WHILE VONDA, LEE, AND SEAN MADE A TEMPO-rary pilgrimage to California in the late 1970s, something stirred among the restless youth of America. Something that, for the most part, was overlooked by parents and authorities, or shrugged off as sporadic incidents caused by the emotional Vietnam era. It made itself more tangible in California, rising from the plush, well-manicured expanse of Los Angeles County and mixing with the glamour and glitz of Hollywood.

Something that cast its evil spell throughout the nation.

Satanism was not an unfamiliar concept on the West Coast. For centuries the devil had conjured up images of a gnarled, horned creature with cloven hooves and a spiked tail. A terrifying monster that sent sinners rushing to the halls of repentance. During the seventies and early eighties, a resurgence of black witchcraft linked to Satanism built to a rapid crescendo. The peak occurred in 1981 in a grand-scale convergence known as the "Feast of the Beast." This union of dark forces ignited a fire, sparking more frequent gatherings of high priests, witches, and warlocks, and exploding into a network that crisscrossed the United States and parts of Europe.

The occult grapevine spread on wings of fury that put hell's flames to shame. Perhaps it was the drug-infested world of the Manson family that placed much of this behavior into the limelight. Although Manson's Satanic involvements were neither proved nor disproved, murder for pleasure clearly happened. Still, in a search to alleviate the agonizing phases of puberty or simple loneliness, many young adults used the occult to soothe the itch of adolescence.

The craving for the salvation offered by black magic and witchcraft did not, however, limit itself to carefree Californians. Books and literature on various occult subjects appeared across the nation. They could be purchased in bookstores or borrowed from libraries.

The *Satanic Bible* became one of the more popular resources for practitioners. Anton Szandor LaVey opened the eyes and ears of a population starved for his indulgent doctrines and "pursuit of pleasure" theme. While LaVey's First Church of Satan, located in San Francisco, unlocked its dark doors in 1966 to those seeking alternative religious guidance, the rest of the world refused to believe that Satan was alive and well on earth.

One California pagan cult comprised of college students, descendants of Salem witches, and even local public officials, grew to a purported membership of two thousand in the early seventies. Recruits were slowly drawn in by elaborate drug and sex orgies hosted by coven acolytes. Soon, new pledges were dismembering fingers as flesh offerings to their master. The bizarre pleasures that Satanism offered seemed more appealing to some than Christian fundamentalism.

During the summer months of 1977 Satan's gospel found its way into Sean Sellers' young world.

Though only eight years of age, Sean *knew* that he must not tell *anyone* about the books shared by the teenage girl who watched him one afternoon while Vonda and Lee were away. As he flipped through page after page, he gobbled up the words and pictures as though his imagination had not been fed in years. A feast lay before him. His curiosity alternated between a longing to absorb the information and an intuition that he was doing something *wrong.* And the more he studied and read, the stronger the urge became. The sketches of nude women portraying human altars, and the charcoal interpretations of spirits that glided invisibly across the earth, held a fascination unlike anything he had ever known. Their effects awakened a dormant, electrical current that flowed through him.

Sean's science fiction pastime took a back seat. The aesthetics of occult literature were much more colorful than star worlds and androids. The exotic ideas dangled temptingly before him; adhered the messages behind the ideas like subliminal *secrets*—recipes for power and control. Sean's artistic talents now focused on beasts and magic. His renderings of Salem's gallows resembled the sharp illustrations by book artists. His literary flair merged with a dark inspiration that gave birth to prose and poetry.

During the six months that Sean and his parents

resided in California, the seeds of hedonism were sown, the queer, foreign words and hooded faces etched into his memory. The stories he'd read explaining the path to happiness, prosperity, and success appealed to him. When the Bellofatto family returned to Oklahoma in the fall of Sean's fourth-grade year, the bizarre ideas began to incubate in his mind.

Another year passed in Sean's simple but well-organized life. He was a healthy, active child with an intellect that fed on his insatiable curiosity—forever questioning the whys, the hows, and never receiving a satisfactory answer. In Oklahoma, Vonda and Lee signed on as drivers for a truck line in Cushing, and Sean was transported back to the home of his grandparents in Ravia. While he accepted the move as part of his lot in life, he began to question the constant moves.

Sean *appeared* to understand his parents' motives for looking for more prosperous work. He never doubted the love of Lee and Vonda, even when they forced him to adapt to another home and school. Neither did he complain when he again confronted the familiar, stony faces at Ravia School.

In 1979, when Lee and Vonda's employment with the Cushing truck line ended, their plans for the future were reevaluated. Over the past few years, the Bellofattos had saved enough money to gain a financial edge. Their hard work, although separating them from Sean, had provided for comfortable security—a nest egg. But there had been a price. At nine years of age, Sean had lived with his parents a total of six months. He was growing up before their eyes, slipping into preadolescence, which would ripen into young manhood. While his blond hair and blue eyes were like

Vonda's, the face that hid a thousand unasked questions belonged to a stranger.

The Bellofattos and their son returned to McAlester as Sean prepared to enter fifth grade. For the second time Jim and Geneva Blackwell bade farewell to their grandson—the child they had practically raised as their own. Sean hugged his grandparents good-bye, though not without a feeling of elation. He had grown close to them, but was delighted to be living with his parents once more.

Replanting his roots for the fourth time, Sean was the new kid in town. Undaunted, he assumed the same role in a different scene of still another play. New kids had to prove themselves or fade when the curtain closed between acts. New kids *stayed* new kids for what seemed an eternity. For Sean, the role had grown tiresome. He walked among strangers in the hall, sat beside them in class, and they remained strangers.

Although jobs were few in a community where the principal job lure is Oklahoma's state penitentiary, Vonda and Lee shared a sentimentality about the place where they had met. The friendly, hometown milieu of McAlester welcomed them like long-lost family. Lee found work with a tank-truck outfit, recovering excess oil for redistribution to oil-related companies. The hours were long and the work was sweaty and difficult, but he finally earned a salary that would allow his wife to remain at home with their son. The Bellofattos could, at last, become a typical American family.

Jim and Geneva Blackwell separated in 1979 after twenty-three years of marriage, but Sean seemed unaffected by their divorce. Now he awoke each morning to a new atmosphere. There were occasional breaks of dawn when he lay still in his bed, struggling to remember where he was. Hushed voices drifted from the kitchen—voices he at first wouldn't recognize. He'd shut his eyes and turn up the volume in his memory until the faces of his mother and Lee raced to the foreground. Vonda called him to breakfast in a singsong hum, but Sean would lay for a moment longer, relishing the soft plushness of the bedcovers, wishing he could freeze the moment.

"Okay, Mom," he would say to her. Then a sudden chill would drift through him. Had he only *imagined* the delicate voice floating through the door to his room?

Sean would rise and pad out to the kitchen where Vonda and Lee sat drinking coffee at the table. He would join them for a hot breakfast of fried eggs and sausage, while in the back of his mind a frightening thought occurred. Would he really be able to stay with them forever? Each day, he calculated. If he set his mind to it, he could *find* ways to make them love him more, so that he would never be sent away, never have to leave. He could *invent* ways, if he had to. Sean would become everything his parents had ever wanted.

In McAlester, the Will Rogers Elementary School students took no special note of Sean Sellers. In the six months Sean spent in California, he'd been noticed. He hadn't been treated as a child, not even by the older kids. He'd seen things—*knew things*—that his present classmates could never imagine: a combination of magic and witches that he'd learned in California, a higher plane of existence. While he missed the excitement of the West Coast, he could not say that he missed any friends. Sean hadn't stayed in one place long enough to develop relationships from which he could draw memories.

In his bid to be accepted by the group of faceless strangers at school, he vowed to project some outstanding trait from within himself, something the others couldn't ignore. He began by creating a certain smile, an almost permanently set, ever-so-slight upturning of the lips, and a sheepish but polite manner. His voice became whisperlike and calm. Eventually they *would* notice him.

Sean sailed through middle school like a feather in the wind. His above-average intellect tended to make many of the other students seem slow by comparison, and in correctly answering the teacher's questions so easily, he intimidated the other youths. Nevertheless, the smile remained intact as his grades climbed to ranks that pleased his parents. The smile also never wavered when he learned that he was expected by his mother to perform menial chores around the house. Sean saw her demands as merely another opportunity to foster the maternal link so that she would always want him around.

During the McAlester days, Vonda's happiness soared to new heights. She had her family together, and Lee's higher income showed no signs of ebbing. She was proud of Sean, who compensated her for her two marriages, the family traumas and numerous moves. His schoolwork reflected nearly straight A's, and his artistic talent displayed tremendous promise. She smiled at the drawings she found among scattered school papers in his room. Sean's abilities reminded her of Jason Sellers, but with his deft intelligence, she was certain her son would eclipse Jason.

Lee's innate fondness for children provided Sean with a loving father who was gentle yet strict. He had a son and daughter from his first marriage, and they lived with their mother in Elgin, Oklahoma. A career in the Army had taught Lee the importance of rules and discipline, but his compassionate nature mingled with this, and his tenderness won him affection from Sean. Lee encouraged his stepson to keep himself physically fit and to face each day squarely and with a positive attitude. He treated Sean well, and his high expectations were those of a father toward his own natural child. In addition, Lee's Italian descent led him to value a strong and loyal family unit. He worked hard to keep his family going—to provide the best life for them that he possibly could.

In the jostle of daily routine, Lee's intention to legally adopt Sean was delayed. If the subject of adoption was present in the minds of the Bellofattos, it was not mentioned during the McAlester days. But neither was it forgotten. The family silently understood that one day Sean would assume the Bellofatto name.

In 1981, just as Sean had adjusted to his new town, just as the faceless strangers had begun to smile at him, Lee's job led to another move—this time to Piedmont, Oklahoma. With an isolated structure of concrete boardwalks and modest homes, Piedmont lies at Oklahoma City's back door. At dusk the sun sets in a fiery triangle, silhouetting the city.

Junior high school began with the same schedule for Sean. As algebra and biology courses loomed, he prepared in advance to keep his grades intact. His academic achievements continued. Still small in stature, he leaned toward literary recreations. To nurture his body, and undoubtedly to try and establish friendships, he joined the football and track teams. In a desire to become totally accepted by his peers, he also lifted weights.

As puberty drew nearer, Sean lost all prepubescent fat. He grew taller, more slender, and his physical characteristics changed dramatically. Although his features approached maturity, his nose seemed too large for the rest of his face. Acne sprouted across his cheeks and chin. His hair and skin glistened with secretions of oil. But his eyes reflected a luminescent blue that softened his otherwise gangly appearance.

In the awkward throes of adolescence, Sean scrubbed his face with acne medications, shampooed his fine, blond hair every day. The boy that looked back from the mirror wore a peculiar expression. An odd mixture of boy and man. A face that stood alone among the junior high school crowd and hid a complexity no one else saw. There were times when he felt as if he were about to tumble into a deep, dark crevasse.

Each afternoon, Sean straightened the house and began a regimen of doing laundry, preparing dinner, then retiring to his room for homework. His mother's attention and supervision of his domestic responsibilities gave him a sense of security. She *needed* his help. She needed *him.* But an emptiness opened inside him, which good grades and pleasing his parents couldn't close. When the emptiness gnawed, he recalled the books he had read in California. Their magic hovered like apparitions, popping in, then evaporating just as quickly. There had to be some way to recapture the stimulation he'd experienced in California.

If girls had never entered Sean's mind before the age of thirteen, they suddenly took on meaning. Bouncing up and down the halls of Piedmont Junior High, they giggled and wiggled to class in a manner Sean had not previously noticed. Their gleaming hair, veils of perfume and makeup, and tiny waists, sent confusing messages to his body. He practiced eye contact, hoping that one day the prettiest girls in school would smile and stop to talk. But he seemed to always be the latest arrival, always the low man on the student-body totem pole. They sensed his struggle to fit, his awkwardness. After much contemplation, following vain attempts to make friends, Sean decided to share his *secret*. Revealing the more intriguing aspects of life that he had learned in California would surely attract the attention of his peers.

Jim Mathis must have felt a lag in his own teenaged life. Though not particularly handsome, his dark eyes, black hair, and shy demeanor set him apart from the students who clustered in groups in the halls and school cafeteria. An unusual bump on the bridge of his nose earned him the nickname of Klinger, a reference to a popular character on the television show *M*A*S*H*. Jim had never been an academic prodigy. Although his efforts prompted him to complete his homework assignments on time, his persona was that of a follower, the shadow that could never quite step out of the dark and take charge.

Sean didn't attract the attention of Jim right away. In the guarded realms of junior high cliques, neither boy created many friendships that would have brought them together. But similarities in their makeup led them to single each other out. Sean tried to be assertive, and finally a few words led to conversation that revealed common interests in several areas. They both ran track and played football. They both enjoyed science fiction and tales of the supernatural. They both liked to ogle the cheerleaders. They ate lunch together in the school cafeteria, exchanging ideas and opinions until the laughter and chatter of the other socializing students receded. After school they hung out, visiting each others' homes as though they were Siamese twins —inseparable.

One day, when the usual topics of conversation had worn thin, Sean remembered overhearing some of the other kids talk about a new game which resembled one he'd learned in California, a game with which Jim admitted to being slightly acquainted. Dungeons & Dragons had replaced the video games that had meteored across Piedmont, consuming teenage allowances and imaginations. D & D had become popular at the beginning of the eighties. Its players literally assumed the identities of mythical beings, acting out suppressed feelings that many adolescents were unable to vent in reality. In addition, after the initial purchase of the rule books, D & D had no further expense. The boys hoped the game would expand their circle of friends.

Minutes after the afternoon school bell, Sean and Jim shed their inadequacies for a voyage into make-believe. Beasts, demons, and monsters pulled them into a world where fantasy intertwined with reality. Under the guise of sorcerers and demons, the two were swept into a magical universe that revolved day after day.

As Sean stepped into the shoes of his soothsaying character, he felt a quickening of his pulse, the same warmth he had clung to in McAlester when Vonda had called him to breakfast. His stomach clenched in anticipation. Feelings of emptiness and loneliness disappeared in a rush of adrenaline, his pulse throbbing as the strategy of another campaign in a mythical land began. He donned his telepathic and telekinetic roles with a shield of superhuman power. The element of bonding with other players provided an emotionally satisfying interconnection which was lacking in his real world.

In the aura of the magic circle, which sheltered him from the ennui of chores and homework, Sean forgot his parents, forgot his adolescence. The litany of questions that no one could *ever* answer retreated to the basement of his mind. He reached inside himself and discovered an inner fabric of strength and dominance, then stitched his character with its threads.

Dungeons & Dragons grew as addictive as it did adventuresome. Saturdays and Sundays were set aside for continuing episodes of Sean's and Jim's passage into another dimension. A few classmates, most of them boys, joined them for sword and sorcery games that began at daybreak and lasted until any hour that parents would allow. But Sean's fascination with Dungeons & Dragons went beyond the afternoons he played with his game companions. His imagination urged him to learn more about the characters, the worlds, the magic and persuasion he held in the palms of his hands. His perseverance quickly led him through star-studded gates to the rank of dungeon master. Now he told the others where they must begin, and allowed them only the freedom to die—unless they were extremely clever at the game.

Sean had tasted the first sweet aperitif of power and control. And it was good.

The game Dungeons & Dragons got me started. I wanted to learn more about it, so [we] went to the library and stole some books about dragons, witches, wizards and Satanism.

—Sean Sellers, January 1987

FOUR

THEY CAN'T MAKE ME DO THIS AGAIN!
  Yes, they can. They've been making you do it all of your life. How many times has it been now, four, five, maybe?
  No. Not anymore. I won't go. I'll live with Jim.
  No, you can't. They won't let you.
  Then I'll kill myself. I swear I'll do it.

The summer of 1982 torched Oklahoma with heat. The rusty whirl of air conditioners could be heard everywhere, at any time of day, if one had occasion to stop and listen. For miles pastoral land lay burnt and ashen from the heat's destruction, its wild flora shriveled. Men and women fanned themselves as they ventured from the coolness of their homes, and children reduced their outdoor frolics to early morning and twilight.

It was during June that Vonda Bellofatto detected

more than a passing fancy between her son and Dungeons & Dragons. As she watched game companions file into his room, it seemed to her that his curiosity had grown obsessive.

While Vonda never demanded that Sean cease his game-playing, she suggested that he divide his time among other interests. Sean complied with his mother's request, assuring her with his persuasive smile, then transferred his D&D campaigns to another location.

In the wake of school's summer break, many Oklahoma churches answered the prayers of parents overwhelmed by the company of their children all day, every day. Vacation bible schools and church camps offered regimented, two-week alternatives to video arcades and other teenage congregations. The Bellofattos had never considered themselves devout in matters of religion, although Lee had been raised as a Catholic, but neither were they averse to attending an occasional mass. When Vonda learned that a neighborhood parish sponsored a summer camp for teens, she decided to temporarily slay her son's dragon.

Jennifer Highland had regularly attended summer church camp for the past three years. Her family had deep religious convictions, and Jennifer had been tutored as an obedient Catholic girl from infancy. She had never met Sean before that first day of camp, had never seen him in mass or participating in any church functions. But her family had taught her the value of exhibiting kindness to new attendees. And on the June morning that Jennifer caught sight of the blond-haired boy fidgeting in his pew, staring wistfully out the window, she welcomed him with a smile.

From the age of six, Sean had experienced auditory

hallucinations. Voices that soothed and coddled him like secret friends. He never questioned their presence or their sympathy. As anger, resentment, and depression festered in his subconscious, the voices protected him like an invisible shield.

Sean's first tangle with puppy love rendered him vulnerable and starry-eyed. Whenever he was near Jennifer, his stomach turned cartwheels. His moods fluctuated between gales of laughter and bouts of depression. He was too short, too plump. His clothes were all wrong. His hair was too straight. It was then that the voices intervened, lending him confidence, replacing his fears with assurance.

During his stay at summer camp, Sean pushed aside his obsession with the forbidden arts. He lay in his bunk, clumped in with the crowd of teenage boys who reluctantly surrendered to the lights-out curfew. Blinking wide-eyed into the night, he sealed a pact with God. He prayed for Jennifer to love him. He promised to be good, sweared to obey his parents' every demand, pleaded to do *anything* if God would grant him her love.

Vonda noticed a strange transformation in her son when he returned from church camp. Dungeons & Dragons no longer dominated his conversations or his time. Jennifer Highland had replaced Sean's former preoccupation, and Vonda wondered whether she had made a serious mistake.

Sometime during September, when school doors reopened, God smiled upon Sean Sellers. Although Sean and Jennifer attended different schools, they nurtured the relationship they had forged in early summer. They talked by telephone every evening, sharing their separate school lives and whispering adolescent intimacies. On weekends they took long walks, holding hands and gazing at one another until the sun melted into a glinting jack-o'-lantern. And when the moment was just right, Sean would pull Jennifer close, inhaling the fragrant scent of her skin, then softly press his lips against hers. He guarded those days in his memory, merging images of her hair, her eyes, with his nightly dreams.

It wasn't until November—when God seemed to have suddenly changed his mind—that the voices turned against him.

They can't make me do this again.

From the time Vonda and Lee had begun their careers as team drivers, the Bellofattos discovered a unique quality in their relationship. They worked well together. Not only did they enjoy each other's company as they drove across the countryside, but the doors of communication in their marriage stood constantly ajar. During mile after mile, they dreamt, made plans; it seemed to Vonda and Lee at such times, that they had done nothing any other couple wouldn't have done in the quest for a richer life.

But by the time Sean had reached his thirteenth birthday, the Bellofattos had created a pattern in their work habits; a well-trod circle that led them around and around like a weathervane in a storm. That pattern might have been difficult to break even if Vonda and Lee had not been proficient drivers. Nevertheless, their teamwork had paid off, leaving the open highway their most favored option. Now, when the road beckoned again, Vonda and Lee answered.

In 1982 trucking jobs were available across the country. News of open slots for drivers traveled by word of mouth at truck stops and destination points from coast to coast. A homegrown trucking company based in Greeley, Colorado, had debuted as one of America's fastest-growing young companies. Rumor had it that they sought a reliable team to haul produce from Colorado's rich, agricultural hub. For Vonda and Lee, the weathervane of opportunity pointed westward.

They've been making you do it all of your life. How many times has it been now, four, five, maybe?

Sean sat in a corner of Jim's bedroom, his knees pulled to his chest, his hands clasping his cheeks. The nagging voices ticked in his head, bickering between themselves. He was vaguely aware that Jim had settled near him, although the events of his day shifted in fuzzy spurts of recollection.

"I can't do it," Sean whispered. "I just can't do this again."

Jim struggled to find words, any words that would placate his friend. He searched the floor, the ceiling. "You have to, man. They're your folks. What else can you do?"

Sean's brow darkened. "Lee is *not* my father." His foot shook with a frenzied side-to-side motion. His fingers toyed with a stack of record albums. "I guess I could go live with my real dad."

"Come *on*, Sean. He's never even tried to get in touch with you." Jim's face turned quizzical. "He hasn't, has he?"

"Shit." Sean flipped through the pile of records, not consciously seeing any of them. "So what? I don't even remember the asshole." In a gust of anger, he kicked the albums over. *Dark Side of the Moon* somer-saulted, then slid under Jim's dresser.

"Hey man, that's my Pink Floyd."

Sean mumbled and stood. "I'm just so freaked out about this. I can't think straight. Man, I don't even know anyone in Colorado."

"So? You didn't know anybody here either. You'll meet people. I'll come out and see you."

"You just don't understand, man!" Sean threw up his hands and ran them furiously through his hair. "Things have been so great for me here. I met you. I met Jennifer. I don't want to have to start all over again."

Motley Crüe wailed through the silence. Jim's lips parted, a vacuum of reassuring words racing to his mouth, then closed them just as quickly.

"She likes me, man. I mean, she likes me a *lot.*"

"You can write her. It's not like this is forever."

"But . . ." Sean's voice went ragged. He tried to swallow the fleshy knot that bobbed in his throat. His eyes stung. "She said if I left, she never wanted to see me again."

"She'll come around. Give her some time."

"I could stay here and live with you."

Jim paused. He scratched his head. "I don't know. You know how my grandfather is."

"Talk to him. Please, man." An urgency slipped into Sean's voice. His eyes turned cold. "You can make him listen." He turned and restacked the toppled record albums.

Jim murmured something that resembled an apology. Sean's gaze burrowed into him like a flashlight in a cave.

"Listen," Sean said, opening the door. "Try to talk

to him. Just try. Then call me later, okay?" And Jim nodded in agreement. Sean knew there was nothing else he could do but go home. His mother and stepfather would be waiting.

On a nippy Oklahoma morning the Bellofattos plucked their son from his warm bed, his friends at Piedmont, his fantasy world, and went west to Greeley, Colorado. In their continuing search for a slice of the American pie, Vonda and Lee embarked on the road which would seal their destiny.

Greeley is located in the High Plains of Colorado along the South Platte River Basin. In the distance, and to the west, the Rocky Mountains scrape the sky.

As the county seat of Weld County, Colorado, Greeley is one third of a metropolitan triangle that includes Denver and Boulder. At the time of Vonda and Lee's move, the city's population stood at approximately 54,000. With the University of Northern Colorado and Aims Community College at its doorstep, nearly half of Weld County's population is under age twenty-four. During 1982 a low unemployment rate and the emergence of several Fortune 500 companies in the Greeley area triggered an influx of newcomers from all regions of the country.

Although farm production in Weld County continues to rank fourth among all counties in the United States, Greeley has been forced to adapt to the sputtering economy in much the same manner as other agricultural communities. The sprawling region has undergone a dramatic transition from a small-town agricultural center to one of the most industrialized regions of Colorado.

With a relatively low average of three feet of snow in

winter, low humidity, and cool summer nights, tourism is another major source of city revenue. But it wasn't until 1987 that a darker side to Greeley's annual 315 days of sunshine came to light.

For those who choose to validate the rumors that Satanism is a growing force in Weld County, there are stories and sightings that have the potential to curl hair. Farmers, policemen, and school students have been witnesses to a disturbing evil. When the sun slips from the sky and a full moon keeps watch over the city, hooded shadows come out to play.

Sean had to admit that Colorado had a beauty, with snowcapped peaks so tall that all of Oklahoma's hills could fit into one Colorado mountain. Ironically hailed as another "City on the Move," its welcoming sign was a far cry from the one that had ushered him into Ravia. Since then he'd turned over many a mile. He wondered how many. Even the voices could not calculate the number.

In 1983, as Sean neared his fourteenth birthday, Vonda and Lee considered him mature enough to be left alone as they returned to cross-country driving. Sean had shown positive signs of handling responsibility, and his independence had grown fierce. There was no reason to believe that he couldn't care for himself for a few days at a time.

As his parents set off in their eighteen-wheeler, steering the rig in the direction of another paycheck, Sean took comfort in the solitude of his room. Since the move, his mood had steadily darkened. It seemed as though everywhere he looked, he saw churches with stiletto steeples perforating the sky. The sight of them drove nails into him. They reminded him of Jennifer. Sometimes he withdrew into his Piedmont memories: he and Jennifer, holding hands in the sunshine; he and Jim, wrestling playfully on the floor. The mental pictures sent jabs to his heart. They flicked off and on like a slide show. He missed Jim so much it hurt. But Jennifer was the spear that twisted in his gut.

On one particular night the pain became too intense. Sean flipped off the light in his room, immersing himself in darkness, and put a record on the turntable. He closed his eyes. The shrieking rock artist became a torch singer whose garbled words taunted him. The vacuity he had felt long before he'd made any memories wriggled back inside him. He was alone. Again. How could this have happened? What had he done? In an attempt to combat the clouds of dissonance, he walked aimlessly through the house, the voices nipping at his heels. God had done this. God had made this happen.

How many times has it been now, four, five, maybe?

Sean closed his eyes and covered his ears, but he could not escape the memories.

"I hate you, God," he screamed. "Do you hear me? *I hate you!*"

The walls seemed to crash around him, cutting off his air. Sean crumpled to the floor. Where was everyone when you needed them? Just where in the hell *was* God anyway? The slide guitar, sandwiched between a shrill of metal, stabbed the silence.

I'll kill myself. I swear I'll do it.

No, you won't. You're a chickenshit.

Running to his parents' bedroom, he yanked the covers from the bed and scattered clothes across the floor. He thrashed inside their clothes closet, tearing back sweaters, slacks, blouses. He reached through the rack and grabbed the barrel of a rifle. *Lee, the great hunter,* Sean thought sardonically. His stepfather had taken him out to practice on occasion, showed him how to load the gun, cautioned him on safety measures. A true father-and-son kind of thing. "Never, under any circumstances, point the barrel at anyone," Lee had instructed.

And now he'd left the gun in Sean's safekeeping. Because Sean could handle responsibility. Because Sean could certainly care for himself.

Sean carried the gun into the kitchen of the small house. Sitting on a chair, he propped the gun beside him. Its barrel jutted skyward. He leaned the rifle toward him, pointed the barrel at his temple, and curled his finger around the trigger. Then he closed his eyes.

Sean quivered; his teeth chattered like a trick set of choppers. Sweat cloaked his right hand. He didn't want to die. Not *really.* He wiped his palm on his jeans and stood, unable to believe that he had actually begun to pull the trigger. There *had* to be another way to end his agony. And he would find it.

Arriving at John Evans Junior High School was similar to parachuting from an airplane and landing somewhere in the middle of the eighth grade. Although Sean's adoption by Lee had never materialized, he went by the name of Bellofatto, thus bestowing a new name on an old face. He joined the football team and readjusted to the lineup of unfamiliar faces on the practice field. While he never gained much in the way of a brawny build, his agility and speed served the team well.

For the most part, acceptance in Greeley came early. As Sean's confidence returned, his attitude grew increasingly take-charge. And his efforts to win the approval of those in authority succeeded. While he discriminated in the choosing of his Greeley friends, he moved toward those who might be followers, toward a timid crowd that would look to him for leadership. He found, for instance, a petite brunette named Tracie and her best friend, Lori. There also was Dutch, an overweight teenage boy who excelled in mathematics, one of Sean's more difficult subjects.

But during the lull in school activities, he took particular note of a quiet, unassuming student. Solhad Muldani seemed to stick out in the midst of other junior high schoolers.

Solhad had never played Dungeons & Dragons, but his open-mindedness made him easy to teach. Sean covered his new friend with layers of praise and applause. And as the two teenagers lounged in Sean's bedroom, listening to rock music and making casual talk, they plotted their first campaign.

"Here, take this and read it," Sean said matter-of-factly, handing Solhad a book.

"What's this?"

"It's about witches and wizards and stuff. You'll understand this game a lot more if you understand the powers of the characters. There's some unbelievable stuff in there."

Solhad stared at the book. Something about it disturbed him. "Where'd you get this?"

Sean grinned his inimitable grin. "Jim and I bought it in Oklahoma. We used to play Dungeons and Dragons all the time."

"I don't know. Sounds a little weird."

"No, no," Sean said. "It's fun."

Solhad grew apprehensive as Sean dug in his dresser and pulled out his D&D rule book. He had visited Sean's house only twice, but found it difficult to believe that anyone from Oklahoma would be reading such things. Still, there was something about Sean that he liked. He also enjoyed the privacy they had at the Bellofatto home. It was almost like being on his own.

Within a short time Sean's loneliness all but dissipated. Solhad began to replace Jim Mathis. And as other girls began to show their interest, the memory of Jennifer retreated further from his mind. The voices had wafted far away. His ego had ripened. He was once again master of his emotions.

As he gained deeper confidence in his relationships with Tracie, Lori, Dutch, and Solhad, Sean freely shared his goals and insecurities, until they felt obligated to return their own. He had deftly scattered bread crumbs along a projected path for his friends to follow.

Since the day they had first met at school, Sean's timid crowd had clung to every word, every breath that he exhaled. Sean was *different* from the other students. He pursued more eclectic interests. His eyes had a fire unlike anything they had ever seen. It was only natural that when Sean mentioned his curiosity in a local group that held secret meetings, the teenagers' minds raced.

In 1983 it was not unusual for townfolk in Kelim, Colorado, just outside the perimeter of Greeley, to catch glimpses of hooded figures circling midnight bonfires. In an abandoned building dubbed "The Witch," which stands in isolation on the High Plains above town, remnants of Satanic services were frequently discovered. Skinned animals were found strung along the grounds. The number 666 had been scrawled in juvenile handwriting across the building's faded brick. A pentagram and the words "Heavy

Metal" and "I sold my sole [sic] for rock-n-role [sic]" were also engraved on the walls.

On the east side of Greeley, in an old building along the railroad tracks, people have claimed to see a strange blend of muted lights and dancing shadows at the windows. In the past, police have confiscated Satanic paraphernalia from teenagers who gathered in the building. Among the items was a notebook detailing their Satanic rites: ". . . dig up graves, run naked through the streets . . . rape, do dope, steal from a church . . ." Other rituals that were described included the Ceremony of Desecration, which involved spitting on a crucifix and bible, then burning them while the thirteenth chapter of Revelations was read. The chapter prophesizes the coming of the Antichrist.

On a star-lit evening, when the moon sat perfectly round on the edge of the sky, Sean attended his first clan meeting. Behind a curtain of secrecy, the blaze of fire gave dimension to black-robed forms that moved like ghosts in the night. The pungent smell of incense drifted in curling tails of smoke.

As Sean's eyes adjusted to the darkness, he visually memorized the artifacts that lay around him. A silver chalice, black and white candles, a pentagram with a goat's head. The excitement drove volts of electricity through him. *This* was what he wanted. He was passed a cigarette that emitted a thick, sweet aroma. He deeply inhaled its smoke, feeling a sudden tingle. He closed his eyes for a moment and allowed the coven chants to toll in his brain. The words were a bizarre mixture of foreign tongues and hypnotic droning.

When a tall, hooded figure bearing a knife approached him, Sean stretched out his hand.

"Look at the story of Adam and Eve," the figure said

in a hushed voice. "The serpent told them they would have knowledge if they ate of the tree, but God told them *not* to eat the fruit. Yet he put it in the garden to tempt them."

The words reeled in Sean's head. His distinction between good and evil began to blur—the angelical white of the holy converging with an impenetrable black. He felt a sharp sting as air met the gash in his arm. The figure pinched his flesh, urging his blood into the chalice.

"Drink," the figure demanded.

Sean tasted his salty-sweet blood for the first time. He leaned back, and under the fog of the drug, watched the others sip from the goblet. Their tongues lapped across their lips, thirsty to catch the final drops. The marijuana kneaded him now, dulling his senses, sending a shiver across his bones.

Maybe evil *was* good. It was *evil* that set the precedent for *good.* Satan represented sin because sin provided knowledge. And for Sean, knowledge was the key to power.

The notion that he could someday become the priest of his own coven was not incompatible with the ideas that passed through Sean's mind. With Solhad as his able assistant, there was nothing on earth they couldn't accomplish.

In the fall of 1983 Sean and Solhad visited the John Evans Junior High School library in an attempt to amplify their knowledge about the occult. They spent their lunch hours scouting through card catalogs to locate books or magazines, *anything* they could unearth, on the supernatural. The two finally determined that the public library would be the more appropriate place, and on the afternoon that the two teenagers walked through its plate-glass doors, every angel in hell must have stood at attention.

The collection of books on magic, demons, witches, and voodoo were more than food for thought. Sean tilted his head, surveying the volumes that caught his attention.

"I've seen this one on TV," Solhad told him, pulling out a Time-Life publication on dragons, witches, and wizards. "You can order a whole series of this stuff."

Sean ran his hand over the colorful illustration of a velvet-cloaked wizard that graced the cover. "Remember the books I told you about that I read in California?"

Solhad leafed through the pages in a semi-trance. "Yeah, all the stuff about the devil."

"It was great, man. It's like I discovered a whole new world. Look." He pointed to a black-jacketed book and slipped it out from its slot. "This," he said, pointing to the title, "is what I want to read."

"Check it out, then." Solhad's attention remained fixed on his dragon book, skimming the pictures with a child's enthusiasm. "I don't know much about that stuff."

Sean broke from his half-hypnotic state and studied his friend. "That's why we're here," he said. "To learn." He slid the book down the inside of his shirt, then tucked it underneath his arm. His breathing grew hard. Sweat gathered in ripples across his forehead. He had never stolen anything in his life, not even candy at the dime store when he was a little boy. But for some inexplicable reason, he *had* to have the book. Not just on loan, but for keeps.

Solhad watched him, shocked by his friend's attempt to smuggle a book that could just as easily have been checked out.

Sean sauntered from the halls of the library, the rap-a-tat-tat of his heart pulsating in his chest. As he met the glare of afternoon sun, Sean was surprised that no librarians chased him to retrieve the pilfered books. He let out a deep breath, spouting the air from his lungs. Their conspiracy had been successful.

As he turned toward home, his memory of the coven meeting returned to him. He relived the chants that had been hummed, the words spoken. All of his life he had been taught *not* to steal, *not* to lie. It was not his fault that he had begun to be tempted. Sin was every-where, even in the Garden of Eden.

Something happened. The temperature in the room dropped about ten degrees. I got a shot of adrenaline and I felt my blood pressure go up. There was an erotic sensation . . . and sharp, clawed fingers touched me. I opened my eyes . . . there was this mist, and I saw demons flying.

—Sean Sellers, January 1987

FIVE

THE FINE PRINT ON A CONTRACT WITH THE devil has not changed substantially since the birth of Christianity. Its execution still requires a signature in blood. The price is still the debtor's soul.

Many church authorities believe that Satan gives man a choice between good and evil, while God provides man the opportunity to be good by refusing temptation. Satanists advocate the devil as the reason the church exists, that without evil, sin, or temptation, the church would not be necessary.

But the struggle between good and evil existed long before the bible recorded its epic conflict. Preceding his fall from heaven, Satan was the holiest, the smartest, and by far the most exquisite of all angels. Although hypotheses differ as to why he challenged God and was cast out of the holy echelons, it is not disputed that the devil took many other angels with him. Some say as many as one third joined the ranks of rebellion.

Soon rumors of the creation of man circulated, which presented Satan with a grand opportunity for revenge. Slithering through the Garden of Eden in the form of a serpent, he flattered Eve into conversation and told her that he had learned to talk by eating of the Tree of Knowledge—a fruit that God forbade Adam and his wife to eat. Eve fell prey to the serpent's diabolical temptation, but she was not alone in her sin. Man continued to stray from God's path, and the devil continued to tempt the whole of mankind.

In the forerunner religions to Christianity, as early as the third century B.C., man found himself lured in opposite directions. Members of these religions were dazzled by primitive magic, which served as the foundation for their practices. Sacrificial rituals, based upon magical beliefs, were conducted to induce sexual fertility for childbearing. Participants relied on the reading of stars—foretelling of the future—and prayer to solve troubles or satisfy curiosities. Magic spells, medical formulae, hymns to the gods, and astrological instructions were devices that provided acceptable answers to unexplained phenomena, such as sickness and natural disaster. The question of whether their religious tenets were right or wrong, good or evil, bore no relevance.

With the revolution of Christianity, however, good and evil became two distinctively separate forces with which man had to reckon. Devils and angels, heaven and hell, emerged with powerful definition. The literal existence of demons also evolved in preachings. These invisible spirits traveled eternally through the air, causing disease, storms, hunger, and feelings of dread for which no logical explanation sufficed. To terrify congregations, the drawings of evil spirits, devils, demons, and Satanic monsters were decorated on church walls. For Christians the devil became a ferocious entity, ready to snatch them up should they waver from the principles of the almighty deity.

Aside from his role as God's adversary, Satan represented rebellion. Power, control, and sexual freedom could be attained through the devil. For those who desired the indulgences that Satan offered, the answer was simple. If a congregationalist no longer seemed satisfied with what the church offered, worshiping the devil became a fulfilling alternative. The mystery religion of the occult was suddenly demoted to the ranks of the forbidden.

For most, that is where it remained.

In late 1983 Sean Sellers' adolescence became his ally. When he peered into the mirror, he no longer felt the thorny prick of insecurity because of a nose that appeared too bulbous or a measlelike complexion. He no longer saw a clumsy misfit who had no friends and struggled to belong. The boy who stared back from the looking glass wore a handsome face, almost virginal, framed by dark blond hair. An innocent sensuality chiseled the corners of his mouth, and his eyes glistened with the afterglow of affection he'd found in Colorado.

The mirror became Sean's comrade, reassuring him at every glance. His body had grown lean but muscular, leaving behind only the faintest trace of his boyhood shell. The eyes in the mirror watched with calculation. The secrets he guarded set him apart from the rest of the world like a rare piece of bone china.

Sean recognized the difference in himself. He possessed a gift for controlling everyone with whom he came in contact. He maintained the posture of a perfect son by day, complying with everything expected of him at school and at home. At night he assumed another identity.

Sean's study of the occult reaped numerous fringe benefits. Drugs and sex were earthly rewards that he'd earned. The more he scanned his books, studied the symbolic drawings, and recited the devil's creed, the richer his compensations became. His sexuality burned with a lightning-quick intensity. At night he gathered together with his fellow disciples, mingling with their warm bodies on the frigid November earth. Female shadows twisted and writhed below him until their energies burst in delirious unison. His sexual prowess sharpened like the edge of a razor. In Satanism, Sean discovered an incredible love.

Vonda and Lee were pleased by their son's independence while they were on the road. He had seemingly blossomed from a young teenager into a responsible young adult. His initiative in taking over household duties reached far beyond that of a fourteen-year-old boy. The Bellofattos were frequently welcomed home to a spotlessly clean house and dinner simmering on the stove. They never worried whether their absence affected Sean's academic disciplines. Vonda and Lee's expectations of their son—both in his chores at home and his schoolwork—were no secret. His honor-roll status gave testimony to their demands that he attain the highest scholastic levels.

In 1984, as spring hastened to the Colorado tundra, the Bellofattos were obliged to make longer road trips. While Vonda and Lee had to adjust to business demands, the week-long and even two-week jaunts across the U.S. placed a growing strain on the family. They discussed the adversities of the trucker's life, the tediousness of double-wide sleepers and cheap motels, and the guilt over the increasingly long stretches Sean faced alone. But Sean never complained about his isolation. He assured them that he had plenty of school and sports activities with which to occupy his time. Nevertheless, he couldn't change their decision to make him move yet again.

Torn between the loyalty to his friends and duty to his parents, Sean packed in March for yet another stopover—this time in Okmulgee, Oklahoma, 25 miles south of Tulsa. The Bellofattos promised him that his stay with Vonda's half sister, Jere Ricks, her husband Doyle, and their two small sons would be temporary.

Although every reason existed for Sean to suspect that Greeley would not be a permanent home, his ties had become cemented in Colorado. During the last year and a half he had made more friends than he ever had over his fifteen years, and any teenager would have envied the freedom he'd enjoyed while his parents were gone. But now he was repeating an old pattern.

The Ricks opened their home and their hearts to Sean. Although Vonda and Jere had had different fathers, they were extremely close to their now deceased mother, and their ties to each other ran deep. But since Sean's previous visits to the Rickses had been impromptu family reunions, he could not help but feel like a stranger to his aunt and uncle—an intruder hurled into a family he hardly knew. Still, he discovered an immediate camaraderie with the children. The squeal and chatter of his cousins, ages four and six, provided him with an opportunity to rehash memories, to relive moments in time that he'd buried years before.

Jere and Doyle were determined to provide a stable, comfortable environment for the teenager who since the age of four had not spent more than two years in any one town. For Sean, life with the Rickses proved to be like the movie *American Graffiti*. There were well-balanced meals, Saturday-night movies and pizza parlors. There were high school drag races along the town's main strip, and nightly assemblies in parking lots. Yet none of these calmed his restlessness. The blandness of eastern Oklahoma made him long for the excitement of Greeley, Colorado.

Even in a rural community such as Okmulgee, teenage vices were readily available for a price. Marijuana, speed, Valium, and beer were in local abundance if one knew the in crowds. Soon Sean revealed his wily talent for sniffing out the proper contacts.

Spring semester at Okmulgee's junior high school was the prelude to a major disappointment. From Sean's vantage point, the students, classes, and teachers were mediocre. He kept to himself, daydreaming about his life in Colorado while the chilly fingers of depression stroked his insides. In between the longing for his friends and his yen for the titillating night life that had scorched him like hot coals, Sean's first drinking binges began.

Alcohol became the substitute for all that he deemed lacking in his teenage life. Booze reinstated his confidence, sealed the cavity that gaped inside him. He ached to hear the master's voice, for he knew that Satan waited for him as well. The scars on his forearms were bittersweet reminders of the knife that had baptized him with his own blood. In his memory he gulped from the chalice, savoring the taste of himself. Wallowing in fantasy, he imagined plunging the dagger into Solhad's flesh, then reeling from the spurts of blood that leaped and splattered across his face. In his fantasies, Solhad thanked him, begged him to drink his blood. Sean licked hungrily, swallowing the liquid that would hallow them as the devil's children.

Each time he snapped to reality, Sean ran his hands over his face, envisioning the crimson beads sluicing down his cheeks. The vision animated him, and soon he had molded and shaped a terrifying plan—one that called for his soulmates in Greeley. But he had to find a way to return to Colorado. Satan wanted him there.

When he awoke from his reveries, sober and solemn, life in Okmulgee seemed more gray than ever. The longer Sean lived there, the more his mind plagued him with unanswerable questions.

Why was he flung from place to place like a boomerang? Didn't his parents care about him? Why had his mother and stepfather dumped him on the Rickses' doorstep like an orphan? Their reasons crumbled like a shaky pillar of Tinker Toys. Still, Sean maintained a facade of charm and bravado. He moved about as though things were as well as they would ever be. But in the Rickses' house, all was not well. With an ever-present smile, Sean examined the Ricks family unit as though he watched from a high balcony—despising their closeness.

A part of the good little boy remained, however. When Jere asked him to stay home more often, he consented, though secretly resolving to escape at every opportunity. The modest dwelling had come to represent a tomb to him. In fact, Sean spent less and less time with his young cousins; he could no longer tolerate their chatter.

In the evenings he paced his room like a caged animal. He visualized cold, metal bars across his bedroom windows. Slices of moonlight beckoned him like peepshows—teasing, yet out of his grasp. He had his music, his schoolwork, his reading material, but he lusted for something more.

Sean had long ago tired of the same old television sitcoms and drama. Watching television with the Rickses sickened him. He preferred movies, especially the horror films that fulfilled his longing for the excitement he could find nowhere else. The plots offered him something far more infectious than the life he had suffered since the Greeley days. He identified with the more carefree characters—such as vampires—who, no matter how sadistic, never had to answer to anyone.

After his dive into a horror flick, the old Sean crept back. The Dungeons & Dragons Sean. It no longer mattered that Vonda had not wanted him to play the game. Or that she abhorred his watching blood magnified in vivid color on the theatre screen. It didn't matter because she was not around.

Spending most of his hours at the Okmulgee public library, Sean pored over books whose topics inoculated him with a new fascination—demonology. Here, he delved into an odyssey of beasts and the circuits of hell's hierarchy. Here, he rededicated himself to Satan, feeding his imagination with infernal delicacies. Of the 1111 legions of incubi and succubi that existed, Sean discovered that each demon retained specific powers. He also learned that if he exercised control over the demons, calling them by both their proper names and their nicknames, the creatures could be subdued to grant the commander his wish. Demons were reluctant to be summoned by mortal man, and often appeared in the form of beast, serpent, or a combination of man and animal, to terrify the summoner.

Sean's interest in goetic or "black" magic had only begun to grow. A new dimension to his knowledge of the occult wouldn't be added in the spring of 1986. During a family get-together, a nephew of Lee's introduced Sean to the Japanese assassin rites of Ninjitsu. As Lee's nephew dressed in the hooded, black costume of the ancient mystical warrior, which left only the eyes exposed, Sean perceived an arousing parallel to the rituals he had experienced in Greeley.

The Rickses were aware that Sean kept in close contact with his friends out west. He obviously cared a great deal for the companions he'd left behind. But that was not atypical of their polite nephew. Sean displayed respect for Jere and Doyle, and they had no quarrels with him while his parents were on the road. They thought that considering their long absences, Vonda and Lee had raised their son well. He cleaned his room without being asked and pitched in with other household taskwork. The Rickses never suspected their nephew's drinking habits, his use of amphetamines and marijuana, or his Satanic interests. Nor could they have imagined the bizarre content of the letters he mailed to Greeley. To them, Sean was the quintessential perfect young man.

At the close of his ninth grade in Okmulgee, Sean welcomed an invitation to visit Solhad in Colorado during the summer of 1984. Vonda and Lee consented to their son's traveling west for a three-week visit, partly because their plans to again move the family to

Greeley were taking shape. It was to be the best summer of Sean's life.

In late June westerly winds that sweep through Colorado are interrupted by tropical air from the south, or by warm, surface chinook winds descending the eastern slopes of the Rockies. A sudden rise in temperature is common, although the average heat index for summer is mild. For days on end a mammoth sun hovers from the roof of a Mediterranean-blue sky.

In 1984 reports of Satanic activity near Weld County's Oklahoma Lake had diminished, but the mysterious movements inside the abandoned building along the railroad tracks increased. Teenage skullduggery was again gossiped about over backyard fences and appeared in reports on the desks of Greeley police. Animals were found bludgeoned; high school students, clutching a *Satanic Bible* to their breasts, preached to fellow classmates; notebooks containing music lyrics that spoke of suicide, pain, and death were prevalent among area students.

The reunion of Sean and Solhad Muldani went better than they had both anticipated. The teenagers bubbled over with smiles and shouts of glee. The sight of the lofty mountain peaks, the feel of the Colorado air, and the joy of friendship all merged. For the past six months, Sean had endured the Rickses' hospitality, biding his time while perfecting his Satanic craft; secretly deriding his parents, whom he could reach neither physically or emotionally. And all along, he had waited.

When Solhad's parents greeted Sean with enthusiasm, he knew that the coming weeks would be full of fun and freedom. He no longer would have to pretend that he was happy and contented with the crimped lifestyle of small-town, U.S.A. He no longer would have to rely on memories, real or imagined. Nor would he have to get high alone or drink himself into oblivion. He was home.

Within a few days Sean and his Greeley friends banded together again. Just past the midnight hour the summer heat dropped to a warm 76 degrees. In the hollows of a shabby, decayed building, Dutch assured the group that they would be undisturbed. Darkness swam in thick, opaque rivers, and distorted, animal-shaped shadows yawned against the walls. Beneath the flicker of candlelight, furry rodents scattered into hidden crevices. Cobwebs sparkled like spun silk. Sour air sank from the ceiling. Tracie lit a joint, inhaled its smoke, and passed it to the others.

Sean readied himself to administer his first Satanic baptism, a ceremony that he had planned while in Okmulgee. He had detailed almost everything for this night in his letters, delegating responsibilities to each of his friends. Most of the items they brought for the baptism were either stolen or borrowed from unsuspecting parents. Sean pronounced the objects religious artifacts that he would retain for safekeeping. He prepared a makeshift altar, adorned the elevated table with a sheet of black cloth, then circled it with black and white candles. He placed a silver goblet atop the black cover, not far from a gleaming, two-sided sword, then dressed in his black robe.

Kneeling before the altar, Sean closed his eyes and silently prayed. Dutch approached him. Sean stood and faced his pledge. "Repeat after me," he instructed. "I swear allegiance to the powers of darkness and desire. Through me, Satan shall reign supreme on earth once again."

Clothed in a long white robe, Dutch bent his heavy, jiggling body. He fell to his knees, repeating Sean's words. He had patiently waited for Sean to return, thirsty to join the covert group who didn't think of him as a mongrel—a fat boy with few redeeming qualities. He'd answered all of Sean's letters, promised to gather the items they would need for the baptism, even if it meant stealing them. Satan would glorify him for his exploits. Sean had told him so.

"No more shall the names of Lucifer be defied. And within this newborn family shall all blossoms of truth unite." Sean held the sword like a samurai warrior; his gaze burned the white-robed pledge. "Strip," he commanded. Dutch disrobed in silence. "Even as my bodily strength wanes shall my mind burst free from proclaiming death to the weak, wealth to the strong."

Dutch held out his arm. He stiffened in anticipation and fear. Sean slid the sword across the teenager's waxen flesh, his eyes wild and venomous. Dutch winced with pain. The hairs on his body bristled as the blade pierced him. Blood raced to the cut in his arm, flushing his skin dark red.

Sean smiled. His teeth glinted a startling white. He pressed the wound and lowered the goblet beneath Dutch's arm, careful to catch each precious drop. "As a group we shall bloom as a flower," he chanted. "The flower shall have thorns, and I shall be one of these thorns to prick out the eyes of those who refuse to believe." He drank from the chalice and passed the cup to Dutch in a Satanic Eucharist.

Dutch quaffed his blood as though quenching a parched throat. The biting sting of his wound subsided as he watched the others sip from the chalice. The iron in his blood would magnetize inside the bodies of his friends and perpetuate the powers now vested in him. They, too, would receive the devil's blessing.

Sean's Satanic devotees convened nearly every night in tribute to the devil. Their interpretations of communions, black masses and baptisms could hardly be considered replicas of the more sophisticated Satanic churches across the nation, but the devotion to their art nonetheless flowed with a zealous faith.

Curious teens who searched for nighttime activities in the break between school semesters were easy recruits for Greeley covens. While twilight fell and stars rose across the sky, unsuspecting parents entertained each other with cocktail parties or reclined with spouses for evenings of summer tranquility. Few gave second thoughts to the evils that hid behind corners and in vacant alleys, waiting for their children. After all, the teens who fell victim to crime and drugs were always someone else's kids. *Their* children, the children of Greeley, went to slumber parties or visits with school friends to giggle over teenage romances and groan over the impending fall semester. The idea that fourteen- or fifteen-year-olds drank to excess and dabbled in drugs amidst devil worship seemed too remote to be taken seriously. The idea that children would mutilate themselves for blood offerings to Satan would have seemed ridiculous.

The covens in Greeley not only enticed junior high and high school students with offers of free drugs and provocative distractions, they reeled them in like fish caught on a trout line.

During Sean's last week in Colorado, he successfully completed each task that he'd planned from his exile in Okmulgee. Dutch, Lori, and Tracie were baptized and proclaimed acolytes deserving of the black robes limited to prescribed members. But the group found themselves short of black material from which to assemble the necessary garments. Although Vonda and Lee had furnished Sean with enough money for his trip, he had spent most of it on drugs. Drastic measures were called for.

Sean Sellers never lacked in creative thinking. He entered a Greeley department store, casually strolled to the notions and material section, and selected a bolt of black cotton fabric. No one would believe that he was anything other than a stock boy transferring merchandise from one end of the store to the other, but he had to be inconspicuous. He looked to either side of the aisle. Shoppers busied themselves with store items or infants. Clerks hustled about, straightening and folding goods and assisting customers.

Sean hefted the bolt of cloth to his shoulder. His heart thumped in frantic rhythm. No heads turned in his direction; no eyes fixed on him as he walked from the department and moved swiftly through the store. Staring straight ahead at the plate-glass doors, he brushed past the bed and bath department, home appliances and kitchenware, his chest bulging with confidence. The front doors approached, urging him on. *Hurry, Sean! Hurry before someone catches you!* Somehow the doors reminded him of his visit to the Greeley public library, where he'd stuffed a book inside his shirt and his blood had pumped with the thrill of danger. He was the Ninja warrior—invisible to the eye, silent to the ear, transparent to the touch.

A voice behind him halted his steps. "Excuse me, sir."

Sean froze. Two hands clamped his shoulders and spun him around. The door swung open so close to him that he felt a breath of wind whish across his face as a customer exited the store. Suddenly his body grew hot and rigid. His mind scrambled for any explanation he could concoct. Traces of sweat beaded across his brow. He gazed into the icy, black eyes of a security guard and surrendered the bolt of material.

Despite the fact that store officials called police, who transported the juvenile shoplifter to the Greeley Police Department, Sean's calm demeanor did not falter. He'd become accomplished in assuming the guise of naiveté. His good looks and intelligence betrayed no signs of a delinquent. Sean maintained that his deed was merely a childish prank that his friends had put him up to. Yes, he was guilty of poor judgment and had exhibited a tremendous lack of prudence. No, he had never considered the consequences of his behavior, but he'd learned a valuable lesson.

The police weighed Sean's admission of guilt and rendered a few stern words. They had little alternative. The teenager was in Greeley on summer vacation. His parents couldn't be contacted, but he had no prior record. In their eyes he was probably a good kid who had tangled with a bad crowd. They notified Jere Ricks in Okmulgee of his misdemeanor, slapped his wrist with a warning, and sent the fifteen-year-old on his way. He was neither formally arrested nor charged.

Sean left the police station without having to make so much as a court appearance.

His time in Greeley was running out.

In less than two days Sean would return to the austere environment of Okmulgee. Back to his aunt and uncle. Back to his purgatory. His summer in Colorado would become yet another memory. His minutes with Solhad tunneled like grains sifting through an hourglass. The echoes of Jere and Doyle, chastising him for his legal entanglement, meshed with the alcohol in his stomach and the marijuana that buzzed in his head.

Sean had not heard from Vonda and Lee during his summer vacation. He supposed they were too busy to be bothered with him. But his parents' concern for him—or their lack of it—no longer bothered him. During his stay with Solhad he made a decision that gave him something to live for. Vonda and Lee condoned his decision making, left his lifestyle to him.

Two nights of pleasure awaited him in Colorado, and his determination to make full use of his remaining hours helped him to prepare. The loneliness and contempt he would face in Okmulgee could be staved off. The climate of the Rickses' home, which suffocated his personality, would be forever altered by his decision. They could not do anything to him once his act became final.

Inside the abandoned building Sean, Dutch, Lori, and Tracie met for a final ode to Satan. That night Sean slit his forearm with the sword and squeezed his blood into the chalice. The others watched with glacial stares, mesmerized by their leader. On a piece of paper he scrawled a sacred oath that would forever unite him with all the powers of hell—powers to transact the devil's work, to invoke fear and trepidation. The power to make him the most *dangerous* person in the world. Sealing an unbreakable bond between himself and Satan, he scribbled his name in blood at the bottom of the page.

Sean Richard Sellers had, in a moment of exhortation and jubilation, sold his soul to the devil.

I don't know why I drank so much blood. I kept a jar of my blood in the refrigerator at home, hidden behind the eggs, and I carried blood with me all the time and drank it a lot . . . I was like a vampire, I guess. I think I might have developed a craving for blood.

—Sean Sellers, January 1987

SIX

ON ST. PATRICK'S DAY, 1988, SOME NINE YEARS after Sean Sellers discovered the devil's mystique, rumors of Satanism emerged from the sleepy, northeastern Oklahoma town of Cleveland. Local ministers contacted an occult expert who traveled from Kentucky to investigate the unholy reasons for Cleveland's gossip. It appeared as though the devil had launched yet another satellite station from his West Coast nerve center.

Amidst television crews and newspaper reporters, residents crowded inside the First Christian Church in an effort to vent fears and satisfy curiosities about an unbelievable practice that had arrived in their town. Doodlings of goats' heads, pentagrams, and inverted crosses on student notebooks, evidence of Satanic material in school lockers, and a consistent withdrawal of library occult books created a climate of fear among residents. Using bibles and Christian faith, parents, teachers, and children were reintroduced to an entity most had only known through biblical preachings.

Whether or not evil had indeed infiltrated Cleveland on March 17, the individuals who huddled on church pews were desperate to understand the hoopla dominating newscasts and front-page headlines across the state. A Satanic fascination had arisen in Oklahoma. How had this happened?

If the less than 3000 residents of Cleveland were skeptical of the existence of Satanism, the occult expert from Kentucky verified the devil's movement in America. In its more organized form of ornate temples and chanting congregations, the concept of Satanism seemed light-years from Cleveland, a lake resort not thirty miles from Tulsa. Local citizens were hardly accustomed to the telltale signs of occult activities. From their viewpoint, Satanism was a religion confined to larger metropolitan cities, far from the values of a God-fearing town. What Cleveland didn't know was that the Satanist philosophy had given birth to an extension of devil worship—one that didn't require a cosmopolitan environment or a tabernacle. The community had no inkling that self-styled Satanism also occurs in the most unlikely areas of the country. In the 1980s it emerged in the Bible Belt.

Teenagers have found this interpretation of the Left Path to be an especially tantalizing route in channeling adolescent energies. Heavy-metal rock and roll, and ritualistic sex and drugs, provide an emotional gratification—a psychological rush—that is the bedrock for new and improved versions of Satanism. With few rules, self-styled Satanism fuels teenage fantasies with a reckless abandon to entice America's youth.

As statistics and media reports prove, there are more than a few young people who actively seek out the extraordinary and the bizarre, including young people who otherwise appear to obey the laws and rules of society. Who even go out of their way to do all the things looked upon with favor and pride. Who struggle to please those in authority so that their real secrets and desires will not be discovered. An internal void—a search for control over that which is missing from their lives—drives them deeper into Satan's clutches. The "rush" they receive becomes far too pleasing to forget. For these individuals, a fifteen-minute bloodletting service is at first satisfying. Then a little more blood is required. Then a little more. As the excitement wears thin, more excitement is needed, until the height of frenzy itself becomes the obsession. The more evil they do, the more evil is necessary to replace the emotional "high." Remorse does not even enter the picture.

Most self-styled Satanic groups limit their evil-doing to lesser acts of aggression—stealing religious artifacts and slaughtering animals. But murder and suicide in the name of the dark lord does happen, and a small percentage of self-styled Satanists have crossed this last barrier and paid the ultimate homage to the devil.

For nearly six years Vonda and Lee Bellofatto had crossed the United States, probing for the opportunity that would advance them financially. Their eyes wide with expectation, they wended the open freeway like pathfinders on an exploration that seemed never to end. The Bellofattos continued to search for that one avenue that would deposit them on the banks of prosperity and secure them a future for the family. Their professional goals were not unrealistic; financial security always lurked right around the corner. But in 1984, no matter how hard they tried, Vonda and Lee could not accomplish their aim. In fact, paycheck figures didn't even offset expenses incurred on and off the road.

When the family reassembled in Greeley, summer brought a final breath of warm air. As northern winds chased August into September, the Bellofattos took up residence in a local two-bedroom apartment. Vonda and Lee were thrilled to have their son living with them again, and readjustment to a stable dwelling proved a surprising relief. Though their original plans for nurturing a close family unit had been delayed, Vonda seized the chance to make up for lost time with her son. The slowdown of freight shipments prompted two- and three-day trucking hauls that permitted the Bellofattos frequent time at home—an extravagance they hadn't known for quite a while. Neither Vonda or Lee could recall ever seeing Sean so happy.

Years behind the wheel of a rig extended few kindnesses, but life had basically been good to Lee Bellofatto. Gentle lines fanned from the corners of his brown eyes, punctuating his forty-one years. Flecks of gray peppered his dark hair, giving him a striking appearance. Lee had managed to retain his lean build despite the minimal exercise truck driving afforded, but his health showed some signs of slippage. The heaviness in his chest and shortness of breath were blamed on greasy diner foods and chain-smoking—two indulgences he found impossible to avoid when on the road.

While Lee's marriage to Vonda had endured miles of endless highway, he was not oblivious to the sacrifices they were forced to make in order to earn a living. That the Bellofatto's livelihood demanded immeasurable travel was a burden that occupied his mind, and nibbled at his conscience. The fact remained that there were few options available for Vonda and Lee in the work world, and the emotional loads that cross-country driving required had become difficult.

With the family together once more, Lee reassumed his position as head of the household, husband and father, closing the fissure that had been allowed to widen between parent and child. Lee was proud of his stepson. He often boasted to family and friends about Sean's high grades and how independent he had grown. It appeared that Sean would follow in Lee's footsteps and seek a military career. The boy looked up to him, depended on Lee for approval and guidance. But Sean's shoplifting escapade provoked a twinge of guilt in Lee as Sean's stepfather. Although Vonda brushed aside Sean's stealing as a teenage problem, Lee saw it differently—that Sean was crying out for attention. And most of the time, the Bellofattos were too far away to hear him.

On August 13, Vonda turned thirty-one. Reflections on the past and thoughts of what might have been filled her with a gnawing disappointment. She wondered if she'd wasted the best years of her life running after a dream she was never meant to attain.

Vonda could not imagine her life without Lee. But over the past months, the Bellofatto's financial situation had ignited more than one argument. Never enough money, never enough time. She also waged internal battles of her own. Self-criticisms plagued her conscience. She should have been a better mother. She should have made better decisions. Yet every choice she had made was for the sake of her son. She wanted to earn a better living so that her little boy could have everything he needed. She wanted him to grow up to be honest, happy, and successful. Still, how could she teach him those qualities if she wasn't with him? What happened to the family togetherness she'd always hoped for?

What had her family become? she must have wondered. There was little Norman Rockwell simplicity there. While Lee was still as handsome to her as the day they had exchanged wedding vows, he had absorbed every ounce of discontent that had seeped into their lives. And Sean kept to himself, damming up his feelings in empty silence. Uncertainty had settled over the family, eroding the promise that Vonda, Lee, and Sean would find their happy ending.

If Sean was aware of his parents' troubles, of their concern for the family's future, he never questioned their plans or motives, never asked where he fit in or if he fit in at all. Instead he thought of himself as a kind of house guest—one who might be allowed to remain with Vonda and Lee if the situation permitted. There was little permanency to life with Mom and Dad, and subconsciously Sean had conditioned himself to accept his parents' decisions with little afterthought. He had numbed himself. For a time he had oscillated between the good little boy who grappled for an affection that couldn't be reached and the barren side of himself that was reconciled to love's absence. Finally the pendulum found its resting point, and Sean emptied his emotions in a vortex of nothingness. He could never, would never, be hurt again.

One desire remained. His move back to Greeley had not only reunited him with his friends, it brought him closer to the master. Relinquishing his soul to the devil had dividends, and Sean had just begun to explore the temptations that awaited him in body and spirit.

His sophomore year at Greeley Central High School held some of his fondest memories. At the suggestion of Lee, he joined the local Civil Air Patrol, a civilian auxiliary of the U.S. Air Force that supports the Civil Defense and American Red Cross disaster relief programs. Since its inception, over half of the Civil Air Patrol participants have been junior high and high school students. At first Sean was reluctant to part with his free time, especially for a stringent, military-type training. But one particular program captured his interest—a mission that permitted cadets to serve in staff positions.

Sean lost no time in becoming qualified under the National Emergency Assistance Training, an achievement he valued highly, one in which he took special pride. His instruction included reacting to dangerous situations and learning life-saving techniques. For all intents and purposes, he could now save a human life. An air of intrigue surrounded his Civil Air Patrol superiors, who Sean imagined protected military secrets in much the same way he safeguarded his own secrets. His attraction to military discipline reflected his conduct at home.

When Sean was promoted to colonel, the highest classification he could aspire to for his length of duty, Vonda and Lee beamed. And when he was honored as Outstanding Cadet, it seemed that he had returned to his All-American boy status. The leader. A winner. In the intimacy of the family unit, the Bellofattos failed to see that their son rotated between a reverent, almost patriotic attitude and a rebellion that skimmed along the fringes of psychopathy.

Not long after his induction into the Greeley Civil Air Patrol, Sean's attraction to Ninjitsu increased. He discovered a bizarre alignment between his responsibility as a soldierly hero and the precision-weighed danger that existed in the Japanese art form. Ninjitsu represented an inflexible concentration of the human senses—a cosmic power that could only be achieved through skill and control. Sean taught Solhad the disciplined exercise, tutoring him with books, magazines, and Japanese weaponry. As the teenagers delved into the Eastern practice, their friendship became even closer.

Meanwhile, Vonda and Lee were determined to teach their son parental respect. This, they believed, could only be taught by firm instruction on the homefront. They refused to allow any outside interferences with his household duties and chores. Dinner was on the table at a prompt hour; laundry was sorted, washed, and dried on certain days of the week; the kitchen and bathrooms were regularly scrubbed.

Sean's outside manner remained subservient, pleasant, without complaint. He complied with every demand. When Vonda lingered on the telephone, chatting with friends or family, Sean ran around picking up clothes, straightening the living room, bringing her glasses of iced tea, just like a good son should. And each time Vonda cited his responsibilities, Sean smiled his Sunday best, tireless and eager to please. Just like a good son.

Yet sometime during late fall, Sean ordained himself

a Satanic priest of his own coven. By the end of 1984, his coven had grown to seven members. Blood never ceased to play the starring role in his secret life, and he eagerly anticipated baptism ceremonies that required the unspoiled blood of a fledgling worshiper. He savored the moment when each member tasted of their new "brother" or "sister" and dedicated themselves as one in the name of the devil. Drugs had become a necessity in rituals, and frequently led to pairings of members who unified their bodies in a sexual delirium. Under the haze of hallucination, Nirvana was born.

Two years later townfolk would report that the hierarchs of the six main northern Colorado covens continued to meet each Sunday. In a Greeley restaurant, the leaders convened to discuss coven activities with an overall leader who called himself Lucifer.

As winter arrived in Colorado, bloodletting and chanting to Satan, even the group orgies, grew mundane for Sean. In shadows and candleglow, he searched for higher planes of eroticism. On one chilly afternoon he browsed through a local bookstore, scanning the occult section. *Necromonicon* leaped to his attention. Offering the dead to the devil was one of the most exciting concepts to ever cross his mind. He could hardly wait to see the expressions on his disciples' faces when he told them of his idea to pillage a grave.

One evening before the coven gathered, Sean discussed his idea with Solhad. He explained the wisdom they would gain from experimentation with the dead, the power that awaited. And, oh, how the master would be pleased. Necromancy fanned embers in Sean's gut—embers eager to burst into flame.

At last he was ready. Leaning against the wall of the coven church, Sean smiled as his acolytes filed in front of him and took their places. When they quieted, he leaned forward. His eyes frosted, locking their gazes.

"I have a very special surprise," he whispered. "For all of you."

I had rituals every night and invited the demons into my body. There was a persona—not a person, but a persona —of another; created by the demons and completely evil.

—Sean Sellers, January 1987

SEVEN

THE ROOTS OF NECROMANCY, OR COMMUNI-cating with the spirits of the dead, can be traced as far back as 730 A.D. to the "Mad Arab" of Damascus, Abdul Alhzared. An early-day sorcerer, Alhzared compiled a diary of incantations and instructions for unlocking "Four Gates," which he believed prevented the dead from reentering the world. Fearful that he might not complete his testimony before his death, the Mad Arab bequeathed to man a horrifying revelation of the evils waiting to rule the earth:

And if I do not finish this task, take what is here and discover the rest, for time is short and mankind does not know or understand the evil that awaits it, from every side, from every open gate, from every broken barrier, from every mindless acolyte at the altars of madness . . .

I have found fear. I have found the gate that leads to the Outside, by which the Ancient Ones, who ever seek entrance to our world, keep eternal watch.

—The Necromonicon

Over the centuries, curiosity about the world of the dead has often appeared; in the ceremonial "magick" of Aleister Crowley, for example, and the tales of H. P. Lovecraft. The Mad Arab's book of incantations for evoking demons and consulting with the dead to foretell the future weaved its way through the lives of both Crowley and Lovecraft, although the two men never actually met.

Aleister Crowley has been considered one of the most famous of all practicing Satanists. Claiming to bear the mark of the Beast, he added the numerals 666 to his name. A magician, Crowley claimed to be the apotheosis of an Ancient One who had received a "message" dictating a new system of life based upon his "magick."

The fiction of H. P. Lovecraft has appealed to the imaginations of millions of devoted followers, who have dubbed him the "Father of Gothic Horror." The author's fascination with primeval forces crept into his bizarre stories of science fiction and the supernatural, culminating with his essay, "A History of the Necromonicon."

The long-lost manuscript that documented Abdul Alhzared's walk with the dead eventually evolved into *The Necromonicon*, a book whose acknowledgments credit researchers, translators, temptors, and even a demon. By those individuals whom the book says "waited and waited for the eventual publication of this tomb with bated breath . . . and something on the stove," *The Necromonicon* has been proclaimed a masterpiece of the occult.

Sean Sellers found the Book of the Dead still another fantasy of danger, and *The Necromonicon* became a prized tool in his collection of orphic literature. His pact with the devil had led him to a menu of forbidden delicacies, but Sean's captivation with demons was the most enticing. He began his ascent up the ladder of the occult, relishing each rung along the way.

But before Sean and his flock could implement their gravesite plans, before any of Greeley's dead could be disturbed from their interment, Vonda and Lee filed bankruptcy papers and announced a move to Oklahoma City. The Bellofattos were eager for a fresh start, a career that would take them away from truck lines, gloomy motels, and days and nights of separation from their son. Lee lined up a job in Edmond, Oklahoma, which promised regular hours and minimal overtime. While his salary would not support a Harvard education for his stepson, it would pay the bills and provide Vonda with a work break. Vonda would at last have her family together. Sean would enjoy a proper home, home-cooked meals, a mother and father.

It would be the last move the family made.

Sean, however, didn't accept the news well. His time in Greeley had been interrupted again. Didn't his parents realize how happy he was in Colorado? Couldn't they understand that he'd made friendships—the only true friends he'd ever known? His feelings about them had changed: Year after countless year, Vonda and Lee sucked him into their motley plans for a better life.

They traipsed across the U.S., stashed him with relatives for months, then transported him to another location as if he were a piece of cargo.

In Oklahoma City the Bellofattos settled in a two-bedroom duplex in a subdivision known as Summit Place. Lee began work as a diesel mechanic for a company less than thirty minutes from home. Vonda enjoyed a brief hiatus from the work world. Content to rest from the endless interstates, she made new friends and reclaimed her duties in the household.

Sean's dismay at the family upheaval did not wane as quickly as Vonda had hoped. Less than a week before Christmas he enrolled in Putnam City North High School. But as the holidays approached, he isolated himself in his bedroom, buried between the pages of books that seemed foreign to Vonda. He resurrected his artistic talents, sketching strange, hooded faces and symbols she didn't understand. His mood brightened only when Vonda's father called to check on the family's move. Jim Blackwell could lift his grandson's spirits with a simple hello.

Unable to ventilate his anger, Sean held his inner bubble of hostility in check, reassured those around him. His dreams became nighttime depositories for the emotions that whirled inside him. Oklahoma City could not compare with Greeley. Oklahoma's icy winter stretched into a miserable eternity. He joined the city's Civil Air Patrol, but that, too, struck him as a cruel joke. To combat his depression he threw himself into his schoolwork, and in particular, a drama class. Sean became one of the best student actors at Putnam City North. When he revived his friendship with Jim Mathis, his anxieties over leaving Greeley eased. The two teenagers were once again drawn together like magnets.

Vonda was relieved to hear the familiar, adolescent clamor of Sean and Jim waft over the Bellofatto home. She could not have chosen a more suitable companion for Sean, and considered Jim a second son, part of the family. Formalities at the house were virtually non-existent. Whenever Jim paid a visit, he casually strolled through the door unannounced. On a few occasions Sean removed the screen from his window on the off chance that Jim might come by late at night.

Jim was ecstatic to have his best friend back. So much had transpired over the years, and Jim's life had been altered dramatically. He now spent an equal amount of time living with his grandfather in Piedmont and his mother in Oklahoma City. His grandfather frequently stayed over at his second home, an apartment in Edmond, thus allowing Jim and Sean reign of the Piedmont house. Jim had saved enough money from after-school jobs to buy a 1976 Chevy Malibu, and had fallen for a girl named Sandy Barlow.

But all was not as well as it appeared. School had never ranked very high with Jim, and he was growing more restless inside the classroom; trapped into striving for grades he couldn't possibly achieve. To make matters worse, Sandy's parents didn't like him, and his efforts to see her were becoming increasingly futile.

Sean had returned to his friend in the nick of time. Clearly, Jim needed a friend to take control and conquer his miseries. Satan provided the clear-cut answer. Sean believed that the devil had given him a calling, ending his duties in Greeley to lay additional groundwork—this time in Oklahoma City. The prince of darkness had delegated a mission for his little soldier.

Tara Duncan would later tell police that she met Sean Sellers by sheer coincidence. On December 31, 1984, Tara visited the home of a school friend who attempted to place a call to her boyfriend but dialed a wrong number. The voice on the other end of the phone, however, seemed interested in continuing the conversation, and the phone was handed to Tara. Tara and Sean spoke for a short time, then made plans to talk again the next morning. After several conversations the two agreed to meet for a date.

A year younger than Sean, Tara was immediately attracted to the blond-haired, blue-eyed teenager. His soft-spoken nature bespoke of a tenderness she couldn't resist. Tara and Sean's dates, which began as twice-a-week get-togethers, soon multiplied. Because they attended different schools and depended on rides from parents or friends, stopovers at each other's homes were natural alternatives when allowances ran short. Tara would later tell authorities that she and Vonda became "friends."

In February Tara listened to one of her psychology classmates give a speech on witchcraft, she later told police. Sean had often proclaimed his interest in the occult, and Tara couldn't wait to share her news with him. According to Tara, Rachel Dean claimed her mother had once employed the services of a clergyman to exorcise the demons that controlled her body. After hearing the story secondhand, Sean promptly asked for Rachel's home phone number.

It seemed only natural to Sean that as Tara became a prominent fixture in his life, she should understand and accept his passions as her own. Sean donned the role of ardent schoolmaster, feeding Tara's curiosity about the occult with his own expertise. Careful not to expose the depth of his Satanic wisdom, he introduced her to the occult world with caution, muting definitions of right and wrong like an artist who blends colors to attain the perfect shade.

One drizzly February afternoon, Sean and Tara visited a local shopping mall and browsed hand in hand through an array of record stores and gift shops. There was little enthusiasm for outdoor entertainment because of the wintry weather. The mall seemed an appropriate weekend shelter away from the eyes of parents. As the young couple neared a bookstore, Sean took his girlfriend aside and whispered in her ear. Tara responded with a nod and a smile, then slipped inside the store. Within minutes she returned, and proudly displayed a copy of the *Satanic Bible* which she was to read from cover to cover, then return to him.

To Sean's delight, Tara learned quickly. She absorbed her reading materials with spirit, then returned to him with questions, to which he promptly provided answers. In a letter to Solhad, Sean remarked on the common bonds he and Tara had nurtured.

> [Tara] and I like all the same things, snakes, animals, ninjas, booze, demons, etc. Everything I like, she does too . . . I know that [Tara] loves me more than I love her. And I love her more than anything.

Sean's relationship with Tara satisfied his appetite for dominance, acceptance, and love, but stopped short of feeding his hungriest needs. Tara appeared intrigued by Sean's experiences with astral projection, voodoo, and séances, but he sensed that her awe of him lay more in the area of romance than in his "secrets." According to Sean, it was Rachel Dean, who called herself "Glazheyon," who became his occult counterpart.

Sean says that Glazheyon permitted few into her private world. Her practice of witchcraft could hardly be exposed to the entire high school student body. Although reluctant at first to pass out her telephone number to a boy she'd never met, Glazheyon soon learned that Sean was no stranger to her arcane talents. According to Sean, their association synergized in a grand occult exchange. After several meetings, the witch Glazheyon bestowed on Sean a prayer that would bring him to the lap of the devil.

Alone in his bedroom one evening, Sean drowned himself in midnight darkness. He torched the last of a joint, inhaled it, then snuffed out the fire. He readied his implements like a meticulous surgeon, positioning the altar in the center of his room, a single black candle beside it. In the black robe he'd brought from Greeley, he knelt before the altar and lit the candle's wick. A long tongue of fire lolled back and forth, then pointed like a blade to the heavens. The flame's shadow flickered across the ceiling.

Sean placed his prayer on the altar. He closed his eyes, reciting the words Glazheyon had given him. The shadow that hovered above him moved across the four walls of his bedroom like a tree sprouting its branchy growth.

"Hail Satan!"

Silence. Sean looked around. He tried to decipher the images he knew to be there—his bed, night chest, the table stand. But they had been swallowed up by the shadow. His closet door stood ajar, parted like a gateway.

The temperature suddenly plummeted. Sean ran his hands up and down his arms, fending his skin from the chilly blast. The hairs on his arms rose. Cold. A brittle cold. He turned to his altar. The candle's flame quivered from side to side. Something had stepped into the room.

Scrambling to his feet, he whispered, "Look upon me, Dark Lord, for I am a child of hell and call upon your guards to make themselves known."

He moved closer to the candle's fire, leaned closer to the flame and wrung his hands above it.

"Hail Satan!"

Adrenaline burst inside Sean, and he felt pulled to the floor. Cold swirled around him as if he had been dropped into a deep-freeze. From behind, he thought he felt a hand fall across his shoulder. Its claws tapped his flesh like spears of metal, lifted his body into the air, then gently lowered him. Sean heaved for oxygen, breathed deeper, deeper.

From the corner of his eye he watched a thin mist spill into the room, seeping from the baseboards and the cracks in the walls. His heart crashed against his chest in a clanging cymbal of excitement. He stood in disbelief as mist spiraled around him.

Then he saw them.

Splotches of blue, yellow, and red gyrated in beams of psychedelic light across the room. Sean shielded his eyes from the blinding intensity, stumbled backward in a spasm of excitement and fear. The dots flew around him in a lunatic dance, elongated like shapeless bands of elastic, then snapped apart. From the saucers of light, demons broke free. They glided toward their summoner, red eyes tearing back the darkness. Whirring vile tidings, the demons sailed in a black wreath around Sean.

Then he thought he heard a voice whisper, "I love you."

At Putnam City North throngs of teenagers coursed through the halls every hour—football players, cheerleaders, brat packs, misfits. Sean Sellers did not fit any of those high school categories. In Greeley he'd been recognized, set apart from other teenage clones. Here he was no one in particular.

To those who had become aware of Sean's sudden transformation, his propensities bordered on the eccentric. Vonda and Lee dismissed his oddities as teenage peculiarities he would eventually outgrow. They interpreted his Ninjitsu fascination as another way of aping Lee and his countless Vietnam stories. Sean's adjustment to Oklahoma City had been fraught with disappointment, and Vonda feared the slightest disapproval would send him back into his shell. When her son refused to have his hair cut and limited his dress to scruffy jeans and T-shirts, she said nothing. When he wore the left sleeve of his shirt rolled up and painted his left pinky fingernail black, Vonda, after a futile argument, gave in. She did not know that his idiosyncrasies were hallmarks of a Satanist.

Ezurate.

The name rolled over Sean's tongue. Now that he had put a name to his demon, his barter with the devil was official. Ezurate.

And there were more demons, each competing for a place in his soul. For weeks Sean invited all the demons of hell into his body, for he now knew that God didn't love him, Satan did. When he glanced into the mirror, his reflection shot back a distorted portrait. But Ezurate had staked his claim. Sean no longer endured his internal torment alone. His blue eyes became a lighthouse for the demon that lurked inside him, his blood a vehicle for the devil's commands—Ezurate and his eternal watch.

Sean now controlled his destiny, from the nightly rituals in his bedroom to the halls of Putnam City North High School. With logic and caution, he experimented with the manipulation of his parents and classmates, suffered no ill consequences, then moved on. Ezurate guided him along this detour with calm and assurance. When the demon instructed him to carry the *Satanic Bible* with him at all times and to flaunt his union with the devil, Sean obeyed.

In early March Ezurate marshaled his little soldier into action. Sean wrote Solhad every week, updating him on plans to commence a recruiting station for Satan worship in Oklahoma City. He described a method to locate abandoned buildings for coven meetings and a formula in which Solhad could muster accommodations for the Greeley "church." The first duty at hand was to attract fresh blood. Both teenagers agreed that a Ninja martial arts club would entice the breed they wanted. Christening their group "Elimination," they established three levels of members: White Beginners, Red Masters, and Blue Leaders.

"The White Beginners won't even know about the Satanist part of Elimination," Sean wrote in his letter. "We'll bring them into it real slow."

When Tara Duncan first became Sean's girlfriend and steadfast companion, she willingly went along with his adventuresome nature, attracted to this young man who seemed so worldly. Tara liked to visit the Bellofatto home, especially when Vonda and Lee were away. Sean's bedroom bulged with unusual trinkets that were just beyond her mind's reach.

On one particular afternoon Tara followed Sean into the kitchen as Vonda finished cleaning up. When Vonda left them to tend to tasks in another part of the house, Sean went to the refrigerator and removed a small vial from behind a carton of eggs. He proudly displayed the vial, which contained a deep vermilion liquid.

"What's that?" Tara asked him, half afraid of the answer.

"What do you think it is?" Sean returned the vial to the refrigerator, careful to replace it in its exact spot behind the egg carton. He turned to his girlfriend and motioned for her to stay quiet. "It's blood," he whispered. "My blood."

Tara opened her mouth but no words came.

"I used a hypodermic needle and drew it out," Sean told her. "Then I drank some of it. I'm keeping the rest in here. To keep it fresh, you know."

Tara felt queasy, but still intrigued by Sean's confession of vampirism. "What are you going to do with the rest of it?"

"I use it to write things. You know, letters and stuff. It's the only way that a true priest does things."

Sean led his girlfriend back into his bedroom and searched a dresser drawer until he came across a manila folder that protected his sketches.

Tara stood mesmerized, gazing at drawings that she now knew to be dedications to Satan, written in Sean's blood. A pentagram laced with crimson. A goat's head smeared with dried blood. "They look so old, Sean."

"Isn't it great? I soaked them in oil then burned them at the edges. See? That's how I can make them look like that. This stuff gets others to join, when they see that I really can communicate with Satan."

In the living room Vonda gave Tara a furtive glance as her son walked the girl to the door and said good-bye. Vonda had held her tongue for as long as she could. Sean and Tara were dating too much. Tara Duncan was just not good enough for her son. Vonda wished he'd see other girls.

Because he helped out at home, and because he had no visible emotional problems, Vonda went about her daily routine, satisfied to be a housewife and mother again. Sean's dress and manner had changed radically, but she'd noted that other teenagers rebelled in much the same manner. His mode of dress was the least of her concerns. If she noticed the blood bank in the refrigerator, she likely assumed it another of Sean's bizarre science projects.

After school Sean straightened the house and put away the laundry, then shut himself in his room. There, he withdrew more blood from a vein in his arm, and replaced the vial in the refrigerator—a fresh supply for the next day. All of this satiated his craving for blood, but he missed Solhad and the Greeley rituals. He continued to write letters to his best friend, begging him to come to Oklahoma City for a visit. His plan to recruit members into Elimination was working well. Sean had discovered an abandoned farmhouse in Piedmont that he hoped to someday buy, and the coven had bred six new members. Lee had bought him a 1973 white Ford pickup for his sixteenth birthday on May 18. The truck, he wrote, would be ideal to get them back and forth.

An excerpt of a letter to Solhad depicts the efficient manner in which Sean carried out his operations. Vials of blood dispatched to Colorado through the U.S. mail became common gifts of friendship.

> You can write things with the blood I've sent and try drinking your own. The needle is sterile and the tip can be reused if you use them *only on yourself* and run alcohol through them to clean them out after each use. Have some guts, try it. The blood I sent you has some anticoagulants in it, so it will keep forever. Don't try to drink it until I make sure the chemicals aren't poisonous.

> Have fun in the blood and I'll see ya later. P.S. Choose a name you like for Satanism purposes and that you'd go for.

At night the demon robbed Sean of his sleep. Twisting, always twisting through his dreams, with ideas and plots and schemes. When Ezurate asked for blood, Sean inducted a new member into Elimination, slashing virgin flesh and drinking hungrily from the chalice. But the demon demanded more.

Mornings, Sean slipped a refrigerated vial of blood into his pocket and toted it to school. At first only his closest friends watched him drink the liquid that supplemented his diet in the school cafeteria. Soon he demonstrated his blood thirst to anyone who would watch. In science class he decided to draw the world a picture. While students sat at their lab tables, preparing to dissect frogs in a study of amphibians and reptiles, Sean waited until he had the attention of his table. When the teacher had busied himself with other students, Sean grinned and held the wriggling frog up for all to see. Then he opened his mouth, and with a steely glint in his eyes, bit the leg off the jerking creature.

The *Satanic Bible*, however, spoke louder than drinking blood or impaling animals. If Sean forgot to stash the book with his other textbooks in the morning, Ezurate reminded him. On one particular day at school, Sean felt especially bold. He took out his bible as the teacher walked into the room, and began talking to a classmate about his pact with the devil. While Sean's conversation distracted some students from their classwork, others ignored him. His drama teacher, mortified, demanded that he put the book away. But one student took serious offense at Sean's blatant admission of devil worship, and an argument broke out between the two teenagers.

Just after the 2:45 P.M. dismissal bell, Sean ran headlong into the student he had angered in drama class. The boy called him names, attempted to rip apart his beliefs. In Sean's view, attacking the Satanic theory could not be tolerated. He'd worked hard to arrive at his present plateau, and no one dared to speak to him with blasphemous words. He was a priest.

Sean's defense of his Satanic devotions brought about a shouting match, followed by pushing and shoving. When the student's fist slammed into his chin, Sean lashed out in fury. Minutes later a teacher broke up the fight and took Sean into the principal's office.

Vonda received the telephone call at home. Shocked by the circumstances surrounding her son's involvement in a fight, she told the principal that there must be some mistake. Anger and bewilderment swelling inside her, she called Lee and asked him to meet her at the school.

In a talk with the school principal, Vonda and Lee Bellofatto listened disbelievingly to a teacher describe the scuffle. Vonda heard words that stung her. Lee asked questions that elicited disturbing answers. Students were upset by Sean's public exhibitions of Satanism. Things had gotten too heated for one student to handle. A fight had erupted between the two boys. Vonda's heart skipped a beat, then sank. She assured the principal that she would "take care of it."

The Bellofattos, settled in the comfort of a quiet surburban neighborhood, were unprepared for the bulldozer that razed their lives. That anything so preposterous as a fight at school over a Satanic bible could shatter their world was beyond belief. Vonda had long ago patched the gaps that threatened to divide the family. How could her only son become involved with the devil?

Lee returned to work, and for the remainder of the day Vonda mulled over several unusual events of the past weeks, all related to Sean. The cold look in his eyes. The whispering with friends behind her back. The nights he slipped from the house without a word. The shoplifting.

She bristled. Maybe there had been something she'd missed. Sean would never steal, not of his own volition. Or would he? For hours thoughts ran through her head. She tried to rationalize what had happened and make connections with Sean's obstinacy. Why had she overlooked those connections? Who had given her son a *Satanic Bible*? Vonda had never invaded his privacy, but now she wondered . . .

With a pang of guilt, she stepped across the hall into her son's room and opened the door. A wave of faded incense assailed her senses. She stared at the assemblage of strange objects on Sean's table. Books. Black candles. A silver goblet. The sword. Her pulse quickened.

When Lee arrived home that evening, Vonda informed him with pale complexion and quaking voice what she'd found in Sean's bedroom. There were things in there, she told him, objects she didn't understand.

Lee rushed into his stepson's room. A no-nonsense veteran who believed in God and country, Lee Bellofatto froze in horror when he saw the parade of items that lay on Sean's table stand. As he gazed upon the scene, the meaning of the Satanic tools slowly took hold in his mind. He fled from the room, shouting. How long had this been going on? Why hadn't they noticed what Sean had been up to? These were no childish games, he told his wife, and they would continue no more.

Lee paced and fumed until Sean arrived home from his martial arts class. His stepson, whom he loved with every fiber of his body, in whom he had faith, who was to grow up to be a man of honor and esteem, strode through the door, wide-eyed and with an innocuous expression of innocence. Trembling, red-faced with rage, Lee confronted him.

Sean stood in defiance, defending his rights, his freedom. He berated Lee for snooping around in his room. Lee replied in a stern voice, demanding an explanation. Vonda attempted in vain to calm her husband even as her anger with Sean mushroomed. And in the end, when the obvious was extracted, when the ultimate nightmare surfaced that Sean had denounced the very God who had given him life and brought the family together, Lee pointed his finger at his stepson and cried out: "You do not exist!"

Why my complete destruction is so important, I don't know, unless it's because Satan knows I don't intend to give him up without a fight.

—Vonda Bellofatto, in a letter
to her cousin, 1985

EIGHT

AT HALF PAST TWO A.M. ON A SATURDAY IN June, Jim Mathis scurried from his car to the Bellofatto home. Sean's window stood half open; the screen had been removed. A tail of white curtain fanned Jim's cheek as he raised the window and climbed inside the room.

His invasion did not rouse the occupants of the house. Sean lay asleep, tucked between early morning dreams. Watching him, Jim chuckled. Jim would soon blow away the notion that Sean was the light sleeper he'd boasted to be.

Jim crept across the bedroom, careful not to bump the furniture. One slipup, one misplaced footstep, and the game was over. He arrived at Sean's bedside with his shadow splayed against the wall, magnifying as he drew closer.

He bent over his quarry, their faces inches apart.

Sean's eyes fluttered once, then twice. Jim extended his right arm then molded his hand and index finger in the shape of a pistol. "Bang! Bang!"

Sean's eyes flew open. He bolted upright, quailing in his bed. When Jim burst out laughing, reality returned with a slap of embarrassment. "God," Sean panted. "You scared the shit out of me."

Jim reeled in amusement at his joke. "I could have killed you, you asshole."

Sean snickered. He shook his head and dragged his fingers through his hair. "What time is it?"

Jim switched on the bedroom light. "I just got off work. It's probably close to three." Still dressed in his restaurant uniform, he plopped on the bed. "I went over to Sandy's tonight before work, and her old man told me not to come back. He doesn't want me to see her anymore." Jim shrugged his shoulders, then turned to Sean. "Man, I haven't done anything to that bastard."

Sean stifled a yawn and wiped the sleep from his eyes. "Forget about the Barlows, man. Just tell Sandy you'll meet her someplace else from now on. Use your head."

Jim's gaze dropped to the floor. "You don't understand, Sean. I really love her." He paused for a moment and swallowed hard. "The Barlows don't think I'm good enough."

The words rang familiar echoes in Sean's ears. For weeks Vonda had urged him to date other girls. He should look around; be more selective. Tara was a nobody. Vonda also had turned up her nose at the mention of Sandy Barlow. Hadn't Jim realized that he was wasting his time on a girl like that? she'd asked.

Sean hid the memory. He planned to break off his

relationship with Tara, but not because of his mother. Tara had begun having nightmares. She told Sean that she didn't want him to talk about the devil anymore. Sean and Tara remained friends, still talked by telephone on occasion, but the romance between them had faded. Overall, Vonda should be pleased, he thought cynically.

Sean measured success differently now. He needed tangible results.

They want to separate us, Sean. They want to destroy me so they can have their puppet back. Don't let them kill me, Sean. You need me now.

Following the incident at school, Sean retreated more and more to the sanctuary of his bedroom. In the wake of the showdown with his parents, he turned to the Satanic books. At first Lee's words of banishment lacerated Sean like a meat cleaver. But Ezurate softened the wounds, applauded his loyalty, and Sean continued to exist.

In the weeks that followed, Vonda and Lee's anger had lessened, but tension mounted in the Bellofatto home. They had forgiven, but they had not forgotten. Whenever Sean left the house, he was the object of a battery of suspicious stares and interrogations. No longer was he the perfect son. He wondered if they knew about Ezurate.

Drugs posed the escape Sean needed. Amphetamines opened a trapdoor that emptied out his remorse and the last relics of guilt. He stayed up throughout the night, poring over Satanic tracts and praying to Satan for strength. When at last exhaustion made him sleep, Ezurate encroached on his dreams, whispering messages that Sean did not understand.

What was the demon trying to tell him? Sean craned to hear the words, but Ezurate's murmur melted into a quivering warp. In time he would know.

The drastic changes in Sean tripped an internal alarm in Vonda and took a physical toll. She began to lose weight. Shadows etched like half-moons beneath her eyes. She attempted to cope with her son, whose gentle, passive nature had turned argumentative and defensive. Yet when she tried to talk to him, he claimed she didn't understand him; she didn't want him to be a man. Anguished, Vonda could not pinpoint the core of her son's distress. She begged him to confide in her, to allow her the chance to help solve his troubles. But communication with Sean was similar to treading on rice paper. He had detached himself from the family. Vonda was losing him.

But in the spring and early summer of 1985, Vonda was not prepared to surrender her son without a fight. She had given birth to Sean. He was not some wicked child taking refuge in her home; he was her son, and she loved him. Someone had led Sean down the wrong path. Vonda knew she must act before he completely alienated himself from the family. Studying her bible and praying for help, the solution struck her: where else but to the house of God? Vonda made an appointment for Sean to see a priest.

Inside the parish Sean scoffed at the Christian literature and religious ornamentation. When his gaze lighted on a crucifix, Ezurate twitched uncomfortably inside him. Sean carried the option to bury his demon in the farthest recess of his mind. Unless he permitted Ezurate to emerge, no one would guess the company he kept. Not even a man of God.

Sean spoke with the priest for less than an hour. He claimed his right to the privacy of his room. His books, decorations, the Ninjitsu sword didn't mean anything harmful, he explained. All the kids his age ventured into practices that parents found strange and confusing. Sean was simply curious.

His pleading worked. The cleric did not find cause for Vonda's and Lee's distress. In his estimation, Sean appeared to be a well-adjusted youth, bright for his age. The boy knew right from wrong. His curiosity was nothing for the Bellofattos to worry about. The priest recommended to Vonda that she give her son's books back to him.

Almost eight years had passed since Sean's first exposure to self-indulgence. Much of that time he'd spent sneaking into pretend danger zones like Dungeons & Dragons or books that were taboo. When he had soaked up all that he could, he'd prowled around for other means of gratification, but those, too, were short-lived. Once Sean had experienced and mastered the forbidden, the thrill disintegrated.

In his search for fulfillment, Sean had been aided and abetted by some of his more misguided peers, a witch, heavy-metal rock bands, and of course, occult literature. But pretending had grown stale.

If they knew about us, Sean, if they knew that you were mine now, we could be free.

No, no. It has to be our secret. We can't let anyone know. Not yet.

When Solhad Muldani traveled to Oklahoma City in July for a ten-day visit, Sean was elated. Marijuana and speed accelerated his joy. His trials with Vonda and

Lee seemed far away. He had settled into regulating life's events from his Summit Place headquarters, and deserting his parents for the farmhouse rituals in Piedmont. With the assistance of Ezurate, he had calmed Vonda's and Lee's anxieties and regained their trust.

Sean's independence through having his own transportation also helped. On a Saturday night, as Sean and Solhad cruised MacArthur Boulevard, high school kids raced along in a summer spree of squealing tires and catcalling. Sean added to the din of northwest Oklahoma City, drinking beer, and growing more daring with every minute.

At one-thirty A.M. Sean telephoned his stepfather from a pay phone and told him that he'd "ran into a bar ditch." He forgot to tell him that he'd been driving sixty miles per hour along a city street. Vonda expressed relief that the two boys had not been injured in the accident. Lee merely told his stepson to save his money for repairs.

Sean's innocent and congenial manner forestalled punishment for many things a more conspicuously errant teenage boy would not have escaped. His shoplifting incident in Greeley had been overlooked; he had walked away undetected from nightly rituals. Although Vonda and Lee had been angry about Sean's fight at school, his visit with the priest had put their minds to rest. And now he'd wrecked the pickup truck his parents had paid for.

All this, and nothing had happened to him. Even more amazing, Solhad had reported that their friends in Colorado had suffered no repercussions for their Satanic devotions. When police raided the abandoned building in Greeley after complaints from area neighbors, black robes and coven instruments were returned to Sean's acolytes with no questions asked. They had broken no laws.

The devil's children were seemingly invincible.

When Solhad left the city, Sean tried to contact Jim. But Jim's attention centered around his girlfriend, the Barlows, and his part-time job. Sean resorted to his old standbys, speed and marijuana, which staved off depression but failed to chase away his loneliness. Maneuvering his artillery of narcotics, he discovered that if he took enough speed and drank enough beer, he mercifully blacked out. The surprise at waking up behind the wheel of his truck while driving fifty-five miles an hour gave him little cause for concern. Ezurate had become his guardian devil.

Sean boosted his use of amphetamines and marijuana until the weeks sped by in a whirl. He alternated between vigorous highs and despondent lows, resigned to sleep only when he could no longer physically stand. With each passing day Ezurate became more difficult to suppress. Whenever Sean drank or drugged himself into oblivion, Ezurate rose from the oubliette in Sean's mind and took over. The demon cleansed his conscience, expunged his memory, and continued to feed him abstract messages.

By summer's end Sean found asylum in a local occult bookstore. The aroma of sandalwood and jasmine welcomed him. Shadowy shelves burst with stories of pagan heroes. At the bookstore Sean encountered a new clique of friends, who introduced him to The Abbey and White Sands, two Satanic stomping grounds where the city's eight major covens gathered for parties and conversation. His late-night escapades led him into the esoteric mania of *The Rocky Horror Picture Show.*

Sean felt quite at home in the tempestuous surroundings of the cult-movie classic, especially in the reminiscent "acting out" of his old Dungeons & Dragons days. *The Rocky Horror Picture Show,* a parody of old-time horror flicks, invited audience participation. Dressed in fright-flash, moviegoers threw props and recited movie dialogue in sync with the on-screen action. The movie's villainous Dr. Frankenfurter, who underscored the creed, "If it feels good, do it," made an indelible impression on Sean. Under the bleat of rock and roll music and the frenzy of Rocky nightwalkers, he discovered sanity.

But Sean's reversal from good to evil, from holy to unholy, was not a question of sanity. Sean had created a substitute for God. While most of his friends considered the midnight rituals and self-mutilations nothing more than a game, Sean adopted his Satanic beliefs as a way of life. He had replaced the Ten Commandments with the Nine Satanic Statements. He had foresaken God and all that God represented.

When Ezurate's cryptic messages came to light, Sean realized that he had reached a turning point. He prepared to make the ultimate commitment.

The ritual began as which had others. Chanting, smoking, and prayers to Satan, all lead to the grand finale: the bloodletting of a raw recruit.

The three cloaked figures knelt over the child's doll as though expecting it to come to life. The doll lay akimbo on the hardwood floor, next to a silver chalice and the sword. At the heart of the room a great black circle decorated the floor. Inside the pentagram a goat's head jutted, its red eyes staring at the onlookers. Candle fire brought definition to the wreckage in the farmhouse. Wooden crates rested like tumbleweeds. Crumpled newspaper and empty bottles decayed on the periphery.

The group of boys, dressed in black robes, stood in a circle like a black halo. Standing off to one side, the pledge awaited his annointment. Electrified with excitement and fear, he noted that the room was void of furniture. Musty odors of dank floorboards and rotting wood beset his senses. As two darkly cloaked figures approached him, static wrenched the hairs on the back of his neck.

"Undress," a voice beneath one of the hoods commanded.

The young man obeyed, first removing his T-shirt, then his jeans. He stood mutely as the figures in black draped him with a white sheet.

"Now hold out your arm so that we may receive the flesh of your flesh and the blood of your blood."

The boy offered his arm. He watched the cloaked figure in front of him writhe slightly. A pale hand slithered from beneath the robe and reached for the sword.

The boy shivered. He glanced across the room. The door to the house was locked and impenetrable. Half-drawn window shades barricaded the moonlight. The dark that waited outside the windows clung to the lower half of the panes of glass, and beyond that the boy could see nothing. "Wait," he said. "I'm not sure I want to."

Sean held the sword at waist level. The blade

gleamed and its shadow leaped to the ceiling. He turned to a fellow apostle. "Hold him."

A hooded figure grabbed for the boy in the white sheet.

"Wait. I'll do it. I want to do it on my own." The recruit lifted his arm toward Sean and squeezed his eyes shut.

Closing his fingers over the boy's arm, Sean tightened his grip on the sword and pierced the pristine flesh with the blade. Blood trickled over the pledge's wrist and into the palm of his hand. Sean siphoned the blood, then pressed the chalice to the boy's lips. "Drink it."

"I can't."

"Do it."

The boy forced a sip of his own blood, then thrust the chalice to the acolyte beside him.

As the others drank from the goblet, Sean placed the doll inside the pentagram. Ezurate jabbed his stomach like a bayonet.

We can show them all, Sean. We can show them what it is like to be free.

Sean raised the sword high. The doll's eyes bore into his soul, communicated the demon's message with its plastic grin.

This is a symbol, Sean. A symbol of what we must do together.

Power coursed through his veins. He plunged the sword into the doll's body.

How does that feel, Sean? How does that make you feel now?

Laughing, Sean raised the sword again and again, hacking at the doll's brains, ripping out its heart. A bright blue eye shattered. Bits of fabric and plastic twirled in the air, then fell to the floor.

Sean sank into the muzzle of the goat. Relief shuddered through him, breaking against his pulse like an undertow. Spent, and lost for breath, he collapsed inside the pentagram and closed his eyes.

The dismembered doll lay in a thousand pieces, its baby smile unrecognizable.

During one of the rituals, we decided to kill someone. I wasn't even Sean anymore. I was Ezurate.

—Sean Sellers, December 1986

NINE

IF SEAN HAD EVER SUPPOSED THAT SATURDAY, September 7, 1985 would be different from any other Saturday, that the events of his evening would forever alter the course of his life, he did not verbalize the thought.

A year later, he would recall the night with all the detail of a finely spun tale—a recollection preserved like an adolescent nightmare that continues to haunt into adulthood.

Jim Mathis would tell a very different version in court, contradicting most of Sean's version of the night and swearing he played no role in the plotting of three murders. Jim's chronicle of the night began early in the evening, when he and Sean picked up Tara Duncan and Sandy Barlow. The two couples drove to a secluded area in northwest Oklahoma City, where they sat in the parked Malibu and visited. While Jim and

Sandy discussed getting married, Sean discussed having a baby with Tara Duncan.

Jim would later testify that, after dropping off Tara, he and Sean stopped by a nearby Circle K store to get something to drink. It was nearing midnight. After dropping off Sandy for the night, Jim and Sean then returned to the Piedmont house, Jim would testify. They considered driving back by Sandy's house so that Jim could talk to her through her bedroom window. Leaving the house, the two teenagers climbed into Jim's Malibu, which Jim noticed was low on gas, Jim would testify. The Circle K was not far out of their way. Somehow, Jim would tell the court, Sean had managed to smuggle a .357 Magnum into the car without Jim's knowledge. Once inside the car, Sean announced that he had the gun and showed it to Jim.

As Sean tells the story, the week had wound its way to September 7 in much the usual manner. His and Jim's teenage lives abounded with school and part-time jobs. For Jim, it also included the pathos of tormented love. According to Sean, while Sandy's father was relentless in his efforts to keep the two apart, Jim's hatred for the Barlows grew more and more passionate.

Sean was not oblivious or even indifferent to his friend's plight. But with an ever-calculating poise, he kept the situation in the back of his mind, assured that its value would soon become apparent.

On Saturday night, it did.

The remainder of this chapter is recreated from Sean's account of what happened and is denied by Jim Mathis.

DEVIL CHILD

* * *

Over a period of weeks, Sean had increased his rituals nearly tenfold. He devoted special times during the day for school displays of Satanic affection and sequestered his nights for communions of Satanic love. During a recent black mass, where he consecrated his coven acolytes and hungrily lapped at their blood, Ezurate had made his purpose known: All Ten Commandments must be broken.

Sean lounged in Jim's bedroom where the air conditioning fought a losing battle. Sean's long, blond bangs, damp with humidity, fell in strings across his forehead. The house in Piedmont was a two-bedroom oven. The Indian summer assaulted the city with sticky, eighty-degree temperatures and little wind. The days had grown shorter, but the nights still held suffocating heat.

To celebrate their weekend, Sean had eaten two hits of speed and snorted rush—a locker-room deodorant that forces all of the body's heat into the head. Although the drugs' effects had been less than gratifying, Sean brushed off his passivity to a mood.

He watched Jim stretch full-length across the unmade bed. Sweat adhered his T-shirt to his skin. Jim's gaze traced the Y-shaped cracks in the ceiling as he discussed the evening ahead. After the Barlows retired for the night, Jim planned to visit Sandy through her bedroom window. But Sean would make the final decision as to where they would go, what they would do, and for how long they would do it. He always did. Jim never argued.

The high-pitched drone of rural tranquility permeated the bedroom, stirring Jim to restlessness. He turned over in his bed and faced Sean, who sat cross-legged on the floor.

"Do you ever wonder what it would feel like to kill someone?" Sean asked. The words sped from his mouth like a discharged shot. He lit a joint and inhaled.

Jim's eyes grew wide in surprise. He sat up in bed. "Kill who?"

Sean chuckled. "I don't know. Sometimes I just get these thoughts, man. And I can't stop them."

"What kind of thoughts?"

"You know, like during a ritual." Sean's voice squelched the quiet. "All these ideas get jumbled up in my head. And I keep thinking about what it would feel like, you know, to have that power over someone. To be so fucking dangerous.*"*

Jim's eyes darted around the room. He wet his lips. His tongue rolled across his mouth like a flat, pink spear. He stood, then joined Sean on the floor.

"They don't go away either," Sean continued. "They just keep getting stronger and stronger and stronger."

Jim appeared to ponder the idea. "Yeah, I guess I've thought about it a couple of times. You know, with Sandy's parents."

The right words clicked. Sean's brain spoon-fed him each syllable. From a corner of his mind, he retrieved the file he had so cautiously stored. Holding the joint between his fingers, he watched embers gobble the papery skin.

"You could do something about it, you know." He shifted a casualness to his voice. "They just can't keep you from seeing her."

"There are times," Jim said, "when I'd like to blow Mack Barlow off the planet."

The heat in the room swirled in stifling layers. Sean leaned against the wall and smiled. "Then let's do it, man," he whispered. "Let's stop talking this shit and do it!*"*

Jim grimaced as though he had been struck with jags of glass. "Just go murder someone? Just like that?"

A long pause.

"Not murder, a sacrifice. Our *sacrifice. Think about it."* Sean closed his eyes, yielding to the drug's comforting haze. *"It would be the fucking ultimate."*

Jim's teeth dragged along his lower lip. "I don't know." He stood and walked to his stereo, flipping switches until music pulsed through the room. "Barlow was a Marine, man. He's one tough son-of-a-bitch."

"For you and me?" Sean asked. "Or your grandfather's .357?"

"Oh, man. Oh, God. I think this whole thing is getting out of control."

"Your grandfather isn't going to know. How the hell is he going to find out anyway?"

Jim threw him an acid stare. "Are you kidding me? Blow someone's head off with his gun and you're asking me how he's going to find out?"

"Calm down," Sean said. "You're getting all freaked out over talk." He held out the butt of the cigarette, but Jim was lost in thought.

Minutes passed before Sean spoke again. He weighed his timing with precision. Careful not to press the issue. Guileful not to let Jim escape his grasp. Jim's longing for acceptance would eventually peek from behind any ambivalence. "That guy at the Circle K, though. Somebody ought to waste him." Three or four seconds passed. "He'd deserve it. Remember when he wouldn't sell us that beer?"

Jim furrowed his brow. "Yeah, I remember."

"And remember when he said those things to Sandy when she bought those Tampax? Remember? Do you remember that, Jim?"

Jim clenched his jaw. Red billows of anger rose to his face. "Yes!" he shouted above the music. He groped aimlessly in his pockets. "I remember, Sean. Okay, okay, so the guy's an asshole. Are you saying that he deserves to die because he's an asshole?"

Sean lowered his head. "Yeah," he shrugged. "I guess that's what I'm saying."

* * *

For Sean, the rest was child's play.

His unequivocal talent for distorting a situation and then manipulating it in his favor blessed him with the many returns for which he'd hoped. Before long, Jim bore the notion that he had ingenued a marvelous plan. Yes, that convenience store bastard deserved to die just as much as the Barlows. Sean agreed that Jim should first spend some time with Sandy. That he would feel much better about the whole situation.

While he explained how Satan would guide them on their journey, protect them as they dedicated their time and services to the master, Jim dissected the scheme bit by bit from an incriminatory standpoint. What about fingerprints left in the store? Sean's answer seemed to appease him: Hundreds of people revolved through the doors of a convenience store every day. What about video cameras? Or electronic buttons that could lock the door and trap them inside? There were none, Sean promised. No cameras, no electronic buttons, nothing.

And just to play it safe, they would wait until after midnight.

Sean says that Jim located a .22 handgun and the stainless steel .357 magnum inside a brief case in Jim's grandfather's bedroom. Both teenagers rummaged through stacks of magazines and loose papers until Jim uncovered six .38 caliber shells for the .357—the gun his grandfather used in security guard duty at the State Capitol. The .22 was already loaded.

Sean caressed the .357 lustily. Ezurate tugged at his loins, echoing his demonic arousal. Pangs of pleasure throbbed until Sean felt himself grow hard with excitement. "They don't fire these guns before they give them out and mark down ballistics, do they?" His gaze never left the revolver.

No, Jim told him, further explaining that police would have to have the gun in their possession before it could be traced. And, of course, that would never happen. Neither would they consider a security guard's gun as a murder weapon.

Together, they concocted what would appear to be a plausible visit to the Circle K store. The clerk, who Jim knew only as "Bower," had been experiencing problems with the clutch in his car. Although Bower rarely fraternized with customers, Jim would offer what little advice he could and mention a friend whose father worked as a mechanic. Perhaps, Jim would then suggest, they could take a look at the car.

Sean liked the idea. But first they would give Bower a final opportunity to remedy his wrong. Jim would try one last time to buy a six-pack of beer. They would offer small-talk until the store was void of customers—then give the clerk his big surprise. After it was over, Sean added, the store money was there for the taking, along with anything else they wanted.

Sean's skin prickled. The night was taking shape.

After collecting the necessary tools for their mission, the two teenagers regrouped in Jim's bedroom. The stream of questions, worries and concerns had run dry. Jim telephoned his grandfather at his Edmond apartment, ostensibly to say goodnight, and ensured that he would not return until the following day. Sean vocalized and dramatized every step, every detail of the plan, and the roles that each of them would play. Satisfied, he lit another joint.

At around 9 p.m., Sean leafed through the pages of his Satanic Bible until he located the appropriate ritual. In preparation for a destruction ritual—a Satanic method used to bring about harm or fatality to an enemy—one of five steps must be selected. Among these, a doll, representing the intended victim, is stabbed with pins; a drawing or painting portrays the victim's demise; a graphic narrative details the victim's destruction; a verbal monologue describes the violence; or infliction of pain or death is summoned by proxy.

The Satanic Bible, which urges its disciples to never turn the other cheek to an enemy, subscribes to the practice that most every indulgence can be attained through ritual. Lust and sex, compassion, even destruction. However, in all rituals, and especially in the case of a destruction ritual, an indulgence is sought symbolically. *Followers of the Left Path depend on Satan's almighty strength to lead the enemy to his ultimate fate.*

Sean decided to go one step further.

Tonight, he chose to sketch the three sacrifices, implementing his artistic talent at its most horrific. On a sheet of paper, he drew the limp form of store clerk Bower, his chest ravaged from a bullet, legs splayed in death.

Ezurate whimpered at the picture. The demon's child-like prattle rustled through Sean.

"Okay, now listen," Sean instructed, reading from his bible. " 'Be certain that you do not care if the intended victim lives or dies before you throw your curse, and having caused their destruction, revel, rather than feel remorse.' "

"Remorse," Jim said. Sarcasm dripped from his voice. He scrutinized the drawing. "Burn it."

Sean flicked his lighter. He lowered the paper to its flame. Fire blackened the page with long, swift licks until the paper curled in ashes. "So it is done."

In pious devotion, Sean and Jim genuflected, throwing back their heads in prayer. They dedicated their time to Satan with the same fervor with which they had planned each murder. Bower would be first. Then the Barlows. But with their limited ammunition, it was imperative that they make each bullet count.

Sliding into Jim's Malibu, Sean placed the .22 and the .357 beneath the car seat. They prayed again, this time for power and strength. In return, they offered three human sacrifices. Sacrifices to the master.

As they sped toward the crest of city lights, Ezurate settled comfortably in the vortex of Sean's fury. And waited.

This is one of the things that really bothers me now:
When the gun went off, it just went *Pop!* And I thought,
Pop? You know, that's *all?* Just *Pop?* I looked at the guy
and I was thinking, "Dead meat! You're dead, turkey!"
And then, *Pop! Pop?* Oh, fuck, I missed!

—Sean Sellers, December 1986.

TEN

BEHIND THE OVERSIZED, PLATE GLASS WIN-
dows of the Circle K convenience store at 122nd
Street and Council Road, Robert Bower had been into
his night shift for less than two hours. It had taken him
minutes to notice that the grocery shelves had not
been restocked. Now past midnight, he had spent the
better part of the past hour muttering under his breath
about the condition of the store.

He had complained to the manager more than once
about the other clerks. Bower complained that he was
left with double duties that made him dread coming to
work every night. But rather than accept his criticisms
of the other clerks, the manager had seemed more and
more displeased with Bower.

Although small in stature and weighing a mere 120
pounds, Bower was a striking figure with his mass of
dark curly hair, cool blue-green eyes, and glasses. His

bushy sideburns joined a full beard and dwarfed the gold earring that pierced his left ear. He wore a silver Seiko watch and a gold neck chain.

An elaborate tattoo of a panther's head below the names "Bob and Cheryl" curved along the brawn of his left upper arm. And the ink imprint of a large snake coiled beneath the hairs of his left forearm. On his right bicep were the words "Mom and Dad." In addition to the unusual decorations on his arms, Bower's right hand sported the letters L-O-V-E between the fingers.

The convenience store job was Bower's fourth since he'd lived in Oklahoma City—or, as he'd told friends, since he'd been *stranded* in Oklahoma City. For a brief period, he'd entertained thoughts of joining his estranged wife in Texas. But after their last attempt at a reconciliation, he wasn't so sure.

He couldn't return to Ohio either. Although his parents had lived in Canton for some time, they had made retirement plans in Florida and would soon join the flock of easterners who migrated toward the sun in their twilight years. Besides, other than a sister, there wasn't much left for Bower in Ohio. He was stuck in Oklahoma City—at least until he figured out what to do next.

Exactly two months before that September 8th, Bower had celebrated his thirty-sixth birthday. With no formal job training and an even less formal education, it was a struggle just to make ends meet. He lived, comfortably enough, in an apartment complex in nearby Edmond. Although he'd lived by himself since he and a girlfriend had experienced an argument, he didn't like living alone. And, since he'd used her car for transportation, Bower had been forced to buy his own automobile.

His salary at the Circle K left much to be desired for a man who had bigger dreams than a paycheck. But there would always be enough drugs to deal for the "extras" he wanted. And, with the profit margin he realized from doing a deal here and a deal there, there was always plenty of free dope to smoke.

Bower's thoughts were momentarily interrupted when the blond teenager stepped into the store to pay for gas he'd just pumped into a red Malibu. Bower mumbled a brief "thanks" and cleared the cash register for the next sale. He might have recalled seeing the boy in the store before, but tonight he seemed to pay little attention to faces. Around 1 A.M., when the customer had returned to his car, Bower prepared to stock the cooler—or face another barrage of accusations from the store manager.

Sean and Jim would later tell very different stories as to what happened at the Circle K convenience store that early morning. As Sean tells it, after paying for the gas, he and Jim continued their cruise along Council Road, planning to return to the store within a half hour. At that time, Sean would wait inside the car while Jim tried to buy a six-pack of beer.

What follows is re-created from Sean's version of what happened when they went back to the Circle K —a version greatly at odds with Jim Mathis's version of events.

Inside the Circle K, Robert Bower abandoned his post behind the counter and headed toward the rear of the store. In the back room, he slipped on a gray jacket that he kept on the hook behind the door. The night was warm, but inside the cooler, the temperature hovered at the freezing mark. The frigid air swirled around him as he dragged cardboard cases of Budweiser and Coors Light closer to the freezer doors, then shoved six-packs onto the shelf. When the electronic buzzer sounded indicating a customer arrival, Bower cursed, ducked out of the cooler, and walked to the front of the store. Not planning on a lengthy stay, he wore the jacket. In the sour mood he experienced on that particular night, he more than likely wanted to deter customers from loitering. The jacket would announce that he had been interrupted from other duties.

"How's it going?" Bower asked, taking his place behind the register.

A dark-haired teenager, who appeared to be fifteen or sixteen, stood at the counter. He wored fade jeans and a T-shirt bearing the exaggerated canine teeth of Ozzy Osborne. "Okay. For a minute I didn't think anyone was here."

Bower didn't reply.

The boy shifted from one foot to the other and dug his hands into his pockets. "My friend and I wanted a beer." He made a gesture toward the parking lot. "We heard you were pretty cool about it."

Bower scoffed. "Well, I don't know who told you that. I gotta see some I.D., man. You know the rules."

"Afraid you'll lose your job?" Jim Mathis laughed and glanced toward the parking lot. "Aw, c'mon, man. It's Saturday night, you know?"

Bower studied him. The kid had been in the store not two days before, trying to buy beer with a face that looked more babyish than adult. "Look, man," Bower said. "I've seen you in here before."

The teenager smiled at Bower's recognition. "Yeah, I was in here last week. Remember? We were talking about your car. I told you about a friend I have who's real interested in cars."

An array of implements for use in Satanic rituals, on display in Sean's bedroom. *(Courtesy Oklahoma City Police Department, Homicide Division)*

The body of Robert Paul Bower on the floor of the Circle-K.
(Courtesy Oklahoma City Police Department, Homicide Division)

The detectives: (Clockwise) Bill Cook, Eric Mullenix, Bob Horn and Ron Mitchell. *(Ray Clark/Oklahoma City Police Department)*

Sean's home, cordoned off by police the day after he shot his parents. *(Courtesy Oklahoma City Police Department, Homicide Division)*

The corpses of Vonda and Lee Bellofatto, who were shot by Sean as they slept. *(Courtesy Oklahoma City Police Department, Homicide Division)*

Sean claimed to have been "born again" in prison and he carried his Bible with him everywhere. *(Don Emrick)*

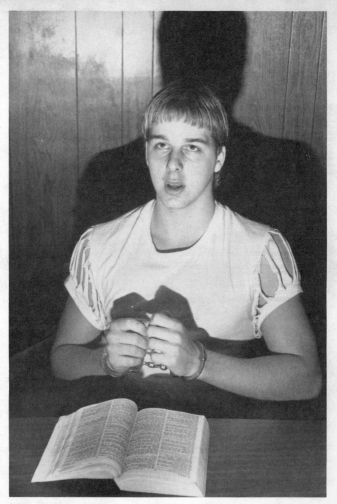
Sean Sellers, the youngest person on Oklahoma's Death Row. *(Don Emrick)*

The Oklahoma State Penitentiary at McAlester, Oklahoma, where Sean Richard Sellers waits to die. *(Cathy Krans)*

"Yeah, well." The clerk tapped his knuckles on the counter. It was the first time Jim had noticed the letters L-O-V-E tattooed in green ink on the back of Bower's hand. *"Sorry,"* the clerk said. *"You're still underage. Come back when you're twenty-one."* He turned and started toward the cooler.

"Wait," Jim called. He fidgeted with packages of beef sticks stacked on the counter. *"Okay, look. It was a joke, man, a joke. We'll just take a Coke or something. Maybe something to eat. We don't have to be twenty-one for that, do we?"*

Bower scowled and started toward the cooler again as another teenaged boy entered the store. He wore dark blond, shoulder-length hair and a smile that seemed molded in plastic. Bower did a double-take. The teenager was the one who had made a gas purchase less than an hour before.

"Hey," Sean said as the door buzzer hissed. *"What's taking so long, Jim? We've got things to do, man."*

"This is him," Jim told the clerk. *"This is the guy I was telling you about. His dad's a mechanic. Remember? I was telling you about him last week."*

"Yeah?"

"Yeah," Jim replied. Then to his friend, *"Let's get something to drink, Sean."*

The blond teenager walked past the counter and toward the cooler section until he was out of the clerk's view. Jim kept up a constant chatter, distracting the clerk with an inane description of his and Sean's earlier drive around the city and plans to go see a girlfriend. But Jim was losing his audience. Bower strained to see what Sean was doing in the rear of the store. He folded his arms and tried to peer around Jim.

Sean could almost hear what Bower was thinking: school punks out looking for a good time on a Saturday night. When he returned to the front of the store, Jim's words slowed, his shoulders eased back. Even the clerk seemed more relaxed. But he said nothing to indicate he remembered their earlier talk.

Surely the guy remembered a simple conversation, Sean thought. Bower had been hitchhiking to work and had mentioned to Jim saving enough money to buy a 1974 Chevy—how there were now problems with the clutch. But Sean's deepest thoughts on the morning of September 8 had little to do with cars, much less the car of a freak like Robert Bower. The pathetically thin, tattooed clerk was the decadent result of a transient life. Bower's filmy eyes spoke of intimacies with chemical abuse and a tutelage with motorcycle gangs. And, as Sean had decided, the clerk was the perfect sacrificial lamb; he had nothing whatsoever to contribute to society.

"Must be kind of scary working here all alone so late at night," Jim said. "I don't think I'd want to do it."

Bower went about his work. "It's all right. No one here to piss me off, you know?" His eyes locked with Jim's.

Sean placed two cans of Coke on the counter. Still wearing the irksome smile, he paid for the drinks. "What would you do if somebody robbed you?"

Bower's eyes narrowed as Sean uncurled his hand and released two one-dollar bills. A long and sharpened pinky nail painted black scraped the clerk's skin. He rang up the sale, then reached under the counter for his cup of coffee. "No one would rob me. There's only fifty dollars in the cash register. It wouldn't be worth the trouble." He began to transfer packages of Levi Garrett tobacco from a cardboard carton to a display box behind the counter. "Look, what else do you guys want? Cigarettes? Candy? Bubble gum, maybe?"

Jim laughed and gave Bower a noncommittal shrug. Sean simply smiled and pocketed his change.

The sultry September heat seemed magnified inside the Circle K. Sean felt it, and Bower must have felt the sting of his own sweat beneath his thick layers of clothing. The clerk removed his jacket and searched for a place to lay the bulky coat. He finally selected a shelf below the register.

The door buzzer sounded, startling Jim. A customer stepped inside the store, glanced at the two boys, then asked Bower for a pack of cigarettes. Sean and Jim exchanged quick looks. The clerk called out the price, took the man's money, then rang up the sale.

When the customer exited, Sean took over. "That your car outside?" he asked. The smile still dominated his face.

"Yeah. Piece of shit, but it runs." Bower appeared at ease when talking to Jim, but each time Sean sauntered to the counter, Bower became irritated. "Why? What about it?"

The teenager shrugged. "Nothing. Jim told me you were having trouble with it. Something about the clutch or something. Thought I could help."

"Well," Bower began, and looked from one boy to the other. "Yeah. The clutch is kind of fucked up."

Jim piped into the conversation. "We could take a look at it for you, couldn't we, Sean?"

Sean's expression never changed. "Sure. We could look at it. Tell you whether you made a sound purchase. That is," he paused and looked around, "if you're not too busy."

Bower stared at the register as though weighing his options. Jim and Sean waited. After a moment, he rapped his knuckles on the counter. "Sure. What else have I got to do?"

Bower's spirits seemed lifted, and the three went out to begin an inspection of his car, which was parked on the north side of the parking lot. Inside the battered Chevrolet, Jim placed the gear in reverse and backed a few feet from the curb. He then drove forward. As the car rocked back and forth, he turned on the stereo. A Deep Purple tune blared in distortion.

"Clutch seems okay," Jim said. "But your stereo sucks, man."

Bower frowned. "I've got a power booster, but I haven't had time to put it in yet."

"Shit. You've gotta get your priorities straight." Jim laughed.

Sean inched closer to Bower who stood beside his car. *"You want to see a kick-ass stereo?"* His words were in hypnotic tones that almost dared Bower to say *"no."*

"Yeah, okay."

Jim left Bower's car, slamming the door behind him. He walked to his Malibu and entered the driver's side like a proud father. Sean crawled into the passenger seat and reached for the door, but a gust of wind tugged at his arm and the door sprung open. Bower stepped back as the door lunged for him, then moved closer to Sean's open window. With one swift movement, Sean extended his right arm toward the floorboard. When Bower looked at him, both men froze.

Despite the curtain of night, Sean detected more than a trace of fear in the store clerk's eyes. For less than a moment, Bower's dark pupils were like those of a hunted deer—confused and foreign to the evils of man. The tiny lines beside his eyes hardened into fleshy rope. The muscles of his cheeks constricted, pulling at the curves of his downturned mouth.

"Listen to this, man." Jim broke the icy atmosphere. From the driver's seat, he tampered with dials and buttons until his stereo wailed to life with a burst of AC/DC. *"Fuckin'-A! This is a stereo!"*

When a pickup truck drove into the parking lot, Bower backed away from the Malibu. *"Shit,"* he murmured. *"I've got a customer. Later, man."* He returned inside the store.

Two teenagers followed Bower into the Circle K. They jeered at each other, name-calling and snickering. Although one appeared more in control than the other, they had obviously been drinking. Inside the store, they piled a two-liter bottle of Coke, two packages of Marlboros and a can of Copenhagen on the counter. Bower rang up their purchases—a $6.42 total.

Inside the Malibu, Sean leaned over and plucked the stainless steel .357 from beneath the seat. The time had arrived.

On their way out of the store, the two customers glanced at the firethorne red Malibu. They noticed the dark-haired occupant idling in the driver's seat. The blond teenager stood by the right front fender as if waiting for someone. No one spoke as the two customers crawled into their truck and sped off into the night.

Sean stood by the car, his legs crossed, arms folded, like a feline studying its prey. Brushing sweat from his cheeks, Jim climbed out of the car and joined Sean on the sidewalk. "They're gone," he said, staring at his shoes, burying his hands inside his pant pockets.

Sean gave Jim a hard look. He knew they would have to act now before someone else showed up. He knew they couldn't afford to waste another second. Rather than share in Jim's anxiety, Sean patted the bulge at his waist. "I'll let you know when it's time," he announced. "Be cool, okay?"

Jim knew what to do. He nodded. No longer perspiring, no longer the loner who had no friends, he slipped inside the store.

Sean Sellers stood by the car a moment longer, remembering the words that he and Jim had delivered to the master earlier in the night. The words hung before his eyes even when they were closed, rang in his ears even as he slept. Words that would heal him, sanctify him, make him whole and all-powerful. But for some reason that he could not fathom, his hands trembled. His head felt as light as ether. Swallowing a lump in his throat, he turned and walked around the corner of the building into the pitch black that waited.

Curling out of the warm night air, an icy finger traced the length of his spine. An isolated wind whipped around the store and rolled toward him, gobbling up stray cups and scraps of paper. Sean crouched. Gooseflesh pricked at his arms and made the fuzz on the nape of his neck stand on end. Ezurate squeezed his chest, forcing him to gulp his breaths.

"I don't know," Sean whispered. "I don't know, don't know."

At first, the snarl was barely audible. An animal's growl twisted through Sean's head, searching for a portal. The demon clutched at his brain and ushered him toward the front of the store. Toward the man. The sacrifice. A fetid stench wafted through the air and swelled inside Sean's nostrils, repulsing him and exciting him at the same time.

Whhhhrrrr . . .

Sean stood, wrapped his arms around his belly and stared out into the night. The darkness gaped like an evil mouth. Its tongue darted out into the black streets, watching, waiting for its next victim. Sean wiped cold sweat from his forehead. The .357 pulsed against his thigh, rubbing his phallus with its cold barrel. Ezurate's bleat swallowed the quiet like a profane vibration.

Sean took a deep breath. Exhaled. The voices in the night pampered him, coddled him. Hot winds washed over him. He steeled himself, bracing the brick wall, and studied the dry palms of his hands. Yes, he could do it. He was ready now.

Sean returned to the front of the store as Robert Bower poured a fresh cup of black coffee and returned to his post behind the cash register. Opening the door of the Circle K, Sean stared at Jim. A silent signal that issued a deadly countdown.

Resuming his stream of animated chatter, Jim took his cue. He pointed to a package of Eveready batteries that hung from the pegboard display behind the counter. "How much are those?" he asked.

Bower recited the price, then picked up his cup of coffee and started to take a drink. The next moment was a blur—a split-second of reality gone terribly wrong. Sean lifted the gun and pointed it at the center of Bower's forehead. The clerk's eyes grew wide, the brown of his pupils darkened. His mouth hung agape.

Bower ducked. His coffee cup toppled from his hand, its contents spilled across the counter.

Sean fired the gun. The bullet pierced the display rack behind the counter.

Bower jerked from the shot's explosion. "All right, man, okay, okay!" As he stepped toward the register, the smile on Sean's face halted him, paralyzed his movement. Their gazes locked. Then a look of futile understanding appeared on the store clerk's face. He bent over and grabbed his jacket.

No one will ever know Bower's thoughts at that precise moment. Perhaps he planned to walk out of the store. Perhaps he hoped that it was all a horrible dream and he would awaken inside the cooler where he'd begun his shift. Bower, in fact, did turn toward the store's rear just before Sean fired the second shot.

The bullet pierced the back of Bower's neck, below his left ear. The store clerk screamed and buckled. Shielding his face and wounded head with the jacket, he sprinted toward the back of the store like a crazed animal.

Jim's reactions were quicker. He blocked the clerk's exit from the counter. Bower reversed his steps, but at the end of the short path he suddenly realized that he faced Sean. Bower's saucer eyes and ghostly pallor exhilarated the blond teenager.

Bower ran back and forth, searching for an exit, somewhere, anywhere. He clutched at counters and displays—anything to escape his attackers.

Relishing their game of cat and mouse, Jim and Sean changed places. Bower scuttled past Jim only to find Sean. An expression of bewilderment crossed his face as he nearly ran headlong into the barrel of the .357.

But Sean grew tired of the chase. "Man, you're being difficult!" he shouted, steadying the gun.

The blood from Bower's head-wound escaped through the store clerk's thick hair. Patches of red patterned the white-tiled floor. The drops of blood were small at first, then dime-sized, then the size of quarters as Bower ran at his frenzied pace toward the restroom.

Sean says that Jim screamed, "Kill him! Do it! Do it!"

Suddenly, Bower slipped and fell forward. His forehead smashed into the restroom door with a sickening crunch. As he wriggled and convulsed on the floor, Sean raised the gun a third time. He fired into Bower's writhing side. Sean's heart thudded at the sight of fresh blood that splashed around him. Adrenaline pumped through him at what seemed ninety miles an hour. He had done it. He was at a height of ecstasy unparalleled with anything he had ever known.

When Sean turned and watched Jim standing over the cash register fumbling with the keys, he looked at his companion with a fiery gaze. "Let's get the hell out of here."

ELEVEN

AFTER A LONG, DRY SPELL IN OKLAHOMA, IT was not surprising that the strong, southwesterly winds of late summer whipped up roiling clouds of dust from the Texas plains. Old-timers vividly recall the phenomenon of the 1930s dust bowl, and some are still uneasy when they awaken to a blanket of dust hovering ghostlike over their town.

The day of September 7, 1985, was reminiscent of the era when winds and heat produced dust devils that inflamed both lungs and nostrils and filled homes with layers of choking dust. A cold front from the north offered no relief from the heat, but provided a slight rise in humidity. Meteorologists predicted a thirty-percent chance of rain.

On the morning of September 8, Sherry Taylor *knew* she would be late for her seven o'clock shift at

Mercy Hospital. It was four minutes past two A.M., and most of the Oklahoma City bars had closed.

From the front seat of the car her friends Scott and Lisa argued over the selection of a local rock station. A disc jockey from FM–100 attempted to announce the station's call letters over a Rolling Stones' tune, with little success. Screeches of a guitar blasted from the speakers as Scott turned up the volume. Lisa groaned loudly and covered her ears.

"Turn that thing down." Sherry shifted position, wishing they'd left Confetti's—a northside dance club —hours earlier. "Scott, we have to find a bathroom soon."

Traffic was light as Scott drove through the outskirts of the city. From her window Sherry watched the streets race by as she searched for a place to stop.

They had driven perhaps two miles when she squinted her eyes at the sign just ahead. The towering red K floating inside a neon circle beckoned in the darkness. Sherry squirmed in anticipation.

When Scott spotted the corner convenience store, he made a left turn onto Council Road. A cascade of light beamed from the store's windows, creating the illusion of a sanctuary in the night. Sherry felt a pang of relief when Scott turned into the Circle K parking lot, cut the engine and turned off the headlights.

The mercury lamps cast an eerie, greenish glow over the parking area. Lisa decided that she, too, needed to use the rest room. The girls climbed out of the car, giggling as they recalled fun-filled hours at the nightclub. Sherry's nursing responsibilities seemed even more remote. So what if she were late? Her patients weren't going anywhere.

She pushed the door open.

The inside lighting sobered the two young women. The store was strangely quiet. Still, they didn't think it unusual that no one was tending the counter.

"Where's the clerk?" Lisa asked, searching the aisles for the store attendant. "Hello? Anyone here?"

Sherry walked toward the counter. "Hello? Hello?"

Only the ping-ping sound of an idle video game in the far side of the store broke the silence.

Beside the displays of gum and candy a Styrofoam cup of coffee had been tipped over and spilled, staining the orange countertop. Sherry peered over the cash register, half expecting someone to lunge forward and grab her. A number of drink cups were strewn about the floor. Spots of blood trailed down the register keys and onto the floor.

"Oh, no," she said, her throat taut and dry.

The electric chatter of the video game mimicked her.

"What is it?" Lisa asked, rejoining Sherry beside the counter.

"Something must have happened. There's blood back here."

More flecks of blood led from the counter and wrapped around the farthest store aisle, then disappeared from view. Beside a row of Formica-topped booths in the snack area a gray jacket splotched with red lay on the floor.

Sherry drew a deep breath. Her pulse quickened as she walked toward the back of the store. She followed the bloody pinwheels that wound toward the rest rooms.

"Don't go back there," Lisa called, cupping her hand to her mouth.

"Someone must be hurt." Sherry sidestepped the

blood-ridden path. She felt as though someone had shaken her from a dead sleep. The pinching in her abdomen was replaced by a throb of foreboding.

The hallway between the front of the store and the rest rooms was immersed in blood. Sherry froze when she saw the man sprawled on the floor in a sea of red. His torso was bent at an unnatural angle, blocking the rest-room doorway. His faded black T-shirt exposed a protruding belly smeared with blood. The man's corduroy-clad legs stretched full length and his dirty-brown cowboy boots pointed like arrows toward the ceiling.

"Oh, my God." Lisa buckled from the sight of blood that had been splashed like paint over the walls and floor. She ran from the hall.

Sherry instinctively went to work. Crouching beside the body, she placed two fingers on his throat. No sign of life. Wiping the sweat from her palms, she slipped one hand under the man's neck and tilted his chin upward. She leaned forward and blew her breath into his mouth.

The man's glazed, half-open eyes stared beyond her. As if to follow his gaze, she turned her head toward the open rest room and watched a vertical line of his blood drip from the wall onto the toilet and floor. The grisly bathroom decoration churned her stomach.

Concentrate, she told herself, and brought her ear closer to his mouth and nostrils. He did not breathe. His pallid skin was cool, his body still and lifeless.

"What happened?" Scott's voice startled her.

"I think he's been stabbed," Sherry said. "Go call the police. He's dead."

Scott recoiled at the sight of the body, ripped and

bleeding with dead eyes staring at nothing and a bluish tinge to his skin. Rivers of blood ran from the curls of the man's hair and branched off into tributaries along the tiled floor. The darker blood had begun to gel.

"Dammit, Scott." Sherry stood, unaware of her bloody hands, which dangled at her sides. "Please, go call the police."

Saliva soured in Scott's throat. He turned and ran toward the store's entrance. Clawing at the door, he rushed outside to the pay telephone.

Oklahoma City police dispatcher Melinda Khamlaksana sipped her lukewarm coffee. Her shift, which had begun at eight P.M. the night before, spilled over into the early morning of September 8. It had been a relatively quiet night in the city. The few incoming calls she had dispatched to the night patrolmen entailed minor incidents or complaints from irate citizens—the more trivial demands in the world of law enforcement.

At 2:16 A.M. the ring of the telephone jarred the communications console.

"Police Department," she answered.

Jumbled voices in the background were in discord.

"Lisa, go get in the car, goddammit," a man's voice shouted. "Just go get in the car. We're leaving." Then, into the telephone, "Hello? Hello?"

"Yes, sir?"

"Who is this?" Scott's voice quivered.

The dispatcher was used to the confusion that surrounded emergency situations. "This is the Police Department, sir."

"Listen, listen," he said.

She waited patiently for him to collect his thoughts.

"I'm at Council Road," he continued. "The Circle K at Council Road and 122nd. We came here to use the bathroom. And there's a man that's been stabbed. He's dead. Nobody's been here except for us, and we just pulled up and . . . somebody needs to get here immediately."

The dispatcher jotted the information on the crime-incident report, but the caller was again interrupted by a woman's uncontrollable crying. He spoke something unintelligible to her, then returned his attention to the telephone.

"I just got here," he said breathlessly. "I don't want to get involved. I just drove up and wanted to tell you, okay?"

The rising panic in the man's voice indicated that he might be about to hang up. "All right," she told him. "Can I have the telephone number you're calling from?"

Scott was near hysteria. "Yeah, yeah," he said. "It's right here," and he read the number into the phone. "Do you want me to stay here or not?"

"Yes," the dispatcher firmly replied. "I want you to stay right where you are."

Scott sighed heavily into the telephone. "Okay, okay."

The line went dead.

Bower didn't have any family or anything like that. He was the perfect kind of person that you would sacrifice according to the satanic bible.

—Sean Sellers, December 1986.

TWELVE

JIM WOULD LATER TELL A MUCH DIFFERENT story in court about what happened the night of Robert Bower's murder. As Jim would relay the story, after leaving Piedmont, he and Sean stopped at the Circle K store for gas. He asked Sean what he planned to do with the gun, and Sean replied that he "was going to kill somebody." But Jim figured that Sean was just acting weird and discounted his remark.

Pulling beside the gas pumps in the Circle K parking lot, Jim says that Sean went inside the store to pay for the gas. When Jim drove to the front of the store to pick up Sean, he recognized the store clerk. Robert Bower was the same man with whom he had discussed car problems earlier in the week. Jim would tell police that he then went inside the store and joined Sean at the front counter, where the three discussed car stereos and clutch problems. Jim offered to check out the "clink" Bower heard in his car, and the three walked out into the parking lot to begin the inspection. Jim says that he then returned to his own car, while Sean followed Bower back inside the store.

From the Malibu, Jim watched as Sean continued his conversation with the clerk. For a moment, it appeared as though Sean had finished his conversation and headed toward the door. But suddenly, Sean stopped and turned around. Jim saw that Sean had the gun in his hand. Sean aimed the gun at the clerk and fired. Jim saw smoke rise from the barrel. He watched Sean follow the clerk to the rear of the store until they were both out of view. After a few seconds, Sean ran out, jumped in the car, and told Jim that he had killed the clerk.

Jim would also say that he and Sean never discussed the murder of Robert Bower in the pre-dawn hours of September 8. He would tell police that he did not aid Sean in unloading or cleaning the gun before returning it to his grandfather's bedroom, and that he could not remember which of them stowed the .357 back into the briefcase.

Sean's account of that morning is somewhat different. He says that after the sacrifice, he and Jim experienced a mixture of excitement and regret. Their regrets, however, were not for the traumatic death they had inflicted upon Bower. Sean, in fact, considered the evening at least a partial failure.

A re-creation of Sean's version follows.

"I fucked up," Sean told Jim as they sped from the store. "How could I have fucked that up so bad? He took three

bullets, man. Three!" He waved the gun in the air. "I can't believe I missed him on that first one. I can't believe it."

"Put that away, man. Somebody might see."

"Dammit, Jim!"

"All right, I'm sorry. I'm sorry." Jim drove erratically through the streets, putting distance between them and the store.

"Can't you go any faster?" Sean wiped the gun on his T-shirt, cleaning it of his fingerprints.

"I've got it floorboarded now, Sean. We'll be in the next county if I keep going like this." Jim raced through the next intersection, slowing only when he was certain no one was on their tail. "Everything's okay." He checked the rearview for the dozenth time.

As Jim headed in the direction of his grandfather's house, Sean placed the gun on the floor and pushed it under the seat, next to the .22. He was grateful that Jim's grandfather had planned to stay the night at his Edmond apartment. It was possible the old man could pay them a surprise visit—but it wasn't likely.

Jim apparently had his own misgivings. "I figure he'll be gone all night. But what if something happens? What if he came back while we were gone?"

"That was your assignment," Sean said. "To be sure he wouldn't come back. It's after 2. He's gotta be asleep by now. He won't come back." Sean sat back in his seat.

Jim sighed. "We just have to hope nobody finds out about this."

"They won't. There's no way."

The night had not been a complete failure, Jim explained. All problems had been reckoned with before the ritual. Satan would take care of all the kinks. The slip-ups. He reminded Sean that the police would never be able to trace the gun.

Sean relaxed. "We did it, man. We did it! And it feels so fucking good." Suddenly, he burst out laughing.

A street lamp illuminated Jim's grin as the Malibu wound its way up his grandfather's street. "What? What are you laughing about?"

Sean grew hysterical with excitement. "Did you see the look on his face? That guy was terrified. We had him so confused." Again, he laughed. "Did you see his glasses fly off?"

"Yeah. It was great."

"He was so dumb. So fucking dumb."

Jim joined in Sean's revelry. "Yeah, he really thought we were his friends. But . . . ." Jim turned the wheel and eased the car into his grandfather's driveway. "We didn't get the money. Or any beer. We could have taken anything. It would have been so easy."

"Yeah," Sean pondered the thought. "I could use a beer. And a joint."

Jim parked the car, turned off the headlights and the ignition. "Let's go inside."

Sean was preoccupied, again wiping the gun against his T-shirt. "I wonder if anyone has gone in there yet."

Jim's expression was blank. "In where?"

"In the store. You know, back there."

"What are you thinking, man?" Jim shot him a toothy grin.

"We could go back. See if anyone found him yet. I'd like to see the look on the face of the person who finds him. Who sees all that blood!"

"Are you crazy?" Jim looked around. The street was deserted. Quiet. Shadows of the night played in the wind. Crickets sang in the silence. "You really think we should?"

For a long moment, Sean and Jim sat in the car contemplating the thought. Somewhere down the street, a dog barked. In a distant house, a light sprang to life. A moment later, the light faded. Jim shuddered. "Sometimes, this place gives me the creeps. We'd better get the gun back where it belongs."

Sean stared at the shadows that swallowed the house. "Okay," he hesitated. "Let's go inside. We have work to do."

Once in the house, Sean unloaded the gun and placed the shells on the kitchen table. Under the careful supervision of Jim, he cleaned the weapon, several times raising the question of what to do with the shells. Then from a window, the teenagers surveyed the unlit back yard. They didn't need light. They knew the terrain by heart.

The yard was a clutter of junk. Their minds relayed an unspoken message to one another, coming to the foregone conclusion at almost the same moment.

"Turn off the light," Sean said in a hushed voice.

Jim obeyed. Then, as their eyes adjusted to the thick black, they silently made their way into the back yard and the maze of debris.

"Over there." Sean pointed to a pile of rotting tires.

"No, wait, over here." Jim walked toward a stack of unfinished wood, then shook his head. No, it still wasn't the right place.

They combed the yard, stumbling over litter in the dark, whispering to each other. Soon, the proper place was decided upon, and together they buried the shells between two pyramids of garbage. After expressing the utmost confidence that the shells would never be found, they returned the .22 to Jim's grandfather's bedroom and the .357 to its case. In Jim's bedroom, the two shared several remarks about the sacrifice. All in all, they supposed, it was a success with relatively few flaws.

Soon it was time to sleep, and Sean and Jim retired from their momentous night with clouded thoughts and a guarded secret.

When they woke, it was morning. Neither mentioned the incident of the previous night. Nothing, they subconsciously concluded, had happened. Jim expressed concern that Sean's parents would be getting worried and offered to drive him home.

Within a few short hours, Jim and Sean had dismissed the previous night's murder. In their careful estimation, Sean had made a noble sacrifice to Satan of a non-contributor to society. A bum. A nobody. And while they had dreamed, their consciences had rejected any wrongful doing.

They exchanged few words until they neared the Circle K store on the way to Sean's house. An unusual amount of bustle in the parking lot turned their heads. Jim slowed as they passed the store. The number of police cars evoked an awed conversation between the two teenagers.

"Wow, I wonder what happened there?" Sean's sarcastic tone prodded Jim.

"Man, I don't know. Must have been something pretty serious."

"Yeah. Must have been a robbery. Maybe something worse."

"Yeah," Jim said. "We'll probably hear about it on the news."

Now bantering lightheartedly, they drove to a sister Circle K store not two miles away. Pulling into the drive, they entered the store and in their continued casual manner, questioned an employee as to what might have happened up the street. They were told that the night clerk had been shot.

"Oh, man." Sean feigned shock and surprise. "You're kidding. When did it happen?"

"Sometime last night," the clerk told him.

"Jesus Christ. It's hard to believe that he's . . . Was he killed, man, or what?"

"Yeah." The clerk looked at Jim and Sean, waiting to see if they had any intention of making a purchase. But the two young men merely stood and stared at him. "Can I help you guys with something, 'cause I need to go in the back for a minute."

"Do you know who he was?" Jim asked. "The night clerk, I mean?"

"Yeah, his name was Robert Bower."

"Gee, we talk to that guy a lot, don't we?" Jim said.

"Oh, man." Sean's eyes were bright. He wore a half-smile. "Yeah. We knew that guy."

THIRTEEN

THE SHARP JANGLE OF THE TELEPHONE WOKE
Oklahoma City homicide detective Bill Cook from a
sleep that seemed to have just begun. He glanced at
the digitals on the bedside clock. Two-thirty A.M. In a
haze of half sleep he picked up the receiver.

"Looks like we got one, Bill," Detective Sergeant
Bill Woodie said. "Robbery and homicide over at the
Circle K at 122nd and Council. Victim appears to be
the night clerk."

Cook dressed in the semi-light of a small table lamp.
His wife groaned in her sleep. His family was used to
the disrupted nights when he slipped quietly from the
house and made his way to yet another crime site in
the city. But to Cook, telephone calls in the dead of
night foreshadowed higher crime statistics and an addition to tomorrow's obituary column—a problem
that nipped at his heels every day.

As he stepped out into the night, the air brushed his skin like warm fingers. The voice of the radio dispatcher crackled a half word as he drove along the quiescent thoroughfare. Cook radioed his position and the dispatcher acknowledged his response.

The Circle K at 122nd Street and Council Road was about five miles from his home. It would take him less than fifteen minutes to reach the store. The stretch of road easily accommodated the light traffic as Cook drove past Quail Creek and Ski Island—two of the more prestigious residential areas. Council Road and 122nd Street intersected in an upper-middle-class neighborhood that spawned housing additions reflecting higher incomes. But as convenience stores and other late-night businesses sprouted in the northwest suburbs, murder inched closer to his own doorstep.

Bill Cook had been an officer for nine years on the city's police force at the time of the Circle K call. In his dress attire, however, he might have been an ambitious businessman, stepping out into the world to close yet another deal, the welfare of his wife and young children engraved in his mind. His genial and affable manner did not fit the archetype of hard-boiled detective.

The expression on his unlined face alternated between stoic seriousness and humor. His premature, powdery-gray hair, neatly trimmed and combed, gave him a look of sophistication that seemed a few years beyond his actual age. Cook was in the prime of his career. He handled his job with aplomb; each step polished and guarded, yet taken with vigor and pride. That, he supposed, would never change.

If his wife and children feared for him, they did not speak of that fear, but went about their daily routines.

They had their own lives to live, and Bill Cook had his job to do. That, too, he supposed, would never change.

At ten minutes past three A.M. he pulled into the Circle K drive. A number of cars—most of them police units—were already on the scene. Red and blue lights illuminated the scene. Three officers had cordoned off the area with the familiar orange police barricade as Cook approached the store. Just outside the perimeter of the mercury lamps' glow, bystanders gawked.

Although advertising posters and displays hampered his vision through the window, Cook saw movement inside. Several police officers were scattered about the store, taking notes and discussing their interpretations of the murder. Off to one side, a man and two women who appeared to be in their mid-twenties talked with Officer Bill Walls, the first uniform to arrive on the scene.

"Hey, Bill," Walls greeted him as Cook walked into the store.

"What have you got?"

Walls joined him by the front door. "Those are the three that found the body and made the call. The victim's in the back, near the rest rooms." He nodded toward the rear wall of the store, then at one of the women. "That's Sherry Taylor, a nurse at Mercy Hospital. She was the first to discover the body, and says she tried to give him mouth-to-mouth."

Cook glanced at the gathering of officers near the rest-room area. "Was anything moved, disturbed?"

Walls shrugged. "She touched the body. I don't think she changed his position, though. She says she tried to listen for a pulse, so chances are she moved his arm. Maybe his head."

Cook sighed. The moving of a crime victim's body was a damaging element in any investigation. "Anything else?"

"I called the store's security and for follow-up personnel."

"Okay, good. Mullenix is on his way too." Cook looked around, taking mental notes of the aisles and shelves that made up the south side of the interior. Everything appeared in order. He walked behind the counter. A number of drink cups, covered with blood, lay on the floor. A pouch of chewing tobacco and a white rag were strewn a short distance from the cups. Red blotches trailed toward the back of the store.

In the narrow corridor Robert Paul Bower lay on his side. His arms rested near his face as though he merely slept. A pair of eyeglasses lay not far from his head. His buttocks and hips were crumpled against the bathroom door. Pools of blood bordered his head and side. On the door facing, wide red stripes dripped. It appeared as though a bucket of blood had been pitched across the toilet and rear wall of the bathroom.

By three-thirty A.M. fifteen police officials crowded the Circle K. Many carried responsibilities that would stretch far into the day. Cook's on-call partner, Eric Mullenix, would assume much of the load.

Upon arrival, he rushed toward Cook. His dark hair appeared to have been combed in a hurry, and undercurrents of sleep still clung to his eyes. "What happened?" he asked, and peered over the counter. "Where is he?"

"Back there." Cook pointed. "A nurse and a couple of her friends found him. Looks like your everyday robbery-homicide." Cook and Mullenix walked toward the rest-room area.

"God," Mullenix breathed. "This is a mess." He crouched beside the body for a closer look.

Cook knelt beside Bower's head where the blood channeled nearly four feet from the victim's long, curly brown hair. "Looks like he's been shot in the side and in the head." He paused. "Kind of strange that he's back here, though. He must have tried pretty hard to get away."

"Somebody definitely wanted him dead, all right. Guess that's an understatement." Mullenix flashed a smile. "Want me to take the witnesses?"

Deciding who would work the scene and who would question the witnesses did not take long.

Cook returned the smile. "Sounds good. I'll call Tom Bevell, then have a look around." He started toward the front counter. Mullenix followed, then branched off into the aisle where the three visibly shaken witnesses waited. Cook telephoned Sergeant Tom Bevell, a blood-spatter expert with the Oklahoma City Police Department. Once on the scene, Bevell would be able to reconstruct the victim's movements from the patterns of blood in the store, and hopefully provide Cook with the answers he needed.

The path of blood that led from the floor behind the counter to the rear hallway demanded Cook's attention first. He studied the large pegboard that displayed batteries, Schick razor blades, Bic pens, and other assorted items. A collector's edition of *Playboy* magazine, which lay beneath the pegboard, was spotted with blood. A clump of brown hair attached to skin tissue was lodged in the metal webbing of a *Penthouse Forum* rack. Next to it, a bullet hole and a bullet fragment. Cook also discovered that a second bullet had spliced a package of Eveready batteries nearly dead center, then perforated the board and wall behind it.

Adjacent to the row of Formica booths in the store's snack area, a gray field jacket lay on the floor. Its lining was speckled with red. The September night had been far too warm for any type of coat, but its bloody decorations led Cook to question its role in the store clerk's murder.

Deductive reasoning also told him that Bower had first been shot while he stood behind the counter. With one final surge of adrenaline, the victim had probably fled toward the rest rooms in an attempt to escape his attacker. Rather than finding asylum, Robert Bower had found death. A gruesome one.

In lieu of breakfast, Sergeant Tom Bevell was faced with the sight of blood. At five A.M. he began his bloodstain interpretation, just as a puzzle enthusiast links the first interlocking pieces of a picture. But as Bevell had discovered, the shapes of the pieces in a murder case were subject to change.

Bevell studied and restudied the spokes of blood that wound behind the counter and dotted the stack of Thirstbuster drink cups. Bower's blood had splattered in the same direction in which he ran. And at a very rapid rate. But the spills of blood that surrounded the victim's final resting place remained baffling.

"What do you think happened here?" Cook asked, staring at the wash of blood in the rest room.

Bevell sipped from a cup of coffee, surveying the dead man. "From the looks of it, he must have hit the door facing. And pretty hard at that. Look at this." Bevell bent beside Bower and pointed to his head.

"His hair is like a sponge," Cook remarked.

"The blood on the door facing and in the bathroom is cast off," Bevell began. "When he hit the wall, all of the blood in his hair was thrown inside the bathroom. Bet you anything the examiner will find some type of blow on his face."

Bevell explained that the blood that ran from Bower's head wound had already begun to separate. Dark crimson rivers, which merged with the pinkish, thinner blood, seeped under the baseboard.

"So he's been here awhile?" Cook asked.

"No, I don't think so. More likely the result of the air circulation in the store, the temperature, and this type of flooring."

Bill Walls interrupted the conversation. "The store's relief attendant is here, ready to go to work," he said. "He's outside with the district manager. I told them you might have some questions."

Sergeant Woodie joined Bevell and Cook as they left the hallway. "The store manager says the victim is Robert Paul Bower. Thirty-six years old. Lived in Edmond. He's worked as the night clerk for about three months."

"Okay," Cook said as he pushed open the front door. "Now we're getting somewhere."

The relief attendant had been prepared to start his morning shift at the Circle K just as he had for the last six months. During his short tenure there had never been any store disturbances, and murder seemed even more remote. "How did it happen?" he asked Cook, straining to see inside the store.

"It looks like a robbery right now. Did you know Robert Bower very well?"

The attendant shook his head. "No, not really," he

said. "He always took about five minutes to wind up his shift and turn everything over to me, you know. But that's the only time I ever even talked to the guy."

"Did he own a gray or silver-colored jacket?"

"Oh, yeah. Bob kept it in the back room when he worked inside the cooler. You know, stocking merchandise and that kind of thing. It got pretty chilly in there. I used it myself."

"Did he always keep it in the back, or would he have brought it up front with him?"

The stocky man shook his head. "No. It would have been real strange for that jacket to be up front. He always kept it in the back room, right next to the cooler."

Cook turned to the district manager. "How do you open the cash register?"

"There's a key already in it," the manager explained. "Turn it to the operation-mode position, then just press the bottom-right button."

Then the attendant interrupted. "When can I get in and go to work?"

"Just as soon as the body is removed. We'll let you know." Cook stepped back inside the store.

The key was already positioned in operation mode. Cook punched the bottom-right key. The cash drawer sprung open. He first noted that there were no twenty-dollar bills in the register. The one-, five-, and ten-dollar slots contained the appropriate bills. A log book, which lay next to the register, had been signed by Bower every time a twenty had been dropped into the vault beneath the counter.

The final transaction on the register's tape indicated that the last purchase totaled $6.42. Fifty-four cents in change on the counter, a penny he'd seen on the floor, and three pennies found outside the store building, totaled fifty-eight cents—the exact amount the last customer would have received if he'd given the clerk a five-dollar bill and two ones for his $6.42 purchase. Cook removed the top five-dollar bill and the two top dollar bills, which he would have tested for fingerprints. He checked the register tape for the time of the last purchase: 2:06 A.M.

The initial telephone call made by one of the witnesses had come into the communications console at 2:16 A.M. Could the last paying customer have been the killer?

At 6:45 A.M., nearly three and a half hours since Cook had first walked into the Circle K, the field medical examiner arrived. Nick Graham also understood what it meant to be on call. And like many of his colleagues, death's timing offered him no choices.

The victim's hands were immediately bagged to preserve possible skin scrapings or strands of hair that might be caught underneath the fingernails. Deterioration of the clerk's fingerprints would also be delayed. Other than a jagged, broken thumbnail, Graham found no wounds on the victim's hands.

Just as Bevell had predicted, Bower had acquired a large purple bruise over the bridge of his nose and lacerations above his right eye. Graham suggested that the victim might have been struck by a blunt object. But the marred bathroom wall indicated that the store clerk had most probably slipped and fallen, then hit the wall before he died.

Graham completed photographing the victim, then removed Bower's wallet. Cook verified the identification and gave it to Mullenix for further investigation.

The tattered brown wallet contained ninety-eight dollars. Bower hadn't been killed for his money.

The first misgivings about the robbery theory crept into Cook's mind. He also had a nagging feeling that there was something unusual about the killing. That the victim had been engaged in some activity other than trying to protect the cash in his billfold.

"Doesn't look like he put up much of a struggle, does it, Nick?" Cook asked, studying the five-foot five-inch clerk.

"Maybe he never had a chance to," Graham replied. "I'll call you as soon as I get the results."

At seven-thirty A.M. Robert Bower was lifted to the waiting gurney and transported to the county morgue for autopsy. The missing piece of thumbnail was discovered underneath his body.

Cook asked the district manager to step inside and check the cash register to determine whether any money was missing. He wasn't surprised to learn that the register was only short $7.87, which the manager pointed out was normal in a twenty-four-hour period. Nearly fifty dollars, the maximum amount of cash allowed outside the vault, remained in the register.

After nearly eight hours of investigative work, Cook and Mullenix returned to the squad room. Sunday morning ushered in a panorama of homicide's aftermath. Cook's telephone rang incessantly.

The officers still on the Circle K scene didn't notice the two young men who cruised along Council Road in a 1976 Malibu. The occupants of the car, drawn to the excitement that surrounded the store, remarked at the number of police cars on the scene and openly expressed their curiosity as to what might have happened to cause such attention.

They had a strong hunch that someone had been killed, and they vaguely wondered whether the victim might have been the night clerk from whom they occasionally made small purchases.

But as they drove by, laughing about the time when the clerk had refused to sell them beer because they were minors, the teenager in the passenger seat smiled. A slight, curved twist of the lips. And thought to himself that the night clerk got just what he deserved.

At eleven A.M. Nick Graham phoned from the coroner's office. His pathological diagnosis concluded that the probable cause of death was the gunshot wound to the clerk's left side. Since the angle of this wound was upward and elongated, the examiner presumed that Bower was probably on the floor when the fatal shot was fired. Secondary cause of death was the first gunshot wound Bower had received. In completing his autopsy, Graham found an underlying linear skull fracture to Bower's forehead region. It was uncertain whether the night clerk had been bludgeoned or struck his head when he fell. Jime of death was estimated to be approximately two-ten A.M.

Cook pondered the information. There were many elements that remained bewildering: What role had the gray jacket played in the last scene of Bower's life? The bloodbath inside the convenience store was a *deliberate* execution, but why? An influx of questions jumped at him, but Cook realized that many of the answers would be permanently entombed with the victim. A movie reel of possibilities flicked through his head, each more complex than the last. It was possible that tonight's robber had panicked and added murder to his repertoire—unintentionally or not—then fled from the store empty-handed. There was even a good possibility that he'd murdered before, and killing another human being was to him like smashing out the life of an insect. Or perhaps the clerk had tried to do something heroic.

In any case, death was a high price for him to have paid.

The first traces of fatigue began to settle in, but Cook's day was far from over. Witnesses waited to be interviewed. Lab reports would have to be analyzed. Family would have to be notified. He realized that before the conclusion of the investigation, he would be deluged with reams of paperwork. His all-in-a-day's-work routine would drift far into the night—maybe into days or weeks.

The aroma of coffee drew him from his thoughts to the area where a fresh pot brewed. He poured a cup for himself as he remembered Bower's ice-cold stare—the unseeing eyes. As he tackled his work load, Cook could not have guessed that the convenience store slaying was only the prelude to an even more abominable tragedy.

Sipping the strong black coffee, he glanced at the words displayed upon the west wall in the homicide room, words that epitomized the life of the homicide investigator: WHEN YOUR DAYS END, OUR DAY BEGINS.

FOURTEEN

SEAN DREAMED ABOUT BLOOD.

Despite the thrill of his sacrifice, its memory evolved into a nagging specter that haunted his sleep. The horrified eyes of Robert Bower plagued his subconscious. In the dream, the clerk darted back and forth behind the counter, his long, dark hair standing on end. Then the clap of gunfire—one, two, three shots. And Jim, fear showing in his eyes, cried, "Do it! Do it!"

In the dream bullets riddled Bower. He bucked from the lead spray. Blood pumped from the holes in his body and fanned around him, flooding the store with red-capped waves. Sean waded through the blood. When he tried to reach for the door, a fresh tide pulled him back and dragged him under. He gasped for breath as the current snagged him. Jim squealed—a chilling vibration that sounded like fingernails scraping a chalkboard. The ocean of blood washed over Sean.

Sean awoke, bathed in sweat. Bolting from his pillow, he clawed at his skin, certain he was drenched in Bower's blood. The face of Robert Bower loomed in his mind.

By daybreak he had suppressed his dreams and recovered his sanity. While Vonda and Lee slept, Sean tried to hide the reality of the sacrifice behind his demon. Then the household came to life with the new day, and the Bellofatto family entered the world that existed beyond the duplex on N.W. 115th Street.

Sean's junior year of high school had begun well. Everyone noticed him and seemed to love him. He made many friends, and his days were filled with things to do and places to go. That year he guarded the darkest of all secrets.

Drugs rendered Sean immune to Bower's recurring death. Amphetamines sped him up, barreled him through the school day in a dizzying blur. Marijuana furnished a repose that took him by the hand and led him to a peaceful sleep. As he increased the amount he smoked, the half-sprung eyes of Robert Bower faded and the clerk's wiry hair—spired in terror—was forgotten. Although blood continued to debut in his dreams, Sean ostracized second thoughts about the murder. He had fulfilled an obligation.

While drugs purged his conscience, they also shut off his psychological power switch. The occasional blackouts he had experienced returned with a ferocity. He dropped in and out of reality. Out of English class, into art class. Consciousness disappeared, then reappeared just as quickly—sometimes during a ritual, other times behind the wheel of his pickup. Time lost its relevance. Days turned into nights. He barely remembered asking classmates if they had heard about the convenience-store killing.

One evening in late September Tara Duncan telephoned Sean at home. Vonda Bellofatto acted friendlier to her now that she and Sean didn't date regularly. And his mother didn't object to their occasional phone conversations.

Tara had not seen or spoken to Sean since the beginning of school. It wasn't like him not to call. She missed the sound of his voice and comparing notes on movies and music. But on the phone that night he sounded fidgety. Much of what he said, a jumble of words, barely made sense to her. But Tara clearly understood when Sean asked if she'd heard about the shooting at the Circle K store, and the question caught her off guard.

She thought for a moment. "Sean, why are you talking about that?"

After a long silence, he whispered, "I did something real stupid."

Tara drew a quick breath. The break in his voice filled her with dread. Sean began to babble then, asking if she had seen the broadcast of the murder on the TV news, not stopping to let her answer before he skidded to another question.

His words dizzied her. "Sean, what have you done?" she asked, breaking in.

He faltered. "I can't tell you," he said. Seconds slipped by. Sean explained that if he divulged what he knew, and Tara ever got mad at him, she could use the information against him.

"Well, if you're not going to tell me," Tara said, "just shut up about it."

Another silence. Then, in a flurry of words, Sean told her how he and Jim had stopped by the Circle K store to buy a six-pack of beer. How the clerk had refused to sell them the beer because they were minors. How he'd intended to leave the store, but instead had walked back to the counter and shot off the gun. The first bullet hit a pack of cigarettes. Tara listened disbelievingly as Sean spoke at breakneck speed, telling her how he'd fired the gun again and this time had shot the store clerk, who then began to crawl toward the back of the store. Jim shouted for him to kill the man. Sean fired and shot the clerk again. Blood, he said, sprayed everywhere.

For a moment, Tara hoped that she'd been strung along in a bad joke and Sean would soon deliver the punch line. But the dead calm in his voice eliminated that possibility.

"Why did you kill him, Sean?"

The last bit of silence. "I don't know."

Tara's loyalty to Sean influenced her judgment when he asked her to never breathe a word of his secret. Afterward, they continued to have telephone conversations, and Tara frequently saw him at *The Rocky Horror Picture Show.* He did not mention the convenience-store murder to her again. But during certain conversations, Sean would flaunt his firsthand knowledge of the murder, reminding her, "Well, you've never killed anyone."

By October Sean's circle of friends from the occult bookstore had increased. He regularly occupied a seat at midnight showings of *The Rocky Horror Picture Show,* where he met up with pretty girls more in tune with his Left Path philosophy and met others who grazed in the devil's pasture. Fellow Satanites were easily recognized by their "evil taint"—a left shirt-sleeve rolled up, a left pinky fingernail worn long, sharp, and lacquered glossy black. Girls and boys greeted each other with the traditional Satanic salute, extending the index and pinky finger of the left hand, akin to the Texas University "Hook 'em horns" cheer. But each showing of *The Rocky Horror Picture Show* was only the beginning for some members of the audience. When Dr. Frankenfurter retired for the night, Rocky followers migrated to Scully's, an Edmond dance club that catered to the more eclectic teenage interests.

Sean's involvement in late-night activities all but eliminated his interest in football, wrestling, and track; he dismissed school sports for the aphrodisiacs that waited after dark. With the exception of his fourth period weight-training class, he abandoned his regimen of athletics. Drama became his favorite subject. He assumed theatrical roles with minimal preparation, jumping into his characters' personalities with the ease of slipping on an old pair of blue jeans. Improvisations by other students were pale extensions of his acting ability, and his teacher was not remiss in pointing out his talents. Sean showed tremendous promise as an actor. Unafraid to perform before an audience, he lost all inhibitions once the spotlight glided his way.

Ezurate accepted much of the credit. Sean never knew when the demon would shove him aside and take center stage. Since the sacrifice, Sean found it impossible to restrain Ezurate, who kept badgering him with demands. The demon wanted him to share their secret.

The murder of Robert Bower had unlatched a deadly gate in Sean. It opened the way to evil for pleasure, and he trampled any obstacles blocking his way. Sean immersed himself in Satanism and the supreme power of human sacrifice. His desire to be the most dangerous person on earth no longer seemed an impossibility. And other kingdoms waited to be conquered. With the help of the *Necromonicon*, he compiled his own Book of Shadows, from which he chanted for strength. His Invocation to Satan characterized a child's prayer for evil intervention in a holy world.

O great desolate one, spawn of the abyss, enemy to the weak, send forth your most glorious blessing and heal the wounds of one of your children. Send forth the dire powers of darkness so that we may do your will. Send to us a burning flare of change so that we may place ourselves to help you.

Cast down the cowardly lies of suppression with a clap of earth-shattering thunder! Let your presence be known, for you are among your most talented. Upon this night, send the soul of mortality to your newfound child and grasp him/her as you would a lover.

We unite to strengthen through the true power of darkness an abandoned god, in all the black glory and richness of truth. Unite among us the powerful force of freedom, and through our power-rise, to someday be free.

Allegiance to your power shall be sworn, as eternity revolves without end.

With the sacrifice of Robert Bower in his portfolio, Sean's recruitment of Elimination members swung into full action. Roger Landis, an acquaintance from

Sean's weight-lifting class and a friend of Jim's, had begun to take an interest in Sean's midnight rituals. Roger was not ready to participate in a Satanic baptism, but he listened openly to Sean, until the two teenagers grew more and more comfortable together.

After Jim was fired from his job in a restaurant, he and Sandy packed what belongings they had accumulated over their sixteen years and ran away to Missouri, where they took a sabbatical from family pressures. With his best friend in another state, Sean drifted closer to Roger. The two teenagers hung out together, exchanging sorrows and heartbreaks, disappointments and victories. Driving along MacArthur Boulevard, drinking beer, they exhausted topics of school, girls, and music.

One conversation meandered to strange things that had happened to them in the past. At first Sean and Roger traded tales in a harmless oneupmanship. Sean hoped to one day become a Green Beret like his stepfather and to enjoy the distinction of being a member of an elite clan of soldiers. His tale of murder, however, froze the conversation. Roger had never heard anyone discuss being a killer as casually as Sean, and disregarded the boast as a lie.

One day in mid-October, when Sean and his friends had progressed from the movie house to Scully's, Sean stopped off at the men's rest room in the club. Ezurate had hounded him the previous night, interrupting Sean's sleep with an infernal whine, aching to be set free. Now, Sean felt the demon beckon him in the distorted mirror, then dance in flames behind his blue eyes. Ezurate wouldn't stop talking about the sacrifice, wouldn't stop making the gurgling sound that reminded Sean of Robert Bower's death rattle.

The demon crawled into his ear, murmuring like a lover. Did Sean recall the stiffness he'd felt in his crotch when he'd pulled the trigger? How the emaciated store clerk had exploded when bullets tore into his flesh? How Sean had rocketed the man into oblivion?

And all that blood!

Sean braced himself against the sink, its porcelain as cold as marble. His vision wobbled. The bathroom swung back and forth, dipping crazily. The thought of Ezurate clenched his gut and knotted his stomach.

All that blood!

Sean felt the demon's rasp echo through his body. He stared at himself in the mirror, searched his face for a hint of the stranger who occupied his mind.

Now he knew.

He felt that the demon had interfered with his thought patterns, just as Ezurate had switched places with him in drama class. It was Ezurate who had made human sacrifices to the devil, then tried to pin the blame on him. It was the demon, he thought, who stretched his lips into a half smile whenever a classmate mentioned the Circle K murder.

Ezurate!

It was the demon who blurted out the story to Tara in a frenzy. Who leaked the news to Roger when Sean's defenses sagged from too much beer or dope. The demon had become a braggart, pushing Sean into killing a man who wouldn't sell them beer.

Just to see what it felt like!

Sean made his hand into a fist, then drove his knuckles through the paper-thin wall, splitting paint and plaster.

* * *

In November 1985 Sean began working at Scully's to make restitution for the damage he had inflicted on the bathroom wall. The manager accepted his offer to compensate for repair costs, and Sean became a weekend bouncer at the club. Vonda and Lee approved of their son's part-time job. His weekend shifts did not infringe on his school work, and the Bellofattos decided that the responsibility of holding down a job was good for him. His grades remained intact, holding steady at a high B average, which satisfied their expectations.

Vonda reluctantly accepted the changes in her son. Sean avoided spending time with the family, no longer cared to share the events of his life. His moods vacillated from day to day. His internal torments, whatever they might have been, raged through bouts of love and hate. The vulnerable, childlike qualities in him had become a bittersweet memory. Sometimes, when Vonda looked at him in the scrutinizing way a mother studies her child, her mind traveled back to the apartment in McAlester—a simpler time, when Sean depended on her for everything. When his sadnesses were easily combatted with ice cream. When the most painful aspects of his life centered around the death of a stray animal or a pig named Charlotte in a children's story. Vonda had paid the price of motherhood: Her son had grown up.

Lee discarded Sean's absences from home as a teenage compulsion for freedom. Sean was an ordinary, restless boy, absorbing every minute of his adolescence before adulthood shook him into a man.

But only a mother could know the escalating discrepancies in her child. The deception in his love.

Sean had become an imposter. A wide, toothy grin appeared on his face as if it were the plastic slash on a mannequin. A smile Vonda didn't recognize. At times his eyes seemed to puncture her like ice picks. Someone had taken away the son she loved so completely.

And it scared the hell out of her.

On the evening that Sean met Angel, he knew that his life would never be the same. When the dark-haired, doe-eyed girl wandered through the doors of Scully's, Ezurate began to feed him bits of information and program his inimical smile. Sean visited clusters of friends and acquaintances in the club, swayed from group to group as an employee gearing up the crowd for a Thanksgiving party. Under the collision of heavy-metal music and teenage banter, a friend introduced him to the girl he had studied from afar all evening. Swapping smiles and conversation, Sean and Angel talked until the dimming club lights announced closing time. As he drove her home, she slid closer to his side, and when Sean kissed her good night, nothing else in the world mattered.

Angel. Even her name was an indication of the way she made him feel. Neither pretty nor unpretty—just a girl. But a mysterious girl, capable of making him happy without uttering a word. Ezurate felt attracted to her sexually, but Sean fell in love with her.

When Scully's closed permanently after the Thanksgiving holiday, Sean accepted a part-time job at a local pizza parlor not far from the Bellofatto home. Repair costs for his pickup had nibbled away at his dance-club salary almost as soon as he collected his paycheck. He worked at the restaurant six evenings a week—the consummate professional server at a family eatery—

then joined the odyssey of *Rocky Horror* fanatics Friday and Saturday nights.

Within a month of Sean's employment at the pizza parlor, Vonda returned to the work world; ironically, as a waitress for the same restaurant. The extra money would allow the family to indulge in a few extras, and she could afford to help her son with his truck-repair bills. Vonda also hoped to tuck away a portion of her salary for a vacation—maybe a second honeymoon for her and Lee. She took an instant liking to her job and to the other employees, but she especially enjoyed working with Sean when their schedules coincided. Sean was the only student labor employed full time at the pizza parlor, and management would later tell authorities that he was an excellent employee—dependable, polite, and hardworking.

Also, Vonda resumed working because she needed a diversion from the troubled waters that rose in the household. Jim's and Sandy's disappearance had, both Jim and Sean would later tell police, sparked a series of irate telephone calls and visits from Mack Barlow, who, according to the teenagers, insisted that Sean knew of his daughter's whereabouts. Arguments in the family grated on Vonda like a rusty saw. But by far the most distressing of her worries concerned Sean's new girlfriend.

When Sean brought Angel home to meet his parents, Vonda could not hide her shock. Her overall assessment of the girl was that she exemplified "white trash." Angel's long, dark hair fell in a ragged curtain over her eyes—hollow spheres that masked the same emptiness Vonda had seen in Sean. The Bellofattos disliked her instantly. There was no question in their minds that Angel was not good enough. Vonda refused to allow her son to become as involved as he had with Tara Duncan. She shuddered to imagine Sean having sex with the girl. If Angel became pregnant, Sean would be forced into a predicament that nauseated Vonda to consider.

The Bellofattos told their son how they felt, expressing their criticisms with subtlety, praying that he would come to his senses. But as Christmas neared Sean continued to date Angel, and Vonda's dislike ripened to loathing.

Everyone hated him.

Everyone. His classmates ignored him. Jim had abandoned him to be with a girl. Roger no longer wanted to hear about Satanism. After Solhad's parents had found a *Satanic Bible* in his bedroom, letters from Greeley had become rare.

And now, Vonda and Lee.

At night Sean lay in bed and pondered a solution to his dilemma. His parents' disdain for Angel would not kill his love for her. Angel had become the only thing worth living for, and neither his mother or stepfather would stop him from seeing her.

Ezurate soothed him. The demon understood Sean, cursed the Bellofattos with an eternal damnation. Angel was a beautiful girl, loving and accepting of Sean, in awe of his sensitivity and talents. She satiated Ezurate's voracious hungers, and the demon loved to caress her skin.

Sean stared out over his shrine—the table stand blazoned with the devil. He comforted himself in believing that everything would work out. That soon, very soon, his parents would change their minds about

Angel. Closing his eyes, he waited to catch the last train to sleep.

Once in a while—every once-upon-a-time in his imagination—Ezurate teased him with the thought that Sean would be better off without Vonda and Lee. And the more Sean's mind toyed with the idea of life without family problems, without disapproval, the more vivid the idea became.

Sometimes he wished they would go on a long, long vacation.

Sometimes he wished they weren't alive.

FIFTEEN

AS WITH ANY HOMICIDE INVESTIGATION, THE complicated jigsaw puzzle that is left behind for detectives often becomes the link to an even greater puzzle. The murder of Robert Bower was no exception.

As Detective Bill Cook soon discovered, Bower's life was as enigmatic as his death. His shady past opened a Pandora's box of promising leads and suspects, a wealth of motives, and just as many dead ends. Although the victim had worked as the Circle K night attendant for little less than three months, he had drawn the attention of a number of unsavory types for varying, and many times intimidating, reasons.

The friends, girlfriends, estranged wife, employment history, and less than desirable residences of Robert Bower, culminated in both a bizarre investigation and pieces that refused to interlock.

Born on July 8, 1949, to Wesley and Alberta Bower,

Robert Bower had not remained long in his north Canton, Ohio, home or in the family setting in general. He was thirty-five years of age when his employment application was accepted at the Circle K, and on June 13, 1985, he was assigned to his post at the store on 122nd and Council Road—a position he never planned to keep for long.

Police uncovered little about Robert Bower's life before he drifted into Oklahoma. But his shadowy past caught up with him in death.

Those who knew him described him as a loner, somewhat insecure around women and forever seeking advice about them—usually from other women. His drug use was pronounced, which directed investigators toward the possibility that Bower had victimized someone in a drug deal, then himself became a victim. Friends claimed that his indulgence in LSD and cocaine had escalated since 1984. Others knew him to be quick-tempered and violently argumentative. But it was more likely Bower's parents who suffered the most from their son's brusque temperament. Their final memory of "Bobby" was an argument nearly a year before.

Two years prior to his murder, Robert Bower had left a sick wife in Arlington, Texas. They never divorced. After a brief recuperation from a hernia operation in Ohio, his intention to return to Texas—possibly for another reconciliation attempt—was foiled when he ran out of money. He made it as far as Oklahoma. With no employment and little cash, his first refuge became the Hope Center—a home for the indigent—in Edmond. His roamings eventually brought him to Oklahoma City, where he sought shelter at the Jesus House, another transient shelter.

It was in the city's street havens that Bower formed local friendships. Most of his new friends either were, or were associated with, ex-convicts of one sort or another. One such acquaintance boasted that he had been a former inmate on Colorado's death row for his role in the Adolph Coors slaying.

A cornucopia of interviews began, casting an unsettling light on Bower's character. The likelihood of several suspects was apparent, and the murder puzzle changed shape. Cook and Mullenix unraveled a skein of possible motives. Bower had once been beaten outside an Edmond bar, which landed him in the hospital with a broken jaw. He also received at least one threat to his life.

And in the midst of questions, questions, and even more questions, one name emerged repeatedly. Bower had indeed made an enemy.

John Paul Hinson had been fired from a local supermarket during the summer and had moved in with Bower and Bower's latest girlfriend, Sally Harjo, around the end of July, Harjo told police. But when the new roommate failed to pay his share of the bills, Bower and Harjo agreed Hinson should move. Embittered, Hinson complied but not before he threatened to "get them both," according to Harjo. Harjo and another witness also said Hinson frequently talked about "needing a gun."

While he had a motive for killing Bower, Hinson was soon eliminated as a suspect when he was found to be living in Ardmore with his mother, nearly a hundred miles away. He had no police record other than his previous detention as a murder suspect, and once again Cook and Mullenix faced a false lead.

Despite his less than attractive appearance, Bower

thought himself to be quite the ladies' man. He had floated from the domicile of one woman to another until arguments erupted over children or use of his latest girlfriend's car. His attempts to room with male friends almost always ended in arguments, many of which were violent enough for Bower to fear physical harm.

Harjo provided Cook with a darker glimpse into Bower's personal life. She had met him at the supermarket where they both had worked in January 1985. Although Bower was a quiet individual and seemingly introverted, they moved in together the first week of May. Bower had worked as a doughnut fryer in the grocery store before they decided to seek other employment, this time with the Circle K company.

But living with Bower was difficult. He was tight with his money, had a terrible temper, drank heavily, and smoked marijuana. Her small children annoyed him, she told Cook, which prompted their split in early August. She hadn't spoken with the night clerk for several weeks.

When Cook asked Harjo what Bower would have done in the event of a store robbery, she maintained that he was basically a coward and would unquestionably have given the robbers everything.

Upon checking Edmond police records, Cook discovered that Harjo's father had recently brought charges against Bower for three stolen and forged checks. No one but Bower, the man claimed, had access to the checks, which were missing from his home and later returned by his bank marked "insufficient funds."

"He was an odd-turned individual," Mike Landry, the owner of a security business, told Cook. Landry patrolled the Circle K area during Bower's shift and would often stop in for coffee. "He'd been working at the store nearly three months and *still* had problems operating the cash register."

"Did you ever talk to him about his problem?" Cook asked.

"No," Landry replied. "But it was plain to see that he was either a doper or had some type of mental problems. Sometimes he would stand behind the counter and just stare off into space."

Just after eleven A.M. on September 10, a telephone call to the Norman Police Department Crime Stoppers line appeared to be the break for which the investigative team had hoped.

A teenager reported that he and a friend had driven to the Circle K at 122nd and Council Road to purchase a bottle of Coke, two packs of cigarettes, and a can of tobacco. When the register tape that recorded their purchase at 2:06 A.M. confirmed the sale to be minutes before Bower was shot, Cook grew hopeful. And when he learned that one of the teenagers had been spotted with a .38 caliber pistol, he became even more optimistic. Ballistics experts had discerned that the bullets spent in the Bower slaying were Winchester .38 Special, 95 grain, silver tips—ammunition used only in a .357 or a .38.

It was time to question the two young men.

The teenagers' respective parents, however, objected to Cook interviewing the minors and borrowing the pistol for a ballistics test. When a search warrant was obtained, the .38 was taken into police possession. But after pertinent testing, the gun was eliminated as the murder weapon. Cook's highest hopes to date for uncovering a tidy solution to the crime proved to be false.

Over the next week other phone calls were received by the police department in response to the Circle K murder. Customers who had made purchases the evening of the homicide offered what little information they had. Some reported suspicious-looking cars or people around the store, while others saw or heard nothing out of the ordinary. Among the many callers was a young man named Jim Mathis, who had stopped by to purchase gas at eleven-thirty that evening. Although he couldn't be sure, he thought he had seen a two-toned pickup at the Circle K during the time he was pumping gas. While he could provide nothing further, he thought the information might help.

With the steady parade and subsequent disqualification of all suspects, the murder files on Robert Paul Bower joined other manila folders containing unsolved killings. The murder of another convenience-store clerk might shed new light. A witness would be a godsend. A confession seemed remote. For now, leads were becoming cold, if not nil, and the motive seemed more intangible than ever.

It was as though the killer—or killers—had been plucked from the face of the earth. Only Bower knew the identity of those who had ended his life so brutally. If it hadn't been someone he knew as an enemy, then surely, as he drew his last breath, he looked his killer in the eye—and wondered why.

SIXTEEN

SINCE HER DIVORCE FROM JIM BLACKWELL, Geneva had maintained her residency in Ravia, opting for the uncomplicated attitude of a small town. Over the years, she stayed in touch with her ex-husband, frequently gathering with him and family on holidays, and especially to spend time with her grandson. The Blackwells' mutual love for Vonda, Lee, and Sean had not changed with the separation.

Geneva remembered the Christmas of 1985 in particular. On December 23 an arctic wind blew around the Bellofatto duplex, whistling through the window chinks like a banshee. Clouds the color of pewter had covered the midday sun. Now it was twilight, and the sky promised an icy rain. A below-zero wind chill penetrated winter coats with relative ease.

In the living room Geneva studied the festive scene with reminiscent eyes. Lights winked red and green.

The aromas of nutmeg, orange, and Scotch pine embraced. As if to match her spirit, ice cubes tinkled in glasses, laughter swirled from room to room, and kitchen utensils clanged amid the scurry of padding feet. Jim relaxed on the couch with Lee, where their discussion of truck driving mingled with the drone of the dishwasher. As Vonda cleared dishes and wrapped leftovers, Sean fine-tuned holiday music from the stereo.

Geneva absorbed the Christmas clatter in silent observation, threading the day into another fond memory. Her grandson had grown into a fine young man, dutifully helping his parents with the demands that came with hosting company.

For a moment Geneva thought back to a day in late October when she had driven to Oklahoma City to spend the afternoon with Vonda and Sean. Summit Place lawns, enflamed with autumn foliage, presaged colder days. But inside the duplex there was a toasty warmth, and an outsider would have recognized the special love between a mother and son. Sean's attempt to show his mother the correct way to exercise turned into a friendly wrestling match. Afraid one of them might hurt the other, Geneva watched the playful bout with a reserved smile. When Vonda suddenly strong-armed her son and pinned him to the floor, laughter boomeranged across the house. Geneva would never forget the sound.

Neither would she forget the Christmas of 1985, the last Christmas she ever celebrated with Sean, Vonda, and Lee Bellofatto.

With the onset of 1986, the afterglow of Christmas gave way to the January sleet. From every windshield and window across the city, Oklahoma resembled a monolith of gray still life. Icy rain fell like prison bars, chasing families indoors, chilling the post-holiday cheer. The Bellofatto family returned to their normal routines of work and school, convening for a meal when schedules allowed, waving hello and good-bye in the same breath. The soggy weather caused some glumness, but Vonda endured the shiver of winter with a comforting anticipation: She and Lee had planned a February vacation to the sun and sea. And February could not arrive soon enough.

Vonda's attempts to sever Sean's relationship with Angel had failed. Miserably. He continued to prance his girlfriend through the house as if she were a budding starlet on parade. Vonda had an intuitive sense that the girl reeked of a bad omen. But her dislike had not stopped Sean's obsession. Rather, he resented her for intruding in his personal life, and claimed she didn't try to understand him. Arguments quickly ignited, sparking accusations. And as the outbursts intensified, cross words replaced good intents. Vonda's anger seethed until finally, as a last resort, she forbade her son to ever see Angel again.

When Jim Mathis and Sandy Barlow returned to Oklahoma, Mack Barlow reluctantly consented to their impending marriage. Sean served as best man at the small wedding; his girlfriend, Angel, was seated in the section reserved for friends of the groom. Marriage immediately affected Jim's friendships. Having tumbled into the awkward period between teenager and adult, he no longer possessed the carefree lifestyle of a normal high school junior. After a two-month estrangement from families and school, Jim and Sandy began work full-time at a drive-through restaurant to pay rent and bills. They flipped burgers alongside their friend Roger Landis. But Jim no longer had time for idle merrymaking with Sean, or pretend rituals to Satan. Responsibility had nabbed him by the scruff of the neck.

Between the animosity that Vonda held for Angel, and Jim's complete surrender to Sandy, Sean's life had been gutted like scrap in a salvage yard. As emotions turned into flared tempers, Sean's communication with Vonda and Lee deteriorated. Doors slammed in exasperation, tongues sharpened, and voices amplified until silence yawned over the family.

For weeks Sean's equilibrium was threatened. He could not permit Vonda and Lee to destroy his love for Angel as they had with Jennifer Highland and Tara Duncan. He conducted rituals in Piedmont with the sanctity of the most devout, and begged Satan for a resolution.

Ezurate appeared in Sean's dreams at night. But the wraith of Robert Bower did not plague his sleep. Instead, Sean envisioned himself walking up the street to his house. Spring had arrived, spilling sunlight across the duplex. Lee's work truck stood on the driveway, its windows reflecting the light in tiny prisms. For some reason Sean knocked on the door, sure that any moment his mother or father would answer. But instead Angel opened the door and invited him inside. Her long, dark hair had been brushed away from her face, and her eyes smoldered topaz. She smiled and kissed him, then slipped something into his hand. The cold steel of the gun tingled. In a wistful voice Angel told him she understood what he had to do.

Sean slinked down the hallway to his parents' bedroom, the gun in his grip. He brushed past the door.

Vonda and Lee lay in bed, their eyes closed in sleep. He looked over their forms, his gaze switching from his mother's blond hair to the gun, back and forth, blond hair, frigid gun. Suddenly Ezurate grabbed the pistol from Sean's hand. The demon's laughter caused Sean's hair to stand on end. Ezurate pulled the trigger, once, twice, again and again. Bullets launched until the white bed sheet flowed red.

All that blood!

Sean awoke, paralyzed from the dream. He wiped sweat from his eyes until mobility returned to his body. When he understood the meaning of his dream, his mind stopped with fear. Ezurate was going to kill Vonda and Lee.

In late February the Bellofattos bid their son goodbye and boarded a plane bound for Acapulco. With their week-long absence, the house had a reassuring tranquility, their echoes condemning "that girl" receding. Sean came home each day from school, completed his homework with serenity, and went off to work with a smile across his face. He performed Satanic masses in the quiet of his bedroom with no interruption or fear of discovery. Later, he basked in the time spent with Angel.

But the week raced. Less than two days remained before Vonda and Lee would return. The dreams of blood plagued Sean's sleep and manipulated his thoughts. As he cut the pattern for the robe and stitched the hem on Vonda's sewing machine, his inner thoughts spun. He worked hurriedly, slitting eyeholes in the matching hood, running his hands across the sleek black fabric. While he soaked parchment in oil and burned the rims of the paper for the blood ritual, Ezurate stood at the helm, navigating with a seaman's eye. Ever watchful of the obstacles along the course, the demon had masterminded a remarkable plan.

The evening before the Bellofattos' plane touched Oklahoma ground, Sean finished his closing duties at the pizza parlor. While one employee vacuumed the carpet, Sean and a waitress cleaned tables and restocked condiment trays. The waitress who frequently worked shifts with Vonda asked Sean about the Bellofattos' vacation. But Sean acted nervous about their arrival. Things had not been going well at home, he told her.

The waitress seemed surprised. "I didn't know you were having problems with your parents."

Sean wiped a table, gathered his supplies, and turned on his heel to leave. "It's okay." He tossed her a grin. "I'm taking care of it."

March 4, 1986

The language-arts teacher at Putnam City North High School could not believe her eyes when she read the essay turned in by one of her students. The impact of its words numbed her to the quick. Rumors of Sean's involvement in the Circle K murder had infiltrated her class more than once. Yet when she picked up the telephone to call Vonda Bellofatto at 3:45 p.m., she didn't realize that the English assignment in her hand implied a warning.

" 'Behold the Crucifix, what does it symbolize? Pallid incompetence hanging from a tree!' These words come from the first book of *The Satanic Bible*. Satanism, the world of the Left Hand path has caught many young people, as well as old, in its maze.

"Satanism made me a better person for myself rather than for the benefit of others; Satanism taught me to reach down into my own heart and mind and soul, to find my true essence and let it permeate my environment . . . I became Ezurate, a Satanist. I found a crowd that would accept me because I was me. . . .

"Satanism has caused me to explore the depths of my mind to ask questions of religion and society and find the truth by asking why . . . Why should I treat others the way I would have them treat me? Why should I not have sex or worship other gods? I treat others not as I would have them treat me, but rather as they treat me. For my beliefs I have been said to be dangerously crazy and confused. Why?! At last, I see my thoughts clearly.

". . . Power is life, power is joy, power is indescribable. The Dragon seemed at first to scramble my emotions until through a twist of fate everything turned clear. The love I felt for everyone around me disappeared overnight, replaced by a strong abhorition [*sic*]. I hated everyone and everything. My family, my friends, plants, animals, even life itself. Slowly my hate for reality decreased and I learned to love my few true friends. Through this love I tasted power for the first time . . . I am free. I can kill without remorse and I feel no regret or sorrow, only love, compassion, hate, anger, pain and joy. Only I may understand, but that is enough.

* * *

". . . I have seen and experienced horrors and joys indescribable on paper. . . . The world of Darkness has touched me as it has touched many. Evil has taught me good, good has shown me evil. . . . All this achieved from an ideal most think to be wrong. How can so much right be achieved from wrong? The Left Hand path has, and will, touch many. May they all learn as I have."

I am free . . . I can kill without remorse, and I feel no
regret or sorrow . . . Evil has taught me good, good has
shown me evil.

—Sean Sellers, in an essay
written in his English
class, March 4, 1986

SEVENTEEN

WITH THE TRIUMPH OF THE CIRCLE K KILL-
ing, Sean Sellers had ceased to feel remorse. By
March, his lack of conscience had rendered him inca-
pable of regret. Sean would soon commit the act of
parricide.

At half past four he strode through the doors of the
pizza parlor, nearly thirty minutes early for his shift.
He ate dinner, frequently checking the wall clock. At
last five o'clock rolled around and he began work.
While he jotted orders for pizzas and rang up dinner
tickets, he thought about the plan with which he had
tinkered throughout the day.

Lee and Vonda Bellofatto had to die.

For sixteen years Vonda had chronicled the life of
her child, reveling in his spurts of growth, astonished
by his innate talents. If she had done nothing else on

earth, Vonda felt, she had borne a gifted son. But in the late afternoon hours of March 4, her thoughts mocked her. The boy who had bade good-bye to her that morning could not be the same person who blatantly defiled the Ten Commandments.

Until the telephone conversation with his English teacher, Vonda thought Sean had kept his promise to her and Lee, thought he'd forever blotted out his dark fantasies of walking hand in hand with the devil. Now she faced the grievous truth: something was terribly wrong with Sean. She reread his diary of self-destructive prose, which she had discovered hidden among the sacrilegious objects in his bedroom. Sean had painted a picture of confusion and unhappiness in words that seesawed with desperation.

In the house where she spent her final hours, Vonda Bellofatto sat heartsick at the dining room table and penned a letter to her son. A letter that, in retrospect, prophesied her death warrant.

> My dearest and most precious son, I love you so very much, and would give my life for you without a second thought.

As Sean checked the restaurant oven, he reflected on his plan. That morning he had risen from a bloody dream, dressed for school, and said good-bye to his mother and father with no particular inflection.

Throughout the morning the halls of Putnam City North swarmed with students. Some students noted the faster pace of Sean's voice, its scalpel edge. Some recognized a more aggressive manner about him; the mysterious air he elected not to explain. The smile on his lips had drawn into a taut, thin line. In English class his teacher returned graded essays, and even though Sean was disappointed by the 79 slashed across the page, his mind's eye was on the night ahead.

But those around Sean had accepted his unpredictable behavior. His charm belied the fact that his conception of the world was skewed. As he jaunted from class to class, few noticed that he walked with a buoyant tempo, as though he had been stripped of a tremendous burden.

Maybe I don't always handle things in a proper manner, but my side of it isn't easy either.

Son, right now you are going through one of the hardest times you may ever face. [I know] what it was like for me at sixteen. . . . But you are fighting this, by pushing it deep within yourself and trying to change your natural personality. If I'm wrong, please tell me, . . . I don't care if you ever talk to me about this, that's up to you.

Sometimes, you and I do better to talk on paper than in person.

They'd not communicated in years. Sean felt that they'd never communicated, and now he could make his own decisions. He could lead his own life without parental advice. And Sean's life had nothing to do with his parents. Vonda and Lee hated what he believed in, and communicating with them banked on the verge of impossibility.

The day you were born was the happiest day of my life. . . . I remember when I brought you home for the first time, I was terrified that you'd wake up hungry *and that tiny little voice of yours wouldn't wake me up, so I put you in bed with me and you slept in my arms. . . . If you were to survive and have any chance in life at all, it was going to be up to me. . . . I became an overprotective mother, maybe too overprotective.*

He had eaten lunch in the school cafeteria, erratic thoughts bouncing in his head like tennis balls. The clock's hands pivoted in slow motion. He devoted thinking time to his mother. But visions of her did not throb in the usual vein. He didn't wonder what she and Lee would discuss at the dinner table while he worked. He didn't concoct an excuse to stay out late on a school night. His mission would be far greater— an episode his memory could not censor. Soon he would be able to go out anytime of day or night without their blessings. They didn't have the right to suffocate him, to try and block the breath from him.

When you were little you used to sit in my lap and cry over things like dogs getting run over, cats getting hurt, people getting hurt, and cartoons like Charlotte's Web because Charlotte died . . . [I'd] cry myself from frustration because I couldn't protect you from life's plain and simple facts. I still cry sometimes when I'm all alone, because I feel so helpless to help you.

Sean had long ago learned to stop his tears. His silent sobs were heard by no one. In his world, even the things that seemed constant were moved around. Like Lee's .44.

He put a hot pizza in a cardboard box as he thought about his plan. Ever the poet, he smiled when he thought of the cartridges spinning and whining. Let the bullets represent his tears.

When you were older, we lost Mother . . . You and you alone kept me going once again. I totally devoted my life and all of its energies to you and your needs.

Satan had taught him the proper emotions—pleasure and pain. Interchangeable emotions. Like good and evil.

The thought popped out of nowhere: What if the umbilical cord still tied him to his mother? What if he hesitated at a crucial moment?

His mind twined back to September, when he had performed the destruction ritual. He recalled how the blood on the bathroom door of the convenience store had sent his own blood racing.

Tonight he would perform a blood ritual to end all others. And he'd wear the costume. Become his own pagan hero. But Lee, aye, there lay the rub. Lee's tours in Vietnam had given him near superhuman senses; he'd wake at the slightest sound. Ezurate's black robe, bulky and rustly, could rouse the dead.

The thought made Sean decide to strip to his underwear. The black pair. Lee would never hear him creep into the room. And he would, of course, kill Lee first.

I struggled to make a living for us, and finally left you at Ravia and went to driving a truck, not because I wanted too [sic] but because I could make better money for you to have what you wanted and needed. Oh, I won't say I didn't enjoy it, but not for very long. I always wanted to be with you, but I made my choice and lived with it, however wrong it may have been.

Over the years, his parents left him here, dropped him off there, scattered him everywhere. But they always returned. And following their vacation, they had again returned. Vonda and Lee knew that Angel had stayed at the house while they were gone. Knew that she had slept with their son. They wanted him to work. Do homework. Get more sleep. Change his girlfriends. Go into the Army. They derided him, his decisions, his lifestyle, and Angel, who was the only one who truly loved him.

Earlier that afternoon, in school, he had not volunteered to answer questions posed by his teachers. Nor had anyone questioned his contemplative silence. Fate turned over the hourglass, and the afternoon sun began its journey westward. But the sand trickled down with agonizing slowness.

Why had he waited so long? He welcomed the coup of the demon, the whir sounding in his ears.

After tonight they would never return.

Right now, I see you suppressing yourself to be something that I've never seen in all of your life. . . .

But I can't help unless you talk to me, and if you decide to, be honest with me and I really will try to help.

Sean, to be strong you don't have to put up a tough outside appearance.

Satan gave him strength, helped him with precise timing. Tomorrow, fate would spell Vonda's and Lee's names across the newspaper headline. Sean had not chosen the night; the night had chosen him.

His mind snapped to attention when a customer stepped inside the restaurant. Sean took the order, his hands working to one beat while his brain waltzed to another.

He knew where Lee had hidden the gun. From a closet shelf within arm's reach, Sean had plucked the gun with ease and checked the cylinders. Loaded. He had fondled the pistol, stroked its bevels with a loving hand, then returned the .44 to its nest. He would retrieve it later tonight.

After school he had driven in a fury to beat his own deadline, to get in and out without being seen. But his mother had been home. She'd asked him about his day, right before the telephone rang. Sean had taken advantage of the interruption by changing clothes. He'd flung school papers on the bed and raced out the door before Vonda could break free. Later he'd sauntered through the doors of the pizza parlor.

Nothing wrong here.

You, my son, are very strong. But you need to release your pain. . . . Emotions are one of the biggest controlling factors in a person's life. . . . Please don't think that it's just because I'm a woman that I say that. Lee will tell you the same thing . . .

When his shift ended at ten-thirty, he planned to drive straight home. By eleven, they'd be fast asleep, curled up inside the last dreams they ever dreamt.

Sean slapped a slab of dough on the prep table. The twinge in his gut was not supposed to be there. He'd stopped all emotions, hadn't he? Easygoing, polite, quiet as a church mouse. There was not a living soul who could read his feelings.

So what was this now? Where was Ezurate?

Friends, my son, are very special, and it's hard to have a lot of real friends. I myself can't say that I have many. But the few that I have are dear to me. It's a tough thing to watch a friend get hurt, and it's tougher still to let a friend go when you want them to stay.

Sean, this past summer vacation has been miserable for you . . . But it's over! Let go of it, son. In fact, you need to let go of several things from the past six months . . . You are hurting yourself more than I think you realize.

There was still the little matter of what to do with the gun when it was all over. Thoughts sorted themselves. Jim would help him. They had been through a lot together. The ultimate sacrifice? Jim didn't know anything. Not yet. But tonight Jim would be his Pegasus. Sean would at last be free to fly away with his Angel.

My son, my son, how can I help you? I think maybe too much responsibility has been put on you for you to deal with . . .

[B]e honest with yourself and try to talk to me, and I will promise to try to listen and hear what you are saying.

You are a strong, good, honest young man, but you are having a problem in sorting things out, and unless you will let me help, what can I do?

He ladled tomato sauce onto the dough, slathered the vermilion liquid across the unbaked crust. He glanced at his watch. Nearly eight-twenty.

After he killed them, he would take the gun and drive to Jim's house in Piedmont. Jim would hide the gun. The trick was to conjure up a plan for tomorrow morning.

Something foolproof. There could be no mistakes.

I see things inside of you that you don't know I see. But son, you have pushed me away, shut me out completely. . . . I guess by trying to show you how to do things the easy way, I've given you a completely different idea. I'm sorry.

Be an artist. Live in the country. With Angel. He'd always had a knack for drawing. Got it from his real old man, he supposed. Who didn't give a shit about him. Lee had something different in mind. Be a soldier. Blow a couple of gooks to hell. Be a real man.

What I'm trying to say to you in all of this is simply put: 1. I'll always love you no matter what. 2. If you'll let me in, I'll help you. 3. I'll always be here when you need me, no matter what, until the day I die.

Tomorrow morning he'd ride back to the city with Jim and Sandy; help them reenroll in school. Sean would lead everyone to think that Vonda and Lee had wanted him home by seven-thirty. But Sean and Jim would oversleep, and Sandy would dawdle, making Sean late for his first class. Jim would stop him by the pizza parlor to get a tardy excuse from Vonda. All of his fellow employees would see him come into the restaurant and ask for his mother. Of course, Vonda wouldn't be there, so they'd have to drive to his house.

He preened. Sometimes his intelligence amazed him.

> Just remember, I am your mother and I love you just because you are my son.

Where had the time gone? Nearly ten. As he swept crumbs from the floor, a mental picture of the patio door flashed in technicolor. His work went into slow motion when he envisioned the doorstop Lee had rigged from an old piece of broomstick. Sean would remove the stick, slide open the patio door, then pull out dresser drawers. Come tomorrow morning the police would think a burglar had broken into the house, then killed his parents.

Ironic that a part of his masterpiece might be credited to Vonda for suggesting Lee secure the door. In the end she would have composed the final lyric.

> Finally, I want to say I'm proud of you, more than you realize. I have every reason to be proud. Your father is proud of you, and I guess he expects too much out of you sometimes because you are something to be proud of. . . . Honey, Lee is just a human, and he loves you so much that he can't help himself sometimes. Don't hold that against him! . . .

> I hope this makes sense to you and will help you to work things out.

> Love forever and always,
> Mother

Her postscript appeared across the bottom of the last page of her letter:

> I wrote this today, because of reading what's under this. If you didn't write this, please say so, but know all of what I've said is still very true.

At the restaurant Sean prepared to clock out at the end of his shift. He would never see his mother's letter.

I stood there and I looked at them. And my mother . . . there was blood running out the side of her head. I stood there, and I laughed.

—Sean Sellers, in a
television
interview, aired
August 1987

EIGHTEEN

SATAN'S LITTLE SOLDIER.

Vonda slept half on her side, half on her stomach. One hand clutched the blanket, which nuzzled against her cheek. Her blond hair spilled across the pillow in a yellow tangle.

Lee also slept on his stomach, one arm curled around the bulk of his pillow. He was deep in slumber.

The shot from the Smith & Wesson exploded. Fire lunged from the barrel as the bullet was hurled toward Lee. The .44 expelled a thunderous crack that nearly caused Sean to drop the gun. A wreath of smoke and the smell of charred flesh clung to the air, mingling with the scent of Vonda's perfume.

The bullet tore into the back of Lee's head like a rocket. He jerked beneath the bedcovers, then lay still, as though a nightmare had jolted him from sleep. Blood spewed from his head like a faulty water spigot, splattering his pillow, the headboard, and wall. Bits of flesh, bone, and hair danced in midair until gravity forced them to the floor and bed. A clump of purplish gray tissue, which the bullet had shattered, now dangled from the gap in his head.

Vonda woke.

Sean lifted the revolver, aiming its barrel at his mother's face. He would have to work quickly. Sweat blanketed his near-nude body and trickled down his face and backside. His lungs raced to catch gulps of air. His trembling hands embraced the gun tighter, tighter.

Now, now!

He cocked the hammer.

In Sean's mind a symphony from hell screeched in the night. Ezurate cheered his protégé, cackling a blasphemous operetta. The demon's voice seared the quiet like a jackal in heat. The darkness was illuminated with fiery eyes that flitted this way, then that. Ezurate nudged him and pointed.

Whhhhrrrr . . .

Sean fired. The burst from the gun conjured new demons—ones Sean had never seen. He watched them dart about the room with frantic delight and hover above Vonda, urging her death.

A mother and her son.

Blood spurted from Vonda's face like a geyser. The red spray cascaded toward Sean and splotched his face and chest with dark crimson. The demons roared orgasmically, swaying their heads to and fro. Gnashing their teeth, they snapped their mouths hungrily at her blood.

Vonda shrieked and raised her head. Blood gushed from her cheek, dribbling onto her chin and neck. The bullet had exited close to her mouth, spouting a second current of blood that dripped onto her lips. Disoriented, she struggled to identify the moving shape in the darkness. As she fought the fog of sleep, her hands searched for the ruptures, for the screaming pain in her flesh. She touched her blood, disbelieving, and strained to see it in the darkness.

Her attacker drew closer.

Vonda flinched, cowering in the bed like a frightened young girl. Where was Lee? She ran her hand across the lump that once was her husband. There was no movement.

Sean forced the bile from his throat. He steadied his finger on the trigger, prepared to usher the final blow to her head. He couldn't—*wouldn't*—wait for her to die like this. It would take too long. The night was slipping from him.

His hands quivered as he lifted the barrel to his mother's head. Vonda watched between the tears and blood that blurred her eyesight. Her sobs waned as the haze of sleep succumbed and a horrifying reality returned.

The shadow of her child descended closer.

Satan's little soldier!

Another shot erupted, wedging a second bullet into Vonda's skull, undamming a bloody river that weaved through her hair. She slammed against the headboard as hot metal lodged in her brain. Vonda Bellofatto blinked once, twice, then slumped.

Sean froze. He waited to see if she would move again. She never did. His heart returned to its normal pace. His breathing slowed. The blood in his veins relaxed. He sat on the bed, shifting his body near his mother, and hypnotically studied the lifeless forms.

Blood still pumped from their wounds, oozing across the sheets in long, red fringes. The task was completed. But his work was far from over.

Vonda and Lee slept, side by side, in a bloody baptismal. Man and wife. Father and mother. Their final communion of love, blotched and battered in violent death. Vonda's blood slid down her blue, cotton nightgown. Fragments of Lee's skull had settled near her fingertips. Her dead eyes watched as Sean reared back his head.

Ezurate laughed.

He stood under the shower and scrubbed the bloody patchwork from his face, neck, and chest. Tingling from the hot spray, Sean watched the remnants of his mother fuse with the gurgling water and spiral down the bathroom drain.

Gone. For good.

He towel-dried himself and wiped the steam from the bathroom mirror. Staring at his reflection, he combed his long blond hair until it hung limply to his shoulders. His eyes searched his face for a visage of remorse. A trembling lip, the twitch of his eye. *Something that would give it all away!* But there was none. *He had done it!*

He dressed in a pink and white cotton shirt and faded blue jeans. He paced his bedroom back and forth, scrutinizing the paraphernalia that lay on the floor, the bed, his dresser. He made note of every object that must be hidden or destroyed.

He gathered the black altar, pentagram, and sword, and carefully replaced them on the two-shelved table stand, where they sat in baleful display. He rinsed the last of his blood offering from the chalice, placed the unused incense in its box, then pushed the items behind his collection of brass candle holders on the first shelf. He stashed his bible and Book of Shadows behind the black and white candles in the farthest recess of the table's second tier. Sean studied his room again for anything out of place. It was time to move on to other things.

In his parents' bedroom he set about his work with the cunning of the serpent. He pulled open dresser drawers to make it look as though a burglar had foraged for valuables. Removing the yellow bar that rested between metal tracks, he unlatched the patio door and slid the glass open. Just enough to invite the frigid air inside the house.

The excitement of his destruction dilated as he completed his work. Sean slipped on his jacket, wrapped the .44 in a bathroom towel, then stuffed it underneath his arm.

He walked through the house once more, from room to room. Reentering his parents' bedroom, he flipped on the light and surveyed the two corpses. Vonda lay in a river of blood. Lee's head was crowned in gore. Sean watched as though he were admiring a true artistic creation. *His* creation.

When he shut off the light, he found it impossible not to laugh.

The ten miles to Piedmont seemed an interminable journey. His concentration was lost, suspended in the warp of time when he crept into their bedroom, aimed the gun at their heads, then blew them both straight to hell. His mind played over and over, like a movie—fast forward, then reverse, then freeze-frame. Vonda, lifting her head in bewilderment, immobile with fear. Lee, bucking from the shot that exploded his brain.

He drove into Jim's driveway, churning gravel chips beneath his tires. The house was consumed in darkness. He scurried from his truck and rapped softly at the front door. Jim appeared almost instantly.

"Hey," Sean whispered. He thrust the towel-wrapped gun at his friend. "Do something with this, okay?" He brushed past Jim into the living room and plopped on the couch.

Still ridden with sleep, Jim rubbed his eyes, then stared at the towel, knowing what lay inside. "What's going on?"

Sean stared at him with an expressionless gaze. "I did it."

Jim joined him on the couch, running his hand first across the coarse brown towel then through his hair. "Did what? You don't mean—"

"Yeah, that's what I mean."

"God." Jim's face went white. He searched Sean's eyes for confirmation. "Holy shit. You did, didn't you?"

The beginning of a half smile contorted Sean's lips.

"How does it feel, man? I mean, how does it *feel*?" Jim asked.

"I feel okay. It's over, you know? No fuck-ups. No complications this time. A lot of blood, though. Everywhere. All over the place."

Sandy appeared in the living room. She yawned and squinted her eyes from the stab of light. "What time is it, Jim? What's going on?" Then, "Oh, hi, Sean."

"Go back to bed, Sandy," Jim instructed. "I'll be there in a minute."

She glanced at Sean, who had stretched out on the couch, then silently returned to her bedroom.

Sean broke the quiet. "I need to smoke a joint or something. I've gotta relax or I'm never going to get any sleep. Hide it, okay? Just hide it."

"We gotta talk about this, Sean," Jim pleaded. "I mean, we've *really* gotta talk." He bolted from the couch and removed the metal screen from an air vent on a living room wall. "You gotta tell me what I'm supposed to do, what I'm supposed to say. There's going to be cops everywhere tomorrow. Just tell me what you want me to do." He shoved the towel-covered gun inside the vent and replaced the screen.

Sean lit the cigarette and inhaled deeply. "Calm down a little. Everything is going to be okay. Here, take a hit off this. *Relax.*"

Jim sat quietly and buried his face in his hands. "I don't know, man. I'm worried."

"Now listen," Sean said. "Tomorrow morning we're going to get up like nothing has happened. We'll drive to my house like nothing has happened. I'll go inside for a minute, come back out, and yell for someone to call an ambulance. It's that simple."

Jim studied his hands. "I don't know," he breathed. "I'm scared about this. I mean, I'm really scared, Sean."

But Sean's words were soothing. "Let's get some sleep. You'll feel better in the morning. Everything will be just fine. I promise."

If there is a devil, it's not an external force. It's something inside of us.

—George Romero, motion
picture director

NINETEEN

A RED RIBBON OF SUNRISE APPEARED ON THE horizon, replacing the gray that blanketed Summit Place on March 5, 1986. A new moon reduced visibility for those who left their homes for work in far reaches of the city. Some had just begun to stir about in the 46-degree morning, drinking hot coffee and enjoying leisurely breakfasts. Others dashed about, readying children for school. Doors opened and closed; car engines sparked to life. Forecasters called for a high of 66 degrees—a warming trend that begged for early planting and the perking of new life in the suburbs. A few miles away, Warr Acres Market Place took advantage of Oklahoma's brief winter with a garden-items sale.

The aura that surrounded the Bellofatto duplex on N.W. 115th Street seemed serene. The Bellofattos' habits had not gone entirely unnoticed. Some would later recall that the couple and their handsome, polite teenage son had moved in during the winter months of 1984. A few recalled the couple's last name, if they took pause to remember. But most Summit Place residents, caught up in their own lives, had no reason to ponder the absence of movement around the duplex that Wednesday morning.

No one questioned the immobile truck, its doors embossed with the logo of an Edmond company, still perched on the white slab of concrete that disappeared beneath the closed garage door.

Sean, Jim, and Sandy left the Piedmont house in plenty of time to make their appointed rounds. Only Sean and Jim understood the importance of their journey. Their eight A.M. departure from N.W. 7th Street in Jim's Chevy Malibu began the rehearsed jaunt into the city.

With meticulous care, Sean had dressed in the change of clothing he'd brought the night before—a long-sleeved, pink and white striped shirt, and blue jeans. Because the early air was still nippy, he wore a black nylon jacket.

Darting in and out of rush-hour traffic, the trio talked about the Mathises' plans to resume their education at Putnam City North High School. They laughed at an occasional remark, most often a jest by Sean. But something rankled Jim. He became irked when Sean urged him for the third time to stop by the pizza parlor first. Sean repeatedly reminded Jim and Sandy that he had to get a note from his mother to excuse his tardiness at school that day.

In Jim's estimation, Sean was making too big a deal of the importance of his and Sandy's plans to reenroll in school. But he played along. And Sandy, still not fully awake and unaware that the conversation was a charade being played out for her benefit, made no complaint about their idle bantering.

When the pizza parlor came into view, Sean became even more jittery. "Mom should be there by now. I'll just run in and get the note, then we can go."

Jim forestalled a frown as he caught Sandy's glance in the rearview mirror. He attempted a smile. "Okay, but hurry up. We're running late."

Sean grinned.

Sandy stifled a yawn with her hand. "Isn't it too early for her to be there? Anyway, I thought I heard you guys say we were going to Sean's."

"No." Sean craned his neck, looking for signs of life as Jim turned into the restaurant parking lot. "We said we were going to get an excuse for me, didn't we, Jim?"

"Yeah." Jim parked the car as his wife let out a sigh. "Just be cool, Sandy, okay?"

She huffed. "I'm cool, Jim, okay? Gosh."

Sean rubbed the palms of his hands on his jeans. "I'll be right back."

Jim shut off the engine, tapped his fingers on the steering wheel. A pain flickered in a recess of his left temple as he watched Sean walk inside the restaurant, then quickly return as though he had spun through a revolving door. With a false smile playing on his lips, Sean motioned for Jim to pull out.

"What happened? Nobody there?" Jim maintained an even keel to his voice, in spite of the fact that his insides were toppling.

"She doesn't come in till nine." Sean hunched his shoulders in a manner meant to stress the unimportance of his error. As if it were an afterthought, he said, "Let's go to my house."

"They . . . yeah, okay. The house." Jim backed the car out onto the street, his face and neck stinging with prickles of heat. He glanced at his watch. "Man, it's eight-twenty, Sean. You're going to catch some shit for not being home on time this morning."

"Nah." Sean didn't look at Jim or Sandy, but stared ahead through the windshield. "I bet my dad's already got my mom halfway to work by now. We'll probably just miss them."

In minutes they turned onto 115th Street. Jim blinked, glancing around as he drove. Except for a few stragglers off to late-morning destinations, the street appeared deserted. They neared the Bellofatto house, which stood in sharp profile under the bright sunlight. The company pickup truck was in the driveway. Jim heard a sharp intake of breath. His—or Sean's?

"They must have overslept." Sean's quick burst of laughter sounded obscene. He glanced at Sandy, who had no way of knowing why Sean was acting as if his remark was a joke. "Shit. I could be in trouble. You guys wait here, okay?"

Jim nodded, parked on the north side of the street, facing west. From there he watched Sean get out of the car, walk around to the front door, and let himself in.

Sandy yawned, stretched, slipped her arm around Jim's neck and began to nuzzle him.

"Don't." Jim shrugged her off, peering toward the front of the house. His fingers drummed the dashboard to no particular rhythm. "What's taking so damn long?"

"What's wrong with you?" Sandy combed her hair, fluffed her bangs. "He's only been in there a minute."

Time stood still. The clicking noises of the cooling engine exploded in Jim's ears. He twitched his foot, then raked his hands through his hair.

Seconds later Sean ran screaming from the house. "Stay here," Jim told his wife, then leaped from the car. At the front door he intercepted Sean, who babbled incoherently, gasping words. His heart pounding, Jim made a hopeless gesture. "What the hell are you talking about, Sean? I can't understand—"

"My parents . . ."

Sandy bolted from the car. "What's wrong?" she shouted.

"Just stay there!" Jim pointed his index finger at her, then followed Sean into the house. He didn't need to reorient himself to the surroundings as he crossed the living room. He'd been made to feel at home many times here by Vonda and Lee. He knew the place by heart.

Sean halted his steps. "Back there." He nodded in the direction of the master bedroom. "They're back there."

Jim's heart pounded as he approached Vonda and Lee's room. He peered inside. The couple, covered by a multicolored quilt, looked to be asleep. Jim sniffed. A strong, coppery odor permeated the room. His mind registered a fleeting thought that at any moment they would rise to greet him. Neither figure stirred.

Lee was stretched on his side, facing his wife. Vonda lay on her stomach, her right hand and arm resting beneath her head. Both faced the back patio door to the bedroom. Jim steeled himself; had gone over this moment hundreds of times in his mind since the night before. He had forgotten the family photograph on the wall—the smiles of Vonda, Lee, and a younger

Sean, their eyes following him as he stepped over the threshold.

His gaze was drawn to the blood that covered Vonda's face and head. He forced the bile from his throat, then stumbled back to the living room, where Sean waited. "Let's get the fuck out of here. I don't like this." He grabbed Sean by the arm and shoved him outside.

Sean knew that his future, his *life* depended on his words and actions over the next few minutes.

He sprinted across the lawn toward a neighbor's house and beyond it. He darted over the sparse patches of green, past one house then another. "Blood!" he screamed. "There's blood everywhere!"

In the car Sandy leaned out an open window and clamored for Jim's attention. "What's going on? Jim? You guys are scaring me."

Across the street a man rushed to the edge of his lawn as the blond-haired boy neared him. "What's wrong? What's the problem?"

Sean flailed his arms. "Call an ambulance. Hurry!"

The neighbor ran back inside his house to place the call.

Whispers spread through the Summit Place addition. Tending to everyday life, neighbors had ignored the newest arrivals to the neighborhood. No reason existed to recall the name of the nice family who had come to live there. Until now. A boy shrieking about blood routed them from their homes. Something terrible had happened at the Bellofatto house.

The morning of Wednesday, March 5, found Detective Ron Mitchell immersed in his shift in the homicide division of the Oklahoma City Police Department. Undistracted by those milling around for coffee and answering calls that filtered in from the switchboard, the blue-eyed, brown-haired Mitchell tied up the loose ends in a batch of paperwork. Having served as a police officer for nearly thirteen years, three of them as a detective, he had become judicious at utilizing his spare time. Details tended to pile up.

At age thirty-three, Mitchell's features and mannerisms were reminiscent of a young Richard Widmark. He withstood the ribbing of fellow officers about his "average" height, and dished out his own potshots when they least expected. His good nature did not inhibit his police work, for which he'd trained since the age of nineteen. His record with the department spoke for itself.

Cracking a case exhilarated Ron Mitchell. And for every case he helped solve, another awaited his scrutiny. Murder took no vacation. Murder acknowledged no leave of absence. Murder favored no particular time of day or night.

There are those who attribute murder to the waxing of the moon; heralding particular calendar days as catalysts for lunacy; blaming evil on the positions of celestial bodies against the heavens. Men who agreed with Detective Mitchell's creed rejected such theories as nonsense. But Mitchell referred to the myths a bit more colorfully: bullshit.

When he received the homicide assignment around nine A.M. to assist detectives Sam Sealy and Willard Paige at the crime site, Ron Mitchell had no inkling that he was about to stumble into a twisted tale of cunning. A tale with twists that rivaled the most intricate plots of Agatha Christie.

Stepping into the bedroom of Vonda and Lee Bellofatto, Detectives Sealy and Paige drew almost simultaneous conclusions. The scene before them, initially labeled by the press as a homicide/suicide, reeked of a setup.

Vonda and Lee Bellofatto had been shot as they lay in their king-sized water bed. Lee apparently never knew what hit him. The Bellofattos, without question, had been shot as they slept.

The attention of the investigative team turned to a back-patio sliding door, where a length of broomstick that appeared to have been used as a doorstop lay inside the room near the metal track. The glass door gapped several inches.

Sealy knelt to inspect the possible source of entry. But the queer placement of the broomstick indicated that the door could not have possibly been opened from the exterior of the house. The area was photographed and the door and broomstick dusted for fingerprints. No other signs of forced entry or any indication of a struggle vied for police examination. Although a dresser drawer hung open, nothing appeared to have been ransacked. A number of coins were piled on top of the dresser. A .25 automatic Raven, which rested on the headboard, remained in a dusty black holster. Valuables lay throughout the house. There appeared to have been no burglary.

Detective Bob Horn, who also assisted in the investigation, was stricken by the same sense as the others. He would later comment that burglars do not enter a house and shoot its occupants as they sleep. Horn's first assignment was to interview a young woman named Sandy Barlow Mathis, age seventeen, who waited outside the duplex with her husband and the victims' son.

Ron Mitchell's arrival completed the network of investigators. At intervals Sealy stepped outside to confer with officers who huddled to receive and trade information. The news that jewelry and money were found in the house trickled to Mitchell, who prepared to interview Jim Mathis.

In his understated manner, Mitchell led Jim from a black and white police car to the unmarked detective cruiser, where he introduced himself. Jim readily answered questions posed to him, beginning with the fact that he'd known the Bellofattos for about five years. The teenager spoke rapidly, jamming words together.

"Sean came over to my place last night after he got off work. Around midnight, I think. We sat around and talked for a couple of hours. My wife Sandy was already asleep when he came by. It got too late for Sean to go home, so he spent the night."

"Tell me about this morning."

Jim sighed. "Okay. We got up at six-thirty, me and Sean. Sandy got up about seven. We were getting ready to go to Putnam City North so Sandy and I could enroll in school. But first we had to get a note from Sean's mother."

"What sort of note?" Mitchell's interest was spurred.

"Well, we were running real late, and Sean had to get a note from his mom because he was going to miss his first class."

The detective occasionally prodded Jim, who explained how Sean had gone inside the pizza parlor asking for his mother, never imagining the atrocity that waited at home. How Sean later entered the house, concerned that his parents had overslept, only to discover their bodies.

"Were the Bellafattos having problems with anyone?" Mitchell asked.

"Well," Jim said. "Yeah. For awhile my wife's dad was giving them some problems."

"And what is your father-in-law's name?"

"Mack Barlow," Jim told him.

After jotting down the information, Mitchell soon permitted Jim to rejoin Sandy.

The Bellofattos' son waited in the police cruiser. The teenager's demeanor was unruffled as he prepared for his interview. The boy who sat in Mitchell's car, his face stoic, displayed an odd look of impatience. His blond hair fell to his shoulders. A few blemishes dotted his baby face; his eyes gleamed like the centers of azure marbles.

In his years of experience, Mitchell could recall from memory the typical reaction of a family member following such a tragedy. He expected panic, fear, hysteria. Sean was soft-spoken, with incredible control of emotion. He did not cry, but hung his head as if pouting when Mitchell asked him to retrace his actions of the day before.

"I got out of school about 2:45 and I went straight home."

"Was your mother there?"

"Uh-huh. And then I had to get ready for work. I had to be there at five, so I guess I left home about four—no, yeah, that would be right. I got off at tenthirty and I went home." Searching for approval, Sean looked up at the detective.

"And what happened then?"

"Well, when I came in, my mom and dad were at the dining room table. Just sitting there, you know, talking, and they said they thought I was working too many hours. They were always worried about me." Sean paused every so often and licked his lips to accentuate a point. "We decided to get my truck fixed. They wanted it running right."

"How long did you talk with them?"

"Well, no more than fifteen minutes. Then I went to my room because I had homework to do. After that, I asked my mom if I could go to Jim and Sandy's. She said I could."

"So everything was okay when you left?"

"Uh-huh. I left about eleven-thirty for Piedmont. But it got so late, I decided to just go on over there and spend the night."

"Did your parents know you were not coming back last night?"

"Yeah. I called my mom from a convenience store in Piedmont. She sounded a little upset at first, but she told me I could spend the night."

"Do you often stay over with your friends on a school night?"

"Well, see, I spoke to Jim and Sandy yesterday, and we were all going to Putnam City North to see if they could enroll. So we could all go together in the morning, that way. My parents wanted me here at seven-thirty." Sean nodded toward his house.

"And your mom gave you no indication that anything was wrong?"

"No, sir."

"Did you speak with your dad?"

"No, sir."

Mitchell, surprised at Sean's recall of detail, was

even more surprised by the ease with which he spoke of his recently deceased parents. The boy's story had a ring of truth—too loud of a ring. "Then this morning you decided to come by here to ask for a note. Is that what happened?"

"No, we decided to go by the restaurant where my mom works first. But I woke up late—about seven, I think. I was on the couch. Jim got up a few minutes later, and Sandy got up around seven-thirty. We left around eight, I think, and drove over to the restaurant. But they said my mom wouldn't be there till nine, so we decided to come by my house." He paused, again hung his head.

"All right," Mitchell said. "Just take your time. Do you remember what happened then?"

"Yeah. We pulled up. My dad's truck was here. I knew then that they'd overslept and that I was in trouble for not being here at seven-thirty.

"So anyway, I got out and I used my key to get in." Sean began to stumble over his words. "I walked into my . . . into my folks' room . . ." He pursed his lips, the pout returning, looked at the floor of the car. "I don't want to talk about it."

Mitchell called on his patience. He lessened the pressure. "Are you okay?"

Taking a breath, Sean nodded.

A surprise crouched behind the answer to Mitchell's next question. "Do you know of anyone who would want to harm your parents?"

"Yes. Sandy's father, Mack Barlow."

Sean went on to explain how Barlow had been a constant problem to the family, having called, and even having stopped by the house twice trying to find Sandy when she and Jim had run away. After Jim and

Sandy returned to Oklahoma, Sean continued, Barlow quit coming around.

Sean consented to being fingerprinted, for "elimination purposes," as Mitchell suggested. In the van that doubled as a technical investigation unit, Mitchell asked whether he might also check Sean's clothes. The teenager consented. Sean removed his black nylon jacket. A spot check of the pink and white shirt and blue jeans followed. The detective found nothing—no spots, no stains.

Sean continued to amaze Mitchell.

"These aren't the clothes that I had on yesterday," Sean volunteered. "I changed over at Jim's and left my other clothes over there."

"Would you mind if we went to Piedmont and looked at the clothes you were wearing last night?"

"Okay."

Such a polite young man, Mitchell thought. *And now, let's go to Piedmont.* And that was it. Sean Sellers was only too happy to lead an expedition to the house where he'd spent a seemingly unremarkable night, chatting about school and then catching a few winks of sleep.

Before they left the crime scene, Mitchell knew he must act quickly to impound evidence from the Bellofatto house. When he asked the teenager whether he would sign a search waiver, Sean faltered; his eyes widened. Mitchell tried to still his palpitating heart.

"I don't know," Sean said. "I'd better ask someone first."

The detective's confidence, as always, sustained him. "Who should we contact?"

"I guess my grandfather, Jim Blackwell." Sean then told the investigator that Jim Blackwell lived in Dallas,

Texas. He didn't know where his grandfather could be reached.

Until Blackwell could be located, Mitchell asked for the name of another relative. Sean could not offer any other.

"Well, Sean, I'll need to advise the detectives that you're not going to sign the waiver," Mitchell said.

Sean's gaze moved from the detective's mouth to his pad and pen. "Well, I guess it would be all right."

"You don't have to sign the waiver if you're not sure."

The teenager looked thoughtful for a moment, then asked whether he might read the form. After scanning the piece of paper, Sean signed his name, thus authorizing the investigators to remove any evidence found in connection with his parents' murders.

Mitchell went lax with relief as he and Detective Horn witnessed the signing of the waiver. He couldn't help but note the jauntiness of Sean's steps as the boy joined Jim and Sandy for the trip to Piedmont.

The arrival of medical examiner Larry Balding precipitated an examination of the bodies of Vonda and Lee Bellofatto and a probe for bullets. Balding folded back the quilt and the left half of a white sheet, then turned Vonda's body over. The smears of blood that stained her face had clotted in her nostrils and across her teeth. Large clumps of jellified blood, almost black in color, had accumulated in the crevice of her left armpit. Lavender striations appeared in her skin above the cut of her blue nylon gown.

Although drained of her life's blood, Vonda lay at peace, her long blond hair shielding the bullet under her pillow. The bullet had not entirely perforated the mattress, but a tiny hole seeped water over the sheet, dampening the front of her gown.

Balding informed Sealy that Vonda had suffered two gunshot wounds to the head area and that there were two exit wounds. But where was the second bullet? Sealy removed Vonda's pillow to the kitchen, where he slashed at the ticking with a knife. Amidst the foam contents, he found the second slug.

The bullet that had killed Lee was discovered between the mattress and the bed's wood frame. The right side of Lee's face had slumped onto the back of his left hand. His left upper eyelid was purple and swollen. Sealy rolled back the sheet that covered his body. Lee wore no clothing. His bronzed back was evidence of the Bellofattos' recent vacation under the Mexican sun. Lee's blood had settled in death, and portions of his lower-right torso and limbs were a discolored, mottled blue.

Considering the violent manner in which the couple had died, officers thought there might have been other shots fired. After removal of the bodies to the county morgue, they drained the water bed in a search for additional projectiles. But no more were found. The three .44 bullets retrieved were bagged and marked for ballistics.

The sign read WELCOME TO PIEDMONT—THE CITY OF OPEN SPACES AND FRIENDLY FACES.

Sean's 1973 Ford pickup was parked in Jim's driveway. Mitchell made a mental note to ask Sean's permission to search the truck. Sandy invited Mitchell and Paige into the house as though she were about to host a cocktail party. Eager to please, Sean handed Mitchell the pair of blue jeans he'd worn the night before, but then changed his mind about the shirt. Now he touted the pink and white shirt he presently wore as the one he had on the night before.

"Do you want me to take it off?" Sean asked the detective.

"Yes." Mitchell collected the clothing, plus a pair of white socks handed to him by Sandy, and placed the items in a paper sack for lab analysis.

When Jim brought out a solid pink shirt for Sean to wear, Mitchell noted light red splotches on the front. "What are those spots?"

"Oh." Sean chuckled. "It's oil paint." Always the compliant one, he stopped buttoning the shirt. "Do you want this one too?"

"Yes." Mitchell, still wary of the thoughtfulness of this trio of teenagers, was not surprised when Sean agreed to a search of his truck. When Mitchell discovered nothing incriminating, he hid his disappointment and reluctantly left the teenagers in Piedmont. He was more convinced than ever of Sean's involvement in the Bellofatto murders.

Darkness fell upon N.W. 115th Street and its dazed residents. Families huddled in the inner sanctum of their homes that night, occasionally taking a peek at the ghoulish circus through closed blinds. Cars drove up, then down the street, flashing bright lights on the Bellofatto house, pausing to satisfy morbid curiosities. But without the parade of intruders, the street would have been fearfully quiet.

The man who'd called the ambulance that chaotic morning had made an observation to a reporter that summarized the thoughts of many. "Is this somebody who's going to start picking this side of town? Is any-body safe anymore?"

A woman who'd consoled the grieving Sean, who had placed comforting arms around him, relived the moments when she'd met him halfway out in the street. That night she couldn't shake the image of how he'd cried while pouring his heart out to her. How he'd expressed his vengeful wish to find those who "did this to my parents."

At the Mathis house in Piedmont, Jim also found sleep elusive. After Sandy retired, he and Sean ex-changed a battery of words and glances. A wall of suspicion had arisen between them. Jim couldn't be-lieve his ears when Sean told him not to "talk about this to anyone." No matter where Jim went in the house, Sean's eyes followed him like two blue telescopes, just as they'd done in the photograph in the Bellofattos' bedroom.

Jim grew tired of the silent insinuations. "Sean, why the fuck are you staring at me like that? They . . . your parents . . . It's not right."

"Remember the Circle K, Jim? Remember, you were there. This is your ass, too, we're talking about here."

Cold fingers gripped Jim's chest. Memories of the Circle K killing had never left him. And now Robert Bower had returned to damn them all. Yes, Jim had been there. But Sean had pulled the trigger. And now look what Sean had done. If he could blow away his own parents . . .

"Okay." Jim pivoted to turn on Sean, who was seated at the kitchen table. "Okay, Sean. So I was there. But I've never breathed a word to a living soul, and you know it."

Sean nodded. "Good. Then we have nothing to worry about, do we?"

His anger not yet exhausted, Jim pounced once more. "What the hell are you going to do if they put this one together, man?"

Sean grinned the half-plastic, half-flesh grin. "I'll plead insanity."

I loved my parents.

—Sean Sellers, in a television
interview with Oprah
Winfrey,
January 1987

TWENTY

THE BELLOFATTOS' DEATHS FRIGHTENED
the principal of Putnam City North High School. He
peered out his office window, the bright March afternoon somehow dimmed by the news, and scrambled
to put the pieces together. The day before, a language-arts teacher brought him a copy of an English
essay written by Sean Sellers in which the teenager
claimed to have no remorse about killing. Rumors of
Sean's participation in the Circle K murder had surfaced over the past months, and at least three other
students—all of them friends of Sean's—leaked information about the crime. After hearing of the Bellofatto murders, an unspeakable thought occurred to
the principal. He instructed his assistant to check
Sean's locker for "evidence." He then called police.

At one-thirty P.M. Sean sat in a booth at the pizza
parlor with Jim and Sandy, acting like a victim with

teary eyes and a quivery voice. For his alibi to work, it was absolutely essential that Sandy never suspect what had actually happened. The Mathises postponed their school reenrollment plans to console their friend, but Jim found Sean's grand display difficult to swallow. Beneath the fluorescent lighting, Sean's face was bathed in a pale, sickly wash, the color of his eyes a dull, murky gray. He rested his head between his hands and, as Sandy Mathis listened, he wondered aloud why his parents had to die. Who possibly could have killed them in such a brutal manner? Could he have prevented their deaths if he hadn't spent the night in Piedmont?

For Jim the act had grown stale. He wrestled with his conscience, avoiding Sean's stare when the cold blue eyes seared him. Sean's recital of grief slipped around Jim like a noose. Sean was attempting to make him an accomplice to the lies. The flawless execution. The absence of pain and regret.

Lacing his fingers around a cup, Jim's memory skipped back in time. Sean charging into the living room with the towel-wrapped gun. Sean rushing from the duplex screaming about blood. Jim had a box seat, but he also had the starring prop in his possession. *What the hell was he going to do with the gun?*

The thought of the gun frightened him. Only this morning he had run from the scene in the Bellofattos' bedroom, terrified. Before he had seen the bodies, rigid and forever stilled by death, Jim had almost sold himself the fantasy that Sean had lied about killing them. The photographic smiles of Vonda and Lee would forever haunt him. They were dead. Sean had killed them. And now Jim had inherited the charade.

At least their stories satisfied the police. Jim had

stuck to his lines like a seasoned actor—the way Sean trained him. No pregnant pauses, no telltale hesitations. Jim would go to his grave with the memories of Robert Bower and the Bellofattos.

Then the recollection hit him like a slab of concrete.

I've got a secret.

Jim would never forget the look on Roger Landis' face a month or so before.

Hey, Jim, Roger had whispered.

How long ago had it been—a month; maybe two?

Hey, Jim. Guess what?

Jim had practically choked on Roger's sarcastic tone, its underlying snag. They'd worked side by side in the restaurant on a night that seemed to crawl on its belly. Jim had sealed himself off from small talk. But Roger would not leave him alone. He'd nudged Jim in the ribs, the dreaded smile on his face.

Guess what? he'd asked. *I've got a secret.*

A dry panic rose in Jim's throat. Roger knew about the Circle K.

For detectives Mitchell, Horn, Sealy, and Paige, the investigation into the deaths of Vonda and Lee Bellofatto was rapidly coming to a close. When the telephone call from Putnam City North High School arrived in the squad room, the status of Sean Richard Sellers rose from suspicious to prime suspect. At two P.M., nearly five hours after Bob Horn had left the Bellofattos' duplex, he drove to the high school to interview the principal.

In talking to school officials, Horn learned that the principal's assistant had searched Sean's locker and discovered seven pages of notes proclaiming the teenager's practice of Satanism. A copy of an English essay had also wound its way into the principal's office. After the language-arts teacher read the contents, she'd made a copy, returned the original to Sean, then passed the copy on to the principal.

"Sean is very intelligent," the teacher explained to Horn. "He has never created a problem in class. But after reading his paper, I became very concerned."

"Did you contact Sean's parents about the essay?"

"Yes, I did. Yesterday around 3:45 or so. I talked to Mrs. Bellofatto, and she told me that she would take care of it."

The language-arts teacher also told the detective that during the previous week she had observed Sean in study hall, but a few minutes later noticed that he no longer was in the room. She called roll to verify his absence. Just before class ended, he reappeared. The teacher advised Sean that she considered him to have missed class and that she would have to contact his parents. He became very upset at the mention of his mother and father, and pleaded with her not to call them.

An interview with the high school drama teacher galvanized the detective. A year before, Sean had become involved in a fight when another student overheard his claim of worshiping the devil. The Bellofattos were called to the school and told about the altercation. Visibly distraught by the news, Vonda and Lee had promised to take care of the problem.

But it was the drama teacher's memory of a private conversation with Sean that made the greatest impression on Detective Horn. Less than three months ago, Sean had appeared fraught with anger at his mother and father, and stated, "I would be better off if my parents weren't alive."

"He's a very bright young man," the drama teacher said. "But I've noticed that he changes moods a lot."

"Really?" Horn asked. "How so?"

"Well, sometimes he has the opinion that everyone loves him. And then at other times, he thinks that everyone hates him."

When Angel arrived at the pizza parlor, Sean's eyes were rimmed with red. His broken voice struggled for words. Angel held his hand, helpless to wipe away his sadness as easily as she brushed away his tears. When Jim and Sandy had first told her of the Bellofattos' deaths, Angel briefly wondered whether Sean could have killed them. His anger with Vonda and Lee had occasionally exploded in threats to "get them both out of the way" so that he and Angel could see each other. But Angel had not taken him seriously. Viewing the pain etched on her boyfriend's face, she dismissed any suggestion that Sean might have killed his parents. He wasn't capable of taking a life.

And Sean reinforced her beliefs, whispering, "Baby, I couldn't do it. Even for you."

As the day slanted toward late afternoon, the lunch crowd in the pizza parlor thinned, and employees busied themselves with tasks that took their minds off the morning's event. Vonda would not be gliding through the door with her famous smile and friendly voice, and the coworkers she'd left behind mourned the loss. Tears were also shed for Lee. He would not be waiting for his wife at home.

At the Mathis house, Jim and Sandy changed clothes in preparation for their night shift. Angel went horseback riding in a neighbor's pasture. In the ensuing quiet, Sean stretched out on the couch for a nap.

In the bedroom, Jim paced, his face stark white.

"What's going on?" Sandy asked him. "I know something really weird is happening."

Jim stared at his wife as if seeing her for the first time. "My God, Sandy. What have I gotten myself into?"

"What's wrong, Jim? Tell me."

"Sean did it. He killed them."

Sandy's mouth fell open.

"I don't know what to do. The gun is here. It's in the air vent in the living room."

Sandy closed her eyes, the words resounding in her ears. Sean's act in the restaurant, his tears—nothing more than a gambit of twisted lies. In a voice that could have cut glass, she said, "I want it out of here, Jim. Now. I don't want it in this house."

"I'm going to get rid of it. I've just gotta think. I've just gotta—"

"Get it out of here!"

A dream jolted Sean from sleep. One loose end remained to be tended. The gun. He had to ensure that the disposal of the .44 would be handled with caution. But he would think about that later tonight. Playing catch with the sandman, he closed his eyes and drifted off again to sleep.

When evening tinged the sky with purple, Sean and Angel drove to the burger restaurant. Inside, the shuffle of customers obstructed Sean's view as he looked up and down for Jim. Spotting him behind the grill, Sean motioned for his friend. Angel sat at a table out of earshot.

When his gaze fell on Sean, Jim ceased his work and stepped from behind the counter. "I can't talk long, man. We're real busy tonight."

"What are you going to do about the gun?"

"I'll take care of it." Jim scanned the restaurant for the watchful eyes of the manager.

The casual response irritated Sean. "Tell me what you're going to do with it, Jim. I want to know."

"Jesus Christ, man." Jim glared, then his eyes darted across the restaurant. More customers filed in. "I don't want to talk about it here. I said I'll take care of it, and I will. All right?"

Sean pursed his lips. His tongue pushed against the soft fold of his cheek. He pierced Jim with a hard stare. "Okay," he whispered. "Okay. But if someone finds it, Jim—anyone at all—you're in this one too."

While Sean performed with consistency, family members who'd learned of Vonda's and Lee's untimely deaths scoured the city for him, baffled as to why he had not attempted to contact them. The empty Bellofatto duplex, locked and cordoned off by police, had already taken on the haunting hues of nightfall. Jim and Geneva Blackwell drove to the pizza parlor to find their grandson, following Jere and Doyle Ricks, who were but one step ahead in the search for Sean. A restaurant employee suggested that they might find him with his friend Jim Mathis, at the burger restaurant.

Geneva had received the telephone call from Vonda's half sister Jere around three p.m. She'd driven the 130 miles to an Oklahoma City truck stop where she'd located Jim, the trip not nearly long enough to plan the epitaphic words deserving of Vonda and Lee. Relaying the news of their deaths was the most difficult task she'd ever had. And now her sorrow stirred the same questions that agonized Jim: Who could have done such a terrible thing?

And why?

The day of March 5 crushed the hopes and dreams of Jim Blackwell. His "little princess" was dead. He envisioned Vonda not in the ugly throes of death, but as the little girl he once bounced on his knee. He treasured the times they'd spent together—times that were far too short. Jim's only child had grown to become a beautiful woman. That was how he chose to remember her. But while he grieved for his daughter, he also felt pain for Lee Bellofatto—the man who'd loved and cherished Vonda. A good husband and father. A good man.

Jim and Geneva found their grandson at the burger restaurant and sat across from him at a small table, searching for clues as to what had happened. Information was sparse. Only the comforting words of Jere and Doyle Ricks helped Jim through the remainder of an evening that destroyed his entire world.

Sean acknowledged Geneva's presence, but spoke directly to his grandfather. She studied the teenager as he explained the events that led to his discovery of the morning. How he'd attended school, then gone to work, then stopped by home before driving to Jim Mathis' to spend the night. Once an integral part of her life, Sean appeared distant to Geneva. She pondered his ill-kempt looks, his brow furrowed with distress. When she'd asked him why he had not called her after his shocking discovery, Sean told his grandmother that he'd remembered she worked alone; he hadn't wanted her to bear the news by herself. His response was indicative of the Sean she remembered —always putting the feelings of others before himself.

No sooner had Geneva consoled herself by this tribute to Sean than a preposterous thought accosted her. A Ravia friend had first asked the question: "Do you reckon Sean could have done it?"

Appalled, Geneva had shaken her head. "No," she'd said. "No way." In her eyes, Sean was practically without fault. Indeed, she would remain one of the last to believe any wrongdoing by the grandson she'd helped to raise.

Jim, too, contemplated the calm complacency of his grandson. He knew that Sean had not been getting along with Vonda and Lee. Just yesterday morning his daughter had telephoned him, the little-girl sound in her voice spilling out with, "Daddy, something is wrong with Sean." Jim had promised to come to the city the next day to have a talk with his grandson, never guessing the urgent nature of the problem. Now, as he watched Sean's lips move like an actor in a silent movie, the possibility that the murders of Vonda and Lee had not been committed by a deranged burglar surfaced, submerged, then bobbed again. Jim listened to Sean's account of the past twenty-four hours, trying to shed the dark notion that his grandson could have been involved. But a blanket of apprehension draped him, threatened to suffocate him.

After Sean and his family left the burger restaurant, Jim Mathis found concentration on work duties impossible. Images of customers ran together like watercolors, their voices thawing into a monotonous bumble. Jim plagued himself with questions. How had he managed to become so involved? Sean had constructed a mousetrap, and Jim had become the mouse. Sean had murdered three people in cold blood without a backward glance. He'd killed his parents with as little indifference as he'd bumped off a stranger. Who would be next? *Who else* stood in Sean's way?

Visions of the gun kept coming back to Jim. He would have to get rid of the gun somehow. Somewhere. The murder weapon must never be found.

That night, the fact that someone else knew the secret of the Bower murder, that he had been inside the convenience store, caused Jim's insomnia. That night the ghost of Robert Bower camped on his doorstep.

On the eve of his parents' deaths, no one trespassed on Sean Sellers' emancipated world. After he'd poured his anguish out to family members at the restaurant, they left him to his Angel. Jim and Geneva had hoped that he'd return with them to Ravia. But Sean imagined his grandparents, aunt and uncle, raking over the sordid details of the crime. He refused to discuss the matter further. He didn't want to hear another word. Sean had talked his grandfather out of dragging him to Ravia. Home was with Angel now, he decided, choosing to milk his newfound freedom to every advantage. Angel's bedroom would be his place of mourning.

That evening in the house where Angel lived with her mother, Sean and his girlfriend watched the late news on television. With an odd sense of distance, he watched the instant replay of attendants removing the bodies of his parents from the duplex to a waiting ambulance. He shivered, then warmed to a fever of arousal.

While Angel showered, he kicked back and drank a beer, weary of the traumatized faces that had paraded before him throughout the day. Vonda and Lee were dead. People would have to accept that fact and get on with life. He certainly planned to.

Reclining in his chair, he basked in the attention lavished on him by his girlfriend and her family. Sean had lured the enemy into a labyrinth from which there was no exit. Had blazed the most intricate campaign of real life Dungeons & Dragons. With what Angel would tell police was the acquiescence of her mother, yet another pawn in his game, Sean and his sweetheart retired to Angel's bedroom for the night.

The morning of March 6 smiled down on the two lovers for the last time.

I was attacked by the demons . . . I had a terrible head-
ache so hard it knocked me down. I was lying on the
floor, curled up in a ball because of the pain. I couldn't
stand. I couldn't breathe. I just rolled up in a ball and
prayed and yelled, "Satan, I rebuke you!"

—Sean Sellers, January 1987

TWENTY-ONE

BY THURSDAY MORNING JIM BLACKWELL'S AN-
ger and confusion over the deaths of his daughter and
son-in-law peaked. Having labored throughout the
night over his decision to talk to authorities about his
grandson, Jim had to find the truth, regardless of its
nightmarish implications. In a conversation with
Detective Ron Mitchell at police headquarters, he
could no longer hide his tormenting question. "Do
you have any idea who could have killed them?"

Mitchell pulled out a chair for Jim, then offered him
a cigarette. "We have a couple of people we want to
question."

Jim quickly read between the lines. "Is it someone
. . . close to home?"

"Yes, it is."

A pained expression swept Jim's face. "I was afraid
you were going to say that."

"I'd like to talk to Sean and Jim again."

Although the detective had not shoved aside pleasantries in light of Jim's grief to bluntly say, *Mr. Blackwell, we believe Sean killed Vonda and Lee,* Jim's hope that Mitchell would name an outsider as a suspect evaporated. The nagging feeling that had interrupted his fitful sleep returned. Sean's performance at the restaurant the day before had confirmed that he would never admit to killing his mother and stepfather.

Jim urged Mitchell to press Jim Mathis for information, and assured the detective that Sean would come in for further questioning.

His worst fears virtually guaranteed, Jim resigned himself to the truth. His grandson had killed Vonda and Lee.

Mitchell remained suspicious of Sean Sellers. He had already planned to reinterview both Sean and Jim separately. He first telephoned Sean, who made an excuse, but promised to come by the station later in the afternoon. At one P.M. Mitchell called Jim, who expressed surprise that the detective wanted him to come in for questioning. When Mitchell persuaded him that he only needed to go over a few details again, the teenager agreed to come downtown.

Jim and Sandy arrived at the station at two-forty P.M. After Sandy was led to a downstairs waiting room, Mitchell escorted Jim into the homicide office on the second floor. There, the teenager repeated his version of Sean arriving at his house around midnight, the planned school enrollment and tardy excuse the next morning. The account varied little from his story of the day before.

Mitchell tired of Jim's cover-up. He listened patiently until a lapse in conversation offered the appropriate moment. "Look, Jim," the detective said. "I know who killed Vonda and Lee Bellofatto. And I think you know too."

In the absence of his best friend, Jim wavered. The color drained from his face. He looked at the floor. "I'm afraid."

The first hint of truth had emerged. "It'll be okay. You can tell me."

"I'm afraid of Sean." Eternal seconds passed. Jim's next sentences were barely audible. "He did it. He killed them."

An intake of breath signaled Mitchell's relief. The gamble had paid off, but his job had just begun. He leaned over Jim's chair. "Where's the gun, Jim?"

The teenager's eyes lowered. "I put it in the trash. At my grandfather's house."

Mitchell relayed Jim's admission to Sam Sealy, who headed the investigative team of the Bellofatto murders. Additional information could later be seized from the teenager, but confiscating the murder weapon took precedence. "Okay, Jim, let's go get it."

The teenager's mouth flopped. "Get what?"

"We'll take you out to your grandfather's house so you can show us where the gun is."

Jim fidgeted. He looked around, his lips pinched. "I've gotta use your phone."

A new game? Mitchell wondered. He played along. "Why?"

"Today is trash pickup day. I need to call and see if it's still there."

The detective's pulse skipped a beat. If city workers had hauled away the garbage, the most incriminating —the *only* physical evidence—would be difficult to retrieve. Fingerprints could be destroyed. He hoped the boy's call was not too late.

Over the telephone Jim's voice took a sharp turn. "Don't let them pick up the trash." A pause, then he snapped. "Just don't let them take it, okay?" He slammed the receiver into the cradle.

In a race to locate the gun, Detective Mitchell and his partner led Jim to their car, only to discover the tank low on gas. They filled up along Northwest Highway, and then drove to the bedroom community of Piedmont. As if to compensate for the delay, Mitchell asked questions. "Let's talk about Sean killing his parents. What did he tell you?"

Without the controlling presence of Sean Sellers, Jim talked. "Well, he came over to my house and brought in the gun. He had it wrapped up in a towel. I never even saw it, really. He told me that he'd taken off all his clothes except for his underwear, and that he'd sneaked into his parents' bedroom and shot Lee first and then shot his mom." Jim drew a quick breath. "But his mom raised up, and so he shot her again. He said that he took a shower and got dressed, then he came to my house."

As they drove the last few blocks to the Piedmont house, Mitchell decided to probe Jim about the Circle K homicide. With a shrewd reel, Mitchell cast his line. "I heard that Sean did the Circle K killing too."

Jim hung his head, stared at his shaking hands. "Yeah. He did it." He peered out the car window. "I was there when it happened."

The fish had taken the bait.

Mitchell wanted to shout that three murders had just been solved. "Why didn't you tell me before?"

"It was hard enough to tell you about his parents. I

wanted to tell you. It's been bothering me for a long time."

Lee Bellofatto's .44 Smith & Wesson six-shot revolver lay just where Jim said it would be. The weapon had been wrapped in a brown bathroom towel and placed in a pizza box stamped with logos advertising the restaurant where Sean and Vonda worked. The box, placed inside a white plastic bag, had been covered by yet another plastic bag and shoved to the bottom of a trash container. The detectives left the gun in the towel wrapping for its journey to the police lab.

On the return trip into the city, Jim agreed to divulge all that he knew. As they neared the police station, Mitchell read Jim his rights. With little coaxing, the teenager recited his tale of the first killing by Sean Sellers. Although he had been aware that Sean carted his grandfather's .357 Magnum from the Piedmont house on the night of September 8, he stressed to detectives that Sean and the clerk were in the store alone when the shooting occurred. Jim only aided Sean in returning the gun to his grandfather's briefcase and in swearing to uphold the sacrificial secret.

Still another coincidence would later be documented in Mitchell's police report. On the return trip to headquarters, Jim recognized his grandfather traveling in his pickup along the same route. Mitchell pulled over the surprised man, who identified himself as a state capitol policeman. After Mitchell explained the situation, the man told detectives that the .357 Magnum, which Jim had indicated to be the Circle K murder weapon, was his state-issued service revolver, loaded with 90-grain silver-tip bullets—the identical ammunition spent in the Bower killing. The security guard agreed to bring the revolver downtown.

For one afternoon Mitchell had netted one helluva catch.

The relaxed atmosphere in which Sean and Angel had indulged over the past hours seemed far away as they drove to the police station. Sean licked his lips constantly, prattling on about how he first thought his grandfather to be mistaken about the detectives wishing to question him again. Then Ron Mitchell had telephoned. And Sean complied. He always did, didn't he? But hadn't he already told the police everything? What was the point in exhuming the same questions? Did they think he'd been able to summon new answers?

Minutes later he sat before Detective Sam Sealy. "I don't know what's happening here. I don't understand any of this. Why am I here?"

Sealy's voice brought Sean's rocking head to a sudden stillness. "Look, Sean, we've already talked with Jim."

Sean's mouth gaped.

"We're placing you under arrest for the murder of your parents."

If the detective expected a sobbing confession, he was nonplussed at the unflappable suspect. Once booked, Sean phlegmatically gave his name and address, and nothing more. Sealy's questions elicited no further response. Sean sat in reverent silence.

When Sealy booked the teenager on two counts of first-degree murder, Sean merely smiled. The detective thought it was an evil smile.

At 5:52 P.M. on the evening of March 6, Jim Mathis

began his first voluntary statement before detectives Mitchell and Paige. He narrated the account of how Sean told him that he had showered after he'd killed Vonda and Lee, looked around outside the house to make sure that no one had heard the shots, then crept into his parents' bedroom one final time to open the patio door.

"Around midnight, Sean brought the gun inside my house in Piedmont, wrapped in the brown towel. I didn't believe his story until he told me the details of the killings," Jim said, adding that he'd followed Sean's bidding, as always, and hid the gun in an air vent. He and Sean talked into the night about how it felt to kill someone. Then, in the morning, they carried out the tardy-excuse theme, driving first to the pizza parlor, then to Sean's house to "discover" the bodies. The .44 remained in the air vent until this morning, when Jim dashed over to his grandfather's house and buried the gun in a trash receptacle.

Thursday, March 6, was to be a hectic day for Bill Cook, who spearheaded a task force of eight detectives. The team had just received a long-awaited break in the murder investigation of an Oklahoma City jogger who'd been raped and strangled in an area park nearly two years earlier. Cook and his men were battling what he referred to as "combat fatigue."

He had just adjourned a meeting when Ron Mitchell appeared in the doorway.

"Hey, Cook, can I talk to you for a minute?"

"Sure. I'm about to wrap things up here."

The respect Cook and Mitchell held for one another flowed like the silent, but forceful undercurrent of a stream. Their shift changes frequently overlapped, but working on different cases left them little time for talk. Cook knew a few sparse details of the Bellofatto case. Today, each man brimmed with his own discoveries.

Mitchell's news proved the more pressing. "I think we just solved the Circle K murder."

Cook gathered his papers. "What are you talking about?"

"If you have time, there's someone in the next room I think you'd be interested in meeting."

Cook shot him a side smile. "I've got time."

Jim's rapport with Ron Mitchell—developed over the past thirty-two hours—prompted him to ask the detective to stay. Mullenix joined in to hear the statement regarding the convenience-store murder. For the next two hours the three officers and a recording secretary listened to testimony that sounded more like a novel. All ears waited, hungry for words—the right words—to put the Circle K case to bed and to solve Bower's murder.

In September, Jim began, Sean had been talking about killing someone to "see what it felt like." After they had taken their dates home on the night of September 8, they drove to Jim's grandfather's house in Piedmont. When they left the house later that evening, Sean had managed to slip the .357 Magnum into the car. Jim recognized the gun as the one his grandfather kept in a large briefcase. The teenagers pulled in to the Circle K store at the intersection of 122nd and Council Road to buy gas. Sean went inside to pay for the gas, then brought the clerk outside.

About a week earlier, Jim explained, he had told the clerk that Sean's father was a mechanic, and now they planned to check Bower's clutch travel, which wasn't working right. After toying around with Bower's car, Jim told the clerk that the clutch appeared intact. Bower discussed his plans to install a new power booster for his car stereo, then Bower and Sean walked back inside the store.

According to Jim, he observed the next few moments from the comfort of his own car. He watched the clerk take a drink of coffee, then saw Sean pull the gun from beneath his shirt. Sean fired at the clerk several times, and Jim saw smoke rise from the barrel of the gun. The clerk ran toward the back of the store. Sean tracked him, the gun aimed at the man, until they were both out of Jim's sight. Then, Sean raced to the car and informed Jim that he had just "shot or killed" the clerk.

Jim hoped that telling his version of the Circle K fiasco released him from responsibility for Bower's murder. He told detectives that after leaving the store that evening, he and Sean returned to his grandfather's house. Jim went inside, but Sean remained in the car a few minutes before reentering the house. In his grandfather's bedroom Jim held open the briefcase for Sean, who replaced the weapon. Jim's grandfather was none the wiser.

His last revelation hardly surprised anyone. Jim told police that Sean would plead insanity if he were ever caught.

Following the Bower statement, Jim was charged with one count of Murder One for the death of Robert Paul Bower. A third count of murder in the first degree was added to Sean's list of charges.

Before retiring for the night, the detectives involved in both cases huddled in conversation. For a sixteen-year-old high school junior, Sean Sellers showed a great deal of cunning. But he had made a grave error. He'd told Jim his secret.

On his way home that evening, Bill Cook could no longer contain his anger. During Jim's statement to police, the teenager admitted that yet another mutual friend had known for several months that Sean Sellers murdered Robert Bower.

The thought gnawed at Cook's insides. For six months a third party had concealed the killer's identity. En route to the grocery store where Roger Landis worked, the detective called for backup. Although he knew nothing about the teenager, one inescapable fact bothered Cook. If the Landis boy had only told someone about the Circle K murder, Vonda and Lee Bellofatto, in all probability, would still be alive.

By the time he arrived at the store, Cook's frustration soared like mercury on a sweltering day. At nine-thirty P.M. he found Roger Landis in the store's cooler, stocking soft drinks. The detective identified himself, read Landis his rights, then placed the boy under arrest.

Roger's eyes, dilating in confusion, suddenly turned cold. He smirked and turned away. "I don't know what you're talking about."

The little son of a bitch, Cook thought. "Listen," he said. "You can cooperate now, or your ass is mine."

"For what?" Roger paled.

Cook fumed. "Material witness to a homicide." He shoved the teenager toward the attending officers. "Take him in and book him." (Roger would be released the next day and he would never be accused of a crime.)

The satisfaction of having solved the Circle K murder was dimmed by the feeling of being too late. Two human lives had been lost. Roger Landis must have known that Sean Sellers had killed "just to see what it felt like."

As he drove the last mile home that night, Cook lamented the times he swam against the tide in his efforts to halt madness. Sometimes the ocean seemed bottomless.

On Monday afternoon, March 10, 1986, an arc of mourners, family and friends, gathered in numbed silence at two gravesites in a small cemetery in Arpelar, Oklahoma. The fragrant aroma of rainbowed wreaths, transported from an Oklahoma City funeral home, encompassed the biers. Vonda and Lee had returned to the community where they'd been joined in wedlock. Loren Bellofatto, the mirror image of his son, stood as a painful reminder of a life cut tragically short. At thirty-two years of age, Vonda Maxine Bellofatto had been reunited with her beloved mother.

One familiar face was noticeably absent from the crowd.

Most police are skeptics. But you have to understand, it doesn't matter what *you* believe, it's what *they* (Satanic killers) believe.

—Curt Jackson, a detective with the Beaumont, California, Police Department, and a Satanic crimes consultant

Satanism didn't have that much to do with it. People have to understand that there are just mean people in the world.

—Eric Mullenix, Oklahoma City homicide investigator

TWENTY-TWO

ON MARCH 7 SEAN AWOKE TO COLD REALITY. Odors mingled; stale urine and the transient pungence of sweat collided as he writhed on the concrete floor of a jail cell. His demons began their journey to find more promising acolytes. Ezurate departed in a grand fury; the evil inside of Sean dissipating with his demon.

In the confines of the Oklahoma County Jail, Sean endured his demon's departure as he had endured his soldiering for Satan. He prepared to make an appearance before the first in a long run of unmoved audiences.

If Sean believed that he was correct in transposing the literal interpretations of good and evil, did Satan serve as the catalyst for that belief? Or was there another, more secular explanation for his behavior? The question of whether Sean killed while under the influence of Satan would sensationalize his case to proportions usually reserved for the most notorious of killers —with one exception. Did the Oklahoma boy who had taken the lives of his mother and stepfather actually ride sidesaddle to the real culprit—the devil?

The occult investigator has become a relatively new phenomenon in police annals, challenging the most steady convictions that Satanic murder *just doesn't happen* in the 1980s. Detective Curtis Jackson, a homicide investigator with the Beaumont, California, Police Department, is but one of a growing number of skeptics turned believer in the reality of Satanic murder. His contention that occult-related murder has become yet another modus operandi in the files of bizarre, unexplained deaths has taken the detective to crime sites throughout the U.S., conducting seminars to open the eyes of police and citizens.

Jackson's revelation has changed more than one non-believer's mind. "I used to think it something to scoff at," he says. "But I've investigated many murders that were direct results of Satanic rituals."

The idea of Satanic sacrifice violates the boundaries of human imagination. Few can, or will, accept its reality. But ritualistic killing has become less of an offering to the devil and more of a message to the world.

Anton Szandor LaVey claims that he chose 1966 to build the First Church of Satan because that year represented the birth of the Age of Fire. The modern Satanist believes that for the length of an age, 1458 years, the world is controlled by one of two powers— God during the Age of Ice, and Satan during the Age of Fire. In his *Satanic Bible,* LaVey writes, "The infant is learning to walk, and by the first working year of his

Age—that is to say 1984—he will have steadied his steps, and by the next—2002—he will have attained maturity, and his reign will be filled with wisdom, reason and delight."

Over the years, Satanists have branched off into "grottoes," or separate affiliations of the same belief. Some have retained the traditional method of worship, and others have reformed into brotherhoods distinctly different from their Satanic kindred. Among these are the inbred Satanist, a family trait passed on to offspring, complete with evangelical modes of recruiting; the organized, nationwide link, such as that which has surfaced in a recent disclosure of the Son of Sam killings. Third, but not least, comes the self-styled Satanist, which Jackson believes is among the most dangerous. "He is more radical; more quickly progressive."

To Satanists, blood represents the "life force" that must be presented to gods and demons in suitable quantities. But the use of blood in self-styled worshiping ceremonies is not always limited to slitting an animal's throat. Some groups carry blood sacrifices a step further. While the aftermath of coven gatherings often resembles pagan ruins, there is little that authorities can do when no laws have been broken. When an infraction has occurred, the Satanists' "Code of Silence" assures police that coven members will go to great lengths to prevent identification. Murder usually guarantees secrecy.

Jackson's theory, "It doesn't matter what you believe, it's what *they* believe," has become synonymous with his job as detective and teacher. "The Satanist cannot drag his sacrificial parent to the woods to be slaughtered," he explains, "so he shoots them in their sleep."

In March 1986 the general consensus of the Oklahoma City Police Department took a 180-degree bend from Curtis Jackson's position. In the case of Sean Sellers, homicide investigators leaned toward a less ethereal explanation.

An undercover detective since 1977, Eric Mullenix hails from a long line of law enforcement officers. His father and grandfather were both members of the force. His wife, a former Dade County, Oklahoma, sheriff, now carries on the tradition as an Oklahoma City patrolperson. Devil worship, Mullenix maintains, had little to do with Sean Sellers' murdering spree. "Sean had a girlfriend," he says, "and his parents stood in his way."

Mullenix believes that Sean could no longer compete with his peers at Putnam City North High School. He no longer stood out in the crowd as he had in Greeley, Colorado. To gain attention, Sean promoted Satanism. And its shock value paid off.

Sean's desire to attract attention to himself, as in his inability to keep silent about the murders, reveals an embryotic narcissism—the first rung on the ladder of antisocial, psychopathic behavior. In the legacy of the Ted Bundys and Captain Jeffrey McDonalds, Sean Sellers could not relinquish the spotlight, no matter what the risk.

"People say he has to be crazy to do what he did," Mullenix says. "And jurors might be persuaded toward that opinion. But the world must begin to understand—there are just mean people in the world."

Without Satanism as a plausible reason, Mullenix's approach to Sean's homicidal motives is by far the most chilling. The calculating mind of Sean Sellers did not allow him to believe that he could not win at his game of murder. Only immaturity and inexperience kept him from victory.

As legal counsel for the defendant, Assistant Public Defender Bob Ravitz filed a motion for a recertification hearing to adjudicate Sean as a juvenile. In preparation for the hearing, the court required a psychological examination and a recertification study, the results of which would be prime elements used to determine whether Sean should be considered a juvenile or an adult. On April 20 and 21, an Oklahoma City psychologist was assigned by the courts to evaluate and test Sean. The appraisal by Dr. Herman Jones was not intended to question Sean's legal sanity, but to determine "his judicial status and to assess his dangerousness to the public."

Dr. Jones' techniques in diagnosing Sean consisted of the Wechsler Intelligence Scale for Children (Revised), the Minnesota Multiphasic Personality Inventory (MMPI), a mental status examination, and a clinical interview.

As family background and personal history are key components in an individual's psychological makeup, Dr. Jones documented Sean's infant and adolescent life with the only tools with which he was given to work. Sean told the psychologist that he was an only child who had lived for a number of years with his grandparents while his parents drove a trucking rig. He listed his chronology of moves, the various schools he attended. At no time did he mention physical or sexual abuse by any member of his family, or injuries that could lead to possible brain dysfunction or a psychosis. In a recertification study prepared by the probation supervisor for the Oklahoma County Juvenile Bureau, additional biographical information was gathered in sessions with Sean, six of his school teachers, the principal of Putnam City North, his employer at the pizza parlor, and the Blackwells. Again, no knowledge of sexual or physical abuse was conveyed.

The results of the intelligence test indicated that Sean functioned overall in the bright-normal range of intelligence. While he demonstrated a focal strength in language skills and a general strength in non-verbal abilities, his scores in arithmetic function were markedly lower, although his most recent school records contradicted this conclusion.

Throughout the two-day session, Sean appeared to be in a "euphoric, pleasant, and cooperative" mood. But the psychologist found Sean's upswing in temperament, despite the austere surroundings, to be transparent. Sean's generally positive outlook—his sunny disposition—represented a "facade that he attempts to project to others. Underlying this is a negative self-image such as that which Sean manifests through his Satanic interests."

The MMPI technique was utilized to determine whether Sean was the product of an atypical personality disorder. The MMPI profile revealed that his anger and hostility were masked by his attempts to "manipulate the situation and portray himself as exceptionally well-adjusted."

"Sean's interactions with others, for the most part, tend to be very controlled and superficial," Dr. Jones reported. "[He] takes great pride in being in 'absolute control' and being able to hide any aspects of himself from others. He does not display good internalized prosocial rules for his behavior, and thus exhibits fluctuating morals, despite his intelligence . . . He has a need to think of himself as unusually self-sufficient, and has great achievement needs, whether as an officer in a youth organization or as the 'high priest' of his own 'coven.' "

The Diagnostic and Statistical Manual of Mental Disorders, or DSM, is the scripture and verse used by psychologists and psychiatrists to categorize an individual's behavioral characteristics. In many cases, overlapping of one group to another occurs, which makes a diagnosis more difficult to pinpoint. On April 28 Dr. Jones concluded that DSM III 301.89, Atypical Personality Disorder, Sociopathic with Histrionic Features, accurately classified Sean's propensities to Satan worship, manipulation, dominance, and control. The histrionic features, or "acting" ability that Sean possessed, explained his inclination to dramatize. In times of crises his high intelligence and nimble ability to rationalize became chief defenses.

The sociopathic personality, or "psychopath," is not necessarily the product of a mental illness. The psychopath has a clear perception of reality, but holds no moral or social obligations. His mission is one of immediate emotional gratification, regardless of whether his pursuit is at the expense of others. He has no empathy and displays no sympathy for anyone, least of all his victims. To the psychopath, people are to be exploited and then destroyed. He has his needs, and for him only those exist.

Behaviorally, the alignment between the psychopath and Sean Sellers is without any remarkable deviation. The psychopath is usually sadistic. While this reflects Sean's enjoyment in cutting his coven friends for blood offerings, it also characterizes his proclivity to boast about his infliction of pain, whether sharing his secret of killing Robert Bower or professing his lack of remorse in an English essay. Power is of extreme importance to the psychopath, but only the power that exists within himself. Sean's wish to be "the most dangerous person on earth" attests to this obsession; likewise, his description of power in his school essay, "Power is life, power is joy, power is indescribable."

The psychopath tries to be godlike and all that is good because he fears that he is actually the antithesis. But when his defenses fail to protect him, he can only retaliate in violence. Sean swayed from good to evil every moment of the day. His obedient nature toward his parents could only continue for so long, until finally his subconscious could no longer suppress the rage tucked inside by the "good son." The psychopath reacts with hostility whenever his needs are frustrated, and particularly whenever anyone gets in his way. The convenience-store clerk refusing to sell Sean beer might have been anyone. The vendetta Sean held was not necessarily against Robert Bower, but against the roadblock that stood between Sean and what he wanted. When Vonda and Lee forbade their son to see Angel, another red flag waved in Sean's eye, and he could only respond with vengeance.

Sean's harmonious response to structure and supervision also fit the psychopath portrait. His compliant, and often subservient, nature toward authority figures fuels his manipulative tendencies. If he excelled in leadership capacities, maintained a high grade-point average, and completed household duties expected of him, how could he be punished for staying out late or reading a *Satanic Bible?*

In this vein, his declaration, "I woke up in jail one morning and found out that they'd arrested me for murder," was but another example of the shroud Sean wore to disguise the "truth." That he claimed demons attacked him in his jail cell after he'd read from a Holy Bible, was in sync with Dr. Jones' findings. The magnitude of *why* he'd been arrested was far too serious to continue his act of being a child of the devil. The time had arrived for Sean to prove that he had been "saved," and thereby changed. God's salvation had delivered him from the evils that randomly controlled his actions—the actions he could not "remember."

By obliterating the murders from his memory, Sean escaped self-blame for the deaths of his parents and Robert Bower. His Satanism defense refused to bend to reality. Sean pointed the accusing finger at Ezurate —his evil side. Distinguishing the twins that lurked inside of him, he referred to himself—the good Sean, the good side—in the third person. He colorfully predicated this distinction with the remark, "They [the demons] made a separate person in me—someone I called Ezurate. It was him who committed the murders, and not Sean Sellers."

Then did an underlying dementia cause him to kill —a result of the voices and hallucinations that crept in and out of his subconscious?

At the time of the interviews, Dr. Jones did not find any indication of active psychotic process in Sean; that is, an ingrained organic mental disorder or psychosis. He did, however, note the presence of "unconventional" thought patterns, and did not rule out the possibility of a thought disorder. These abnormalities are evident in the area of Sean's Satanic worship, his fascination with blood, and in particular, his visual and auditory hallucinations, which the psychologist believes he did indeed experience.

In sum, Dr. Jones recommended in his evaluation that Sean's atypical personality would be difficult to reach therapeutically, and that Sean's drive to remain in control would eradicate any significant change. In this regard, he suggested that Sean be judicially considered an adult. The psychologist also determined that Sean presented "a mild to moderate risk to others in a community setting at this time, and that he is at mild risk for a genuine suicide attempt but is a moderate risk for a suicidal gesture."

On May 12 Judge Manville T. Buford, associate district judge for Oklahoma County, presided over the recertification hearing of Sean Sellers. The issue of whether Sean presented a future threat to society was discussed, and these discussions became acrimonious.

Assistant Public Defender Bob Ravitz employed the only strategy available to him. By factoring in Sean's high intelligence and the absence of any serious prior legal entanglements, he attempted to show the court that Sean's best interests rested in the area of treatment, not imprisonment. This could only be achieved, he argued, by adjudicating Sean as a juvenile and remanding him to the Intensive Treatment Center (ITC) in Tulsa County, a maximum security facility for juvenile offenders.

Ravitz's ammunition consisted of an arsenal of witnesses who testified that the adult system was the improper solution for Sean—and possibly detrimental. He hammered home that rehabilitation prospects in the ITC unit were excellent. Sean's intellectual stature made him atypical of the other residents housed at ITC, and could only be advantageous for his eventual release back into society. Experts in the fields of criminology and sociology illustrated the physical and mental marring that occurred for juveniles in penal institutions. Dr. Thomas Murton, professor of criminology at Oklahoma State University, explained that Sean would be "placed in with somebody at random and subjected to violence, homosexual attacks, and finding himself lost in an adult chaotic world."

Jim Blackwell knew firsthand the type of men turned out by Big Mac—McAlester Penitentiary. His grandfather had served as a prison guard on death row at the penitentiary for twelve years. If Sean were to stand trial as an adult and be convicted, Jim explained, the prison environment would abuse and destroy him. Even though Sean might be convicted of murdering his daughter and son-in-law, he would lend his grandson every means of physical and moral support, and encourage further treatment if warranted.

Ravitz secured ITC's chief psychologist, Dr. John Hurlburt, who testified that the center's one- to three-year therapeutical program was specifically designed for the one-time violent juvenile offender. While Hurlburt endorsed the ITC program to treat the behavioral patterns of Sean as portrayed in Dr. Jones' psychological evaluation, he found difficulty accepting the diagnosis. The evaluation, Hurlburt explained, rendered an adult diagnosis, was limited in its procedure, and did not accurately reflect Sean's emotional makeup.

The state found little value (or solace) in placing Sean into a treatment program whose duration could last only one or two years. Assistant District Attorney Wendell Smith found the conception of a twelve-month stint for three heinous murders outrageous.

Sean had shown a pattern of killing, and the Intensive Treatment Center had no way of promising that he would not kill again.

In closing, Smith explained the considerations for adjudicating Sean Sellers an adult. The considerations in making the decision, he explained, could not be overlooked. The offense was committed in an aggressive, violent, premeditated, and willful manner, and there was not just one offense, but three separate and distinct murders. Secondly, the offense was against property or persons; in this instance, murder. The third consideration of the court was whether Sean had any history of legal trouble. His contact with police in Greeley, Colorado, despite its trivial repercussions, handicapped his case. In establishing the fourth consideration—the prospects for adequate protection of the public if Sean were to be processed through the juvenile system—Smith argued that the defense failed to show that the public would be protected; failed to show that Sean would not kill again. The maximum time Sean could be incarcerated, he concluded, would be two years.

Ravitz had expounded his belief in Sean's possible rehabilitation in his opening statement, and he reiterated it in his closing. A period of intensive treatment for Sean Sellers lay in society's best interests.

Judge Buford's ruling came within thirty minutes. Rather than basing his decision on the conclusions of Dr. Jones' psychological evaluation, he took the gut of the report under consideration. In assuming Sean's guilt of the three murders and the psychological reasoning that Sean appeared to have a personality disorder marked by anger and hostility, any signs of

rehabilitation might only be Sean's continued manipulation of the system.

"The psychological evaluation in this case indicates
that the defendant will be difficult to reach therapeutically," Judge Buford added, "which suggests to this
court that even if the court, on its motion, extended
the juvenile jurisdiction to the age nineteen, there is
no reasonable assurance presented in the evidence
that all of the treatment necessary to protect the public
and to make the changes contemplated under the Juvenile Code could occur.

"The court, therefore, finds that the motion of Sean
Richard Sellers to be certified as a child should be
denied." Judge Buford also found the state's evidence
sufficient to bind Sean over for trial in the adult division, with formal arraignment to take place on May 19,
1986.

When news of the impending trial made headlines,
some parents in the city shuddered. A boy of sixteen
had murdered his parents while they dreamt safely in
their beds; their fatal error was to fall asleep. Rumors
had it that the boy dabbled in devil worship, but most
would not concern themselves. If an unspeakable evil
paced within the mind of Sean Sellers, authorities had
caged that beast.

The odd smile adhered to his blemished face, Sean
fully expected to spring that cage door.

They say I have no mercy and they want to give me death. And I ask: Who is the merciless one?

—Sean Sellers, November 1987

TWENTY-THREE

ON SEPTEMBER 24 INDIAN SUMMER SUPERIMposed rectangles of sunlight on the walls of the Oklahoma County Courthouse. Sitting between assistant public defenders Robert Ravitz and Kindanne Jones, Sean felt the ambience of the courtroom. Fluorescent lamps burned above him, dimming what he knew to be a fair sky just beyond the windows' perimeter. Sean had not seen, touched, or smelled the outside world in over six months; had not left the orbit of his jail cell without the restrictive clamp of handcuffs and an arm grip. For the next eleven days of his trial, he would sit mute.

Oklahoma County District Attorney Robert Macy and Assistant D.A. Wendell Smith readied their presentation at the prosecution table. Jim Mathis had agreed to a plea bargain—a five-year deferred sentence on a reduced charge of accessory to murder—in exchange for his testimony in all three homicides. Other witnesses in the prosecution's corner included Sean's former girlfriend, an employee at the pizza parlor, a friend who had discussed with him methods of parricide, and detectives involved in both cases.

Dressed in his ebony, western-cut suit, cowboy boots, and signature string tie, Macy was an intimidating symbol of the state he represented in a court of law. His silver hair complemented liquid-blue eyes. In his eight years as district attorney, Macy had sent twenty-seven men to the Oklahoma State Penitentiary F Cell Block, better known as death row. But of all the men he had encountered in a courtroom, Sean Sellers disturbed him most.

The blond boy's former shoulder-length hair had been cropped short. He wore a light-colored shirt and dark tie. Sean glanced at the great seal of the State of Oklahoma—a pentagram in its own right—then transfixed his gaze on a side door that opened for jurors.

Jury selection in the trial *The State of Oklahoma versus Sean Richard Sellers* had begun on September 22, the day after Satanists celebrated the Autumn Equinox. As the men and women filed in and took their seats, Sean studied them, hoping to catch a glint of expression on the twelve stoic faces.

The final preparations of Ravitz and Macy wound down as spectators prepared for a view of the highly publicized proceedings. Curiosity seekers squeezed into pews; reporters crammed into vacant seats near the door, their ink pens drawn and ready. The world awaited the truth: Had the devil slipped behind the blue eyes of a child and instructed him to kill? Or had the child committed murder, plain and simple.

The D.A.'s decision to ask for the death penalty

came after he and his staff had made their own post-mortem of the murders. Had Sean killed but once, execution would not necessarily have seemed the punishment befitting the crime. But in Macy's estimation, the murder of Robert Bower was a "test" killing in a plot to ultimately kill Vonda and Lee Bellofatto. The prosecution believed Sean had experimented with the *feel* of murder, and if set free, would kill again. Macy planned to engrave on the minds of the jurors that the teenager's motives could not be disguised as the domination of the devil. The state had no intention of losing, and every intention of putting Sean to death. A Satanic defense was about as watertight as the *Titanic*.

When the bailiff called the court to order, a hush fell across the room. The Honorable Judge Charles Owens emerged from his chambers and took his seat. The court session began.

In his opening statement Macy considered each juror, his pale eyes and soft voice holding their attention easily. "The defendant Sean Richard Sellers has entered a plea of not guilty, which casts upon the state the burden in proving all of the allegations to your satisfaction beyond a reasonable doubt. And this we will gladly do." He paused for a second, his words confident. "Sean Sellers is guilty of three counts of murder in the first degree, and we're going to expect your verdicts to say so."

As Bob Ravitz rose from his chair and buttoned his jacket, conversation interrupted the quiet. His life-long advocacy of banning the death penalty was well-known. But Ravitz's condemnation of the death penalty was never presented in a more articulate manner than in the Sellers' trial. The fact that Oklahoma set no minimum age for execution, or weighed age as a mitigating factor in a capital offense, made the task of pleading for a life all the more difficult.

The conflicting views of Ravitz and Macy stretched to opposite ends of the globe, occasionally erupting on the courtroom floor. The trial of Sean Sellers was no exception. Ravitz's later remark, "Only a sick society would send a teenager to death," provoked Macy's rebuttal: "No, only a society that's sick of killings would sentence a sixteen-year-old to death."

In the courtroom, the legal scrimmage between prosecutor and defense attorney intensified. A heated moment during the Sellers' trial brought Ravitz's emotions to the surface, along with several unexpected remarks to Macy. Out of earshot of jury and judge, the district attorney invited the public defender to "step outside."

In molding a defense to save the life of his client, Bob Ravitz faced a harsh battle. The prosecution had a strong case: an eyewitness to the Bower murder, damaging testimony by several other witnesses, and two murder weapons. Ravitz's only hope for securing a not-guilty decision in the death of Robert Bower lay in discrediting Jim Mathis' account of what happened the night of September 8, 1985. Satanism was to be blamed for all three allegations, and, the defense believed, constituted insanity.

When Ravitz faced the jury, his eyes searched for a sympathetic resting place. "I think you'll come to the conclusion that if Sean Sellers did this, and that's a big if, he did not know what he was doing, because someone or some force was forcing him to do it." A moment's intermission punctuated his argument. "I think when all the evidence is in, you *will* have a reasonable doubt, and you *will* vote not guilty."

* * *

For the next two days the prosecution played its trump cards. Testimony by Tara Duncan and Roger Landis acquainted the jury with a boy—Sean Sellers—who boasted about his murderous escapades. On September 25 Jim Mathis related his version of the convenience-store murder and how Sean wanted to "see what it was like to kill somebody."

Macy directed Jim to the night of the Bellofatto murders: "What did he say to you that night?"

Trying to avoid Sean's relentless stare, Jim shifted in his chair. " 'I did it.' And I said, 'You did what?' And he told me—he said, 'I killed them.' I said, 'Who?' And he told me his parents."

"What did he tell you that he did?"

Jim began to speak too quickly. Judge Owens asked him to slow down and take his time. But Jim continued to speak rapidly as he related how Sean had described the shooting of his stepfather, then his mother.

"He said his mom had blood pretty much all over her," Jim said. "Then she raised up. And he didn't know if she raised up because he missed her or because she was in pain, and he shot her again."

"Did he indicate anything about any laughter at the time?"

"He said after he—I don't know if he said he laughed out loud or he slapped himself. He was real pleased with what he had done, though; how he had done it so far."

Debra Wilson, another friend of Sean's, had also been subpoenaed to testify for the prosecution. Now fourteen years of age, Debra had recently completed a detoxification program for alcohol and chemical addiction and abandoned her beliefs in Satanism. Her startling account of several bizarre telephone conversations with Sean stunned the court.

"Did you and Sean ever have discussions about your parents or his parents?" Macy asked.

"Yes," Debra said.

"And what were the natures of those conversations?"

"He'd be angry a lot. He had a lot of anger."

"Did he tell you who that anger was directed to, who he was mad at?"

"It was sometimes his mom and his dad," Debra said. "Just depended really. It was just sometimes that he'd get really angry at them."

"What else did he tell you about his parents, his thoughts toward his parents?"

"When they'd get into a fight sometimes, he would —he'd just tell me how much he hated it, being told what to do. And we talked about—he said, 'I want to kill my parents sometimes.' And I would say, 'No, you don't.' "

"Did he ever mention anything to you about trying to kill his parents or his mother?"

"Yes."

"What did he tell you?"

"He said the previous summer that he had poisoned either a Coke or a hamburger and he tried to kill her with that, but that it didn't work."

On cross-examination of Debra Wilson, Ravitz steered the jury back to Satanism. If Sean told someone that he'd tried to poison his mother, then Satanism, once again, was the reason.

"What is the Code of Silence with regards to Satanism?" Ravitz asked.

"Really, it's just like you have your Satanic friends, and they know, and no one else knows," Debra said. "You don't break anonymity of any of your Satanic friends. You don't go around talking about it. It's a very quiet deal."

"So, if you knew names, you wouldn't give them to me; correct?"

"Yes."

"What would happen to you if you gave them?"

"I don't know. It's inner fear."

"You fear that you or someone you loved could be killed?"

"Yes."

Ravitz walked back to the prosecution table, picked up a paperback book and handed it to Debra. "What is that?"

"This is a *Satanic Bible.*"

"Talks about killing people, doesn't it?"

"Yes."

"At some of these meetings, do they talk about killing people?"

"Yes."

"Almost brainwash them?"

"Yes. It's a lot like taking over their brain, and the person is so much into fear and admiration of the other person that they would be willing to do anything that they say."

Macy again approached Debra, determined to bring the court back to the issue at hand. "Do you recall, about three weeks before Sean's parents went to Mexico, that he was talking to you?"

"Yes," she said.

"And what was he talking to you about?"

"I don't really remember. We started in on the Satanism and killing parents."

"If you told the police that he was talking about killing his parents, would that have been right?"

"Yes."

"Do you remember describing to the police the kind of weapon that he would use?"

"Yes."

"Tell them that he would blow them away?"

"Yes."

When Julie Schille, a former coworker with Sean at the pizza parlor, took the witness stand, Assistant District Attorney Wendell Smith spilled the deck. "Do you remember having had a conversation with Sean sometime in the fall of 1985 concerning the homicide at the Circle K?"

"Yes, I do," Julie said. "He was upset. And I asked him what was the matter."

"And then what happened?"

"And he proceeded to tell me that he was mad at society and mad at people pushing him around and telling him what to do, and that he had killed people for less than that. I didn't believe him, and I told him that what he was saying couldn't possibly be true."

"And then what did he say?"

"He said, 'I don't care what you say; I know I did it.'"

"Did he ever display any of his artwork to you?" Smith asked.

"Yes, sir. One afternoon—maybe it was evening, I'm not exactly sure—we were working together, and we were sitting at the break table, and he showed me pictures of his parents."

"Could you describe the picture he showed you?"

"There was—it was just a blank piece of paper, and it was sketched upon. And there were two people, and they appeared to be dead. The woman in the picture looked like Vonda. She had blond hair."

"What was it about the picture that made you think the persons looked to be dead?" Smith asked.

"Because there was blood," she said. "There was a lot of blood."

On Monday, September 29, as Sean practiced his Code of Silence, testimonials by the defense were put before the court. Everyone leaned toward the witness stand as Bob Ravitz began his presentation.

The case against Sean had received a lot of media attention. Newspapers and television newscasts had splashed his picture and the story of his alleged crimes across the state. But Sean's defenders also used the media to state his case. Surviving family wanted to reveal his loving side and the abiding respect he held for his parents. School teachers would testify to his rank as a star pupil. Expert witnesses on the practice of the occult were called in to strengthen the teenager's claim that the devil had made him do it.

Now, Ravitz planned to introduce evidence that would rock the jury. After hearing the contents of a letter Vonda had left for her son, the court would know for themselves what Satanism had done to Sean Sellers.

The language-arts teacher of Putnam City North High School declared that Sean had never been a disciplinary problem. He was an excellent student, intelligent and talented. His English essay illustrated the twisted authority the devil had on even the brightest of pupils. In calling the school drama teacher to the stand, the defense determined to show that Sean was an exemplary teenager, and not the expert "actor" he was made out to be by the prosecution.

When Macy cross-examined the drama teacher about Sean's acting proficiency, testimonials continued to swing in Ravitz's favor. "Well, I wouldn't send him to Broadway," the teacher said, "but he was a fine actor for the classroom."

In light of the testimony by Angel's sister Rebecca, there were those who later commented that perhaps Sean should have sought a Broadway audition. Immediately following his parents' murders, Sean played an award-winning scene. On the eve of March 5, when Rebecca arrived home, Sean was there. "He opened the door, grabbed me, and told me that he couldn't believe it was true, that his parents were not dead. He was almost in tears."

Macy seized the moment. He inquired about Sean's composure in an attempt to prove that the fair-haired thespian had fooled even those closest to him. Rebecca described Sean as usually very placid, but on the afternoon of the murders he was "too in shock to be excited."

"He was as white as he could possibly be," she said. "There was no blood in his face at all."

When Ravitz called Jim Blackwell to the stand, whispers flew through the courtroom. Jim painted a portrait of mutual respect and admiration between his grandson and Lee Bellofatto. Sean idolized his stepfather.

"I don't know of any natural father that had thought any more of his son than Lee did of Sean, and Sean of him," Jim said.

If any fault rested with the Bellofattos, he told the court, it was the perfection that they demanded from their son. Sean was nothing more than a timid, beaten-down kid forever trying to please his parents, but never managing to do enough. As a mother, Vonda had been a strict disciplinarian, but she'd loved her son more than life itself. Jim explained how Vonda had recognized the discrepancies in her son; how she'd asked his teachers if they had noticed his strange behavior. Sean was not the boy he'd once been.

The defense hoped that introducing Sean's diary of prose, found beneath Vonda's letter, would convince the jury of his deep-seated problems.

> I've got a problem lying deep within me, far too deep to find. It's causing people to drive away. Everybody tells me it's my attitude.
> I once told a story to a friend, asking for advice.
> The story spoke of a lover's choice to die.
> He hurled himself off a cliff to be with his girl again.
> He left his friends at the shore, his body to carry in.
> When I finished the story, I looked up at her as a tear ran down her cheek.
> She smiled at me, she touched me hand, she said, "I guess I'm weak."

But Vonda's answer to her son was Ravitz's ace in the hole. He began to read aloud her epistle of undying love. By the time he reached her ironic proclamation, *I would give my life for you without a second thought,* the public defender was convinced that Vonda's words had had the desired effect. The length and context of Vonda Bellofatto's posthumous testimony affected the audience, who pictured a ravaged mother sitting at her dining room table, trying to somehow reach the son she no longer knew.

Wendell Smith would later recall that by the end of the letter not a dry eye could be seen in the courtroom. For the first time to anyone's knowledge, Sean, too, broke down.

The idea struck most people that perhaps Vonda had interpreted her son's poem as warning of intended suicide. But the weight of Vonda's sorrow in the hours preceding her death would never be fully appreciated. As Jim Blackwell listened to the letter from his daughter, his body was racked with sorrow. He may have been the sole person who understood that on the afternoon of March 4, his daughter had reached the end of her rope.

The defense now prepared to expose the Jekyll and Hyde personality that had come over Sean when he began to play the Dungeons & Dragons game, which eventually flourished into Satanism.

George Proethal III, a former Orlando, Florida, criminal investigator, had spent fourteen months investigating the case of six teenagers implicated in a murder during a campaign of Dungeons & Dragons. Proethal related his findings of a game that not only influenced, but *cajoled*, its participants into killing. Convinced that Sean was obsessed with the game, Proethal told the jury that the teenager's D&D "character" was still very much alive inside of him, and that unless it "died" in an active game episode, Sean could "bring it back immediately if he wanted to."

Defense witness Patricia Pulling, president of the Richmond, Virginia-based organization BADD (Bothered About Dungeons & Dragons), knew from experience the adverse reactions caused by the game.

Pulling's son had committed suicide as a result of his enslavement to D&D. When the prosecution inquired as to the kind of problems caused by D&D, she described her interview with Sean. The teenager admitted that when deeply involved in the game, he believed that Satan was more powerful than God.

"It's a systematic type of brainwashing," Pulling told the court, "that changes values about good and evil."

The most provocative testimony came on September 29 from Virginia Meyers, a Fontana, California, homemaker, whose sons had been seduced by Satanism. Meyers' testimony revealed directives by cult leaders who threatened death to members if they ever "talked" or thought of withdrawing from the group. Her research had also uncovered data regarding Satanic rites of human sacrifice.

Kindanne Jones prodded Meyers about cult-related mind control. "What kind of impact does it have on these kids?"

"Very strong, because they make it what they want," Meyers replied. "It's a mind game. If a child plays Dungeons and Dragons and they are into that power structure, they read Anton LaVey's book, they find that they can achieve power through selfishness and possibly violence. In the ritual book (*The Satanic Rituals*) it never *says* to kill anybody. But there is a ritual that takes a human arm bone. Now, where do you get that arm bone from?"

Meyers went on to describe the brainwashing effect on children who become entangled in the Satanic net. The only possible way someone could escape, she said, is to "leave and hope they don't catch up with you. And you never say a word, because if you talk, they might kill you."

"What if you do?" Jones asked. "What if you violate a Code of Silence?"

"If you violate it to the point that you go out and tell people who the other members are, then possibly your outcome could be death."

Meyers next talked to the jury about two occult holidays that struck familiar chords in all those who had followed the Bower and Bellofatto slayings.

"Is there a holiday on September seventh?" Jones asked.

"Yes, there is."

"And what is that holiday?"

"It's a Marriage to the Beast of Satan."

"What is that?"

"It's a dismemberment holiday," Meyers explained. "There are blood sacrifices. If the group is into human sacrifice, there would be a human sacrifice."

Jones made a similar connection to the Bellofatto murders. "Is there a holiday on March fourth or fifth?"

"No," Meyers said, "but there's one on March first."

"And what is that day?"

"St. Eichardt's [sic] Day. That day is also a blood sacrifice."

On September 30, having spared no effort to show that Sean had been the innocent pawn of Satanism, the defense rested. Closing summations followed. Both prosecuting attorney and public defender reiterated their belief in Sean's guilt or innocence before the jurors.

Macy thundered, "I hope and pray that in the last few seconds of [Vonda's] life, she didn't realize that her husband had just been killed and she was being killed by this young man who was so precious to her."

Presented with the task of weighing the evidence and rendering a decision, the jury went to work. Less than twenty-four hours after being charged with their duty, a verdict was reached.

In the morning hours of October 2, 1986, Sean stood, surrounded by his defense counsel, and prepared to hear his destiny. What was that saying he'd heard in jail?—that if the foreman or anyone on the jury glanced even cross-eyed at the accused before a verdict was read, it meant they had voted not guilty.

"We, the jury, impaneled and sworn in the above entitled cause . . ."

No eyes grazed him.

". . . concerning the death of Paul Leon Bellofatto, find the defendant, Sean Richard Sellers . . ."

Now they focused on him.

". . . guilty of the crime of murder in the first degree."

With eyes fixed on the lips of the foreman, Sean heard identical verdicts for the deaths of his mother and the convenience-store clerk.

Guilty. Guilty.

The men and women who found him responsible for three murders seemed to melt out of the courtroom. Sean peered around as his audience scattered for the double-wide doors. He broke his vow of silence and asked Ravitz for permission to approach the district attorney.

With spirited steps, the prisoner approached the prosecutor. Sean asked, "Mr. Macy, do you hate me?"

For a moment the D.A. wondered if this was what it all came down to—love and hate eclipsing right and wrong. He looked into the boy's eyes. "No, Sean. I don't hate you," he said. "I hate what you've done."

I never knew what life was all about until they finally told me that I had to die.

—Sean Sellers on the *CBS News* with Dan Rather, 1987

TWENTY-FOUR

"F CELLHOUSE" IS THE NAME THAT ARCHES over the entrance to death row at the Oklahoma State Penitentiary in McAlester—ironically, it stands three feet from an exit sign. In late October 1986 Sean Sellers became the sixty-fourth member on Oklahoma's death row and the youngest condemned to die.

Lethal injection is the manner by which he is slated to be executed. A humane way to die—when, and if, he makes that last walk to the waiting gurney. When? Because the Oklahoma criminal-appeal process can take anywhere from seven to eight years to exhaust; some inmates have languished ten years awaiting the final signature on their death warrants. And the "if" is because the last man put to death in Oklahoma was in 1966—nearly four years before Sean's birth.

Three times the jury foreman faced Sean in the sentencing phase of his trial on October 14. Three times a stranger rewarded him with death as the ultimate retribution for murder. As Judge Charles Owens read the decision, Sean lowered his gaze. Wearing his new, almost militant look, he stood motionless. It was a bitter pill to swallow. The state wanted him dead.

In retrospect, evidence that the defense believed would absolve Sean—namely, the reading of Vonda's letter—might have in fact sealed the jury's decision to vote for the death penalty.

From his cell Sean has a bird's-eye view of the world he wanted to conquer. A small window teases him with life on the outside. A steel cage prevents him from getting there. The former honor student hoped to take classes to complete his high school education, but "they look at it like this," he explains, "you're not here to be productive one day in society. You're here to die."

He's learned to adapt, albeit reluctantly. The meals are starchy, the showers sparse, the "lights out" curfew descends like a sharp stab in the dark. He looks forward to exercise periods in the death-row yard—a disk of land sequestered from the rest of the prison population. Still another cage to prevent the most dangerous from circulating with the less dangerous. In view of the wire pen, the prison graveyard sprawls.

Dim lighting casts a glow over his long, narrow cell with its single bunk and simple desk, covered with notebooks. As Sean sketches, writes poetry, or reads his bible, there is only the metallic crash of steel doors to interrupt the silence. With more time on his hands than he imagined, he is determined to keep his creative interests alive. "Your body doesn't have a lot of room to move around in or be active," he says, "so your mind takes over and becomes twice as active as it ever was before."

Fellow inmates who caught wind of his crimes dubbed him "Devil Child." His peers perceive him as not as streetwise as they, but a strange breed nevertheless. A killer with the face of a child. While nicknames no longer bother him, the jury's decision in his case haunts him incessantly. For a while he dwelled on what he thought was their callousness. "The jury says they prayed about it," Sean says. "But one of them was an atheist and one was a Jehovah's Witness, and I'd like to know who they prayed to."

Bob Ravitz recalls, "He honestly thought he was going to walk right out of that courtroom."

Almost from the beginning of Sean's residency on death row, he began his own prayer vigil—to the God whom his parents worshiped in life. Jailhouse religion has become his surrogate for Satanism, but most do not want to hear his gospel. Others see his "born-again" Christianity as a ruse to further manipulate the public.

The media spread Sean's story across the nation within weeks of his arrival on death row. The controversy surrounding the Sellers' case, much to the chagrin of Robert Macy, was too interesting to pass up. America sought to execute a child. But this child stood apart from the rest. He was intelligent, intense, soft-spoken. In one newspaper, the Oklahoma County District Attorney lamented the status of victim Sean has attained simply because of his young age.

"By committing the most heinous crimes imaginable, he's becoming a national hero," Macy said. "It makes me sick. He epitomizes everything that is evil. I think the S.O.B. should die."

DEVIL CHILD

In December *People* magazine told the story of the young boy turned Satanic killer. During one interview he asked a journalist, "Have you seen all the articles that have been done on me? Did you know I'm going to be on TV next week?"

He appeared on talk shows and news specials via satellite and telephone. Versions of his story covered the nation and traveled across U.S. borders. On January 11, four days after the first scheduled date for his execution, the articulate teenager made headlines in Colorado. Handcuffed and displaying a baby face, Sean appeared in the pages of the Greeley *Tribune*.

His first national television appearance on the Oprah Winfrey Show near the end of 1986 entertained some and provoked many. Winfrey herself seemed to question his plea in retrospect: "I loved my parents, Oprah." Sean later called the Winfrey audience "bloodthirsty," saying they only wanted to hear about his capacity to kill rather than his conversion to Christianity.

Through a first automatic appeal of his sentence, Sean escaped the syringe of death to reappear in the limelight—a far cry from the March afternoon when he'd retorted to Detective Mitchell, "If I killed them, I don't know it." But in his dreams Sean has not forgotten, and most nights he still grinds the little wheels of death that won't stop spinning. Reliving the murders over and over again, Sean's subconscious has become his enemy. Blood continues to make cameo appearances in his sleep.

In 1987 the American Society for Adolescent Psychiatry and the American Orthopsychiatric Association conducted the first clinical study of its kind on fourteen death-row inmates who had committed capital offenses as juveniles. Sean Sellers was chosen to participate in the study, along with thirteen other inmates across the United States. In what has been termed a landmark study, psychiatrists sought to uncover not the motives behind the killings, but a common denominator concealed in each of these juveniles. Violence, the psychiatrists believed, does not materialize from nothing.

The study indicated that each inmate was "handicapped" by either serious psychiatric problems, childhood trauma such as physical or sexual abuse, or had suffered head injuries sufficient to cause irreparable brain damage. Sean made for the first time allegations unconvincing to anyone familiar with his family, that he had been physically and sexually assaulted as a child and that extreme violence and psychiatric illness existed in his family:

> [Beaten] in infancy by father. Beaten by mother with ropes, shoes, belts, etc. Sodomized by family member when age eight. Sodomized by family friend in early childhood. Possible sexual abuse by female day-care worker. Extreme violence [in the family]; stepfather preferred "hunting men" to animals; stepfather cut another man; brutality to animals. Mother takes medication for nerves.

All fourteen death-row juveniles were found to have experienced serious head injuries as children. Nine of the fourteen showed serious neurological abnormalities. In the area of psychopathology, seven were diagnosed as psychotic, four others had a history of severe mood disorder, and the other three had periodic paranoid ideation.

Within a year of his diagnosis as sociopathic, Sean's psychological label was drastically altered. Symptomatic "auditory and visual hallucinations, bizarre behaviors such as drinks blood daily, sticking tacks in head, and suicidal ideation," were opinions doctors rendered, calling Sean "floridly psychotic," a term that refers to a full-blown, pathogenic brain dysfunction commonly known as schizophrenia. The psychotic diagnosis in this study was in complete contradiction to Dr. Jones' findings of an atypical personality disorder.

Opposing theories have emerged from experts who seek to find reasons why certain people kill. Placing all psychological diagnoses in abeyance, some claim that serial killers and mass murderers have a "mission"—that they premeditate each phase of their "task." Other experts believe that homicidal tendencies arise from mental disease. In notorious cases such as serial killers Albert DeSalvo (aka the Boston Strangler), and mass murderer Charles Starkweather, conflicting diagnoses have been the topic of numerous documentations. In all three cases, the thrill of killing appears to be the prime motivator.

For those who continue to ponder the question of what made Sean kill, there is no clear-cut answer. His impulse to kill Robert Bower, as well as his diligence in premeditating the murders of his parents, cannot be dismissed as the deranged product of a mental illness. Yet the auditory and visual hallucinations he claimed to experience lend credence to the psychotic diagnosis. Just how long Sean played with the idea of murder is another unknown factor. There is little doubt that his fascination with Satanism, in the end, propelled him onward.

Sean is but one of nearly four hundred U.S. children each year who slay their parents. The number who only flirt with the idea of parricide will never be known. Most of these children are brought up in middle-class families that harbor no animosity—at least to the outsider. They are the kids next door. Their crimes are sometimes spontaneous, and other times thoughtfully plotted. The result in each case is permanent.

As Satanism mounts in popularity among teenagers, case histories of kids who kill could possibly assume a new importance. Occult investigators now urge police to check for Satanic evidence when confronted with bizarre crimes, especially family murder and suicide. Many investigators believe these types of crimes are the direct results of Satanic death contracts. Just who are these kids who kill? They belong to everyone. They are the "good" kids—those whom parents least expect. They are Boy Scouts, honor-roll students, class presidents, leaders—all searching for answers to problems induced by a strained adolescence. Satanism lends them the courage to follow through with their fantasies. Sean's death-row confession that he, too, fantasized about killing fits the portrait.

"I was just wrapped up in my own darkness," he says. "I would just lose all compassion. I didn't care about anything. I fantasized about chopping people up in little tiny pieces."

During the first half of the twentieth century, the hands of the executioner sprang to action eighteen times with regard to those under the age of sixteen. Since then the number of juvenile killers has increased to shocking proportions—but the imposition of the death penalty for these offenders has been lax.

"I began to have a dream that I'd killed my parents," Sean says. "Every day for a week, I had the dream over and over again. And one time I woke up, and it wasn't a dream."

Still, Sean views himself differently. He doesn't see himself as the culprit. He cannot comprehend why those around him, why his public, will not accept his change. His mother was "kind of nervous" and "prone to outbursts of anger." He blames his stepfather for not spending enough time with him. He once hated his parents for a reason that today he can't explain. In 1987 Sean told a *CBS News* correspondent, "I don't think you take a teenager and tell him you're not fit to live, you should die. I think you take a teenager and say, 'I love you and I know you've got problems.' "

He has no ill feelings for those who bore witness against him during his trial, and seems to have only affection for his prison "family." In his brilliant command of the English language, sounding more middle-aged than teenaged, Sean philosophizes, "People on death row—they're just people. They laugh, they cry, they feel, they love. They're somebody's uncle. They're somebody's father. Something just went wrong."

Until a resolution can be found to the mystery of what "went wrong" with juveniles who kill, parents today face a frightening verity: Whose children are candidates? The old adage of raising children to the best of one's ability no longer suffices—many of those kids stand at the edge of destruction. In the dead of night, children used to scream out for their parents, pointing to the boogeyman in the closet. To whom can mothers and fathers cry out when, in their darkest night, the bedroom door squeaks open?

Sean Sellers leaves a legacy. Through his recruiting efforts, the Satanist has possibly "parented" devil-children of his own. If the world unwittingly has inherited his deadly heirs, perhaps parents who sleep in the room next to beloved sons and daughters should sleep with one eye open.

EPILOGUE

OF THE THIRTY-SIX STATES THAT ENACT valid death-penalty statutes, only nine—Arizona, Delaware, Florida, Oklahoma, Pennsylvania, South Carolina, South Dakota, Washington, and Wyoming—have set no express minimum age for execution. Oklahoma is currently the only death-penalty jurisdiction holding a juvenile under a death sentence that also does not weigh age as a mitigating factor.

Controversies surrounding the death penalty for juvenile killers have never been as volatile as they are today. In a country that considers itself to be among the most civilized nations in the world, the United States faces worldwide criticism for executing its young, the practice compared to the primitive customs of Rwanda, Pakistan, Barbados, and Bangladesh. Some believe the mere thought of executing a minor to be one of the most abhorrent, barbaric acts imaginable. Others view this realm of punishment as a deterrent to other would-be juvenile killers.

William Wayne Thompson, a five-year tenant of the Oklahoma State Penitentiary F Cellhouse, sentenced to die at age fifteen for the murder of his brother-in-law, is luckier than most. A June 1988 decision by the Supreme Court held that Thompson's death sentence was cruel and unusual punishment, supporting the conclusion that juveniles condemned to die under the age of sixteen offends "civilized standards of decency."

The decision, however, came not as a blanket ruling. While Thompson's death sentence has since been commuted to life imprisonment, other death-row juveniles wait for their chance to be heard by the highest court in the land. They may not have to mark time. The fate of these juveniles and future juvenile killers is expected to be determined by the Supreme Court in the summer of 1989.

In a 1987 airing of the *CBS News with Dan Rather,* correspondent Bernard Goldberg described Sean Sellers as the "central figure in a new death-row debate." American Civil Liberties Union spokesman Henry Schwarzschild believes the nation faces a new moral crisis in the area of juvenile death penalties. "They've done outrageous things, and of course they ought to be punished," Schwarzschild said. "The only question is whether the state of Oklahoma ought to do to *them* what we utterly condemn their having done to their victims—namely, kill them."

The root of this ever-growing concern may revolve around rehabilitation of juvenile killers—an alternative that breeds yet another dilemma: Can society be guaranteed protection when these juveniles are again released into the community? Can they be forgiven for the tragic crimes committed in youth? Sean maintains

"I cannot understand taking a person and telling them that they are so evil and so vile that they don't deserve the chance to change."

On a 1987 *NBC News* special, "Crime, Punishment and Kids," Bob Ravitz declared, "I think it's a pretty strange society that'll say we should kill children. Kids are just developmentally different. They haven't formed the basis to rationally act out everything that they do."

But Bob Macy viewed criminal execution from a different vantage point. "The death penalty to me carries two purposes," he rebutted. "Number one, you see to it that this person does not kill anymore. But the second thing is—and hopefully, Sean Sellers' case sent a message out across the nation—that, hey, even though you're sixteen, that doesn't mean you can go out here and kill and get away with it. That even though you're just sixteen, if you go out here and commit one of these horrible crimes, then it's going to cost you your life."

The Sellers case provokes opinions among family members as well.

Carlos Lindley, Vonda Bellofatto's stepfather, is convinced that Satan brainwashed the eldest of his fifteen grandchildren. He has reconciled himself to Sean's pending execution, saying, "If they put him to death, that's between Sean and God. If he gets out, it'll be a miracle. I say his soul belongs to God, but his tail belongs to the state."

Geneva Blackwell has not seen her grandson since the day of the Bellofatto murders. After watching him on television, she is left with one reverberating thought: "It makes you wonder what it is that he has to appeal."

Jim Blackwell dreams of an idyllic life for his grandson. Now living in the Virgin Islands, Jim fantasizes Sean joining him in the sun and sea, developing his artistic talents, and being left alone to live out a normal life.

But a death-row existence has left Sean with a stark sense of reality. "Society wants me to die," he says. "Period."